Muriel Pulls It Off

An Unofficial Guide
to Country House Manners

About the author:

Susanna Johnston is a former features writer for *Tatler*. Her books include *Five Rehearsals, Collecting, The Passionate Pastime, The Picnic Papers* (with co-editor Anne Tennant) and *Parties: A Literary Companion*. She contributed to *The Enlightenment House*, edited by Alvida Lees Milne, and she also edited *Late Youth: An Anthology Celebrating the Joys of Being Over Fifty*, published by Arcadia to great acclaim in 2005 and now on its third print run.

Susanna Johnston

Muriel Pulls It Off

An Unofficial Guide to Country House Manners

Arcadia Books Ltd
15-16 Nassau Street
London W1W 7AB
www.arcadiabooks.co.uk

Published by Bliss
an imprint of Arcadia Books 2006

A catalogue record for this book is available from the British Library

ISBN 1-905147-24-4

Typeset in Bembo by Basement Press
Printed in Finland by WS Bookwell

Arcadia Books supports English PEN, the fellowship of writers who work together to promote
literature and its understanding. English PEN upholds writers' freedoms in Britain and around
the world, challenging political and cultural limits on free expression. To find out more, visit
www.englishpen.org or contact
English PEN, 6-8 Amwell Street, London EC1R 1UQ

Arcadia Books distributors are as follows:

in the UK and elsewhere in Europe:
Turnaround Publishers Services
Unit 3, Olympia Trading Estate
Coburg Road
London N22 6TZ

in the US and Canada:
Independent Publishers Group
814 N. Franklin Street
Chicago, IL 60610

in Australia:
Tower Books
PO Box 213 Brookvale, NSW 2100

in New Zealand:
Addenda
PO Box 78224
Grey Lynn Auckland

in South Africa:
Quartet Sales and Marketing
PO Box 1218
Northcliffe
Johannesburg 2115

Arcadia Books is the *Sunday Times* Small Publisher of the Year

To Maureen Freely,
with love and gratitude

Chapter 1

Muriel Cottle idled the afternoon at her friend's antique shop, a half-hearted affair that operated within a curve connecting the New King's Road to the World's End. Throwing excursive glances towards the glass-plated door that opened onto the street and through which she saw shoppers whisk by, whilst she hoped that none would enter, she lit a cigarette, cracked each of her knuckles separately and fumbled in the drawer of her desk for chocolate.

Muriel's attitude towards the opening of doors had changed since her youth when, weekend after weekend, she had lain in spare beds belonging to the parents of her friends; had watched and listened, after dark, for the turn of a handle and a 'corridor creeper' to lay claim. It had been exciting and not always had she been correct in her surmises as to who might take the liberty to enter. Sometimes these forays had led to chaos, but for the most part her group lived in a rush, and they were usually ready to escape the consequences by a Sunday afternoon.

A form darkened the glass. The handle turned and a dapper fellow entered the shop. He walked in mincing steps towards an Empire table that stood in the window, the clawed feet of which gave Muriel the creeps. In silence he ran his hand across the marble top, his expression showing it to be in need of dusting. Then he bent to finger every inch of its legs.

Neither spoke but the man's interest in the table did not endure for he left it and walked, past the desk at which Muriel sat, to the back of the shop where he reached towards an oriental lamp that stood, green and mapped in crackleware, upon a shelf. He turned towards her enquiringly, and she winced as the telephone rang.

A strong and unfamiliar voice belted out, 'Tracked you down at last. My name is Delilah. I'm the rector's wife at Bradstow and I've been asked to have a word with you concerning your uncle.'

Muriel did not have an uncle and, lately allergic to intrusion, did not want one.

What was more, other than in the Bible or in a sickly song that went 'Why? Oh Why Delilah?' she had never heard of anyone answering to that name. Nor had she heard of any place called Bradstow. She did know from Lizzie, owner of the shop, and from Ellen, her part-time daily cleaner, that an unknown woman had been trying to get hold of her but had left no name.

The neat man pursed his mouth in impatience to be served and Muriel, speaking into the telephone, said, 'I'm awfully sorry. Wrong number. I mean wrong person. I've never had an uncle of any description. Awfully sorry,' and rang off. Whoever this Delilah might be, she was barking up the wrong tree.

She faced the man who held up the crackleware lamp and awkwardly asked for a discount. She negotiated a sale and agreed to wrap the object in bubbly sheeting as the telephone rang again and the neat man fidgeted. This time it was HRH Princess Matilda, youngest sister of the Queen, born the same year as Muriel and some seven years after Princess Margaret. Muriel said, 'Sorry Mambles,' – 'Mambles' was what Princess Matilda's few friends were encouraged to call her – 'I've got something to wrap. I'll call you back.'

'Don't be a doormat Muriel. Tell whoever it is to wait. Tell them it's me.'

'I can't. I'll ring you back.'

She regretted having to use the same words twice but Mambles was dreadfully demanding.

'I'll be with you in a jiffy,' Muriel told the man. She loved the word 'jiffy'.

There was a walk-in cupboard combined with a closet at the back of the shop and there she searched without success. The shelf where plastic padding and tissue paper normally lay was bare and she flinched as she heard the customer clear his throat and scuffle his feet. In the corner of the closet there was a large wooden chest. In that, with luck, she might find something with which to wrap the lamp.

On opening the lid she saw that the chest was full of old newspapers and guessed that they would have to do. Bending down she saw a photograph of herself in faded colour newsprint, although it might as well have been in black and white considering the paleness of her face and the charcoal blackness of the Chanel suit lent by Lizzie for the memorable occasion. The newspaper was two years old and the headline that accompanied her likeness ran 'Revenge of Cheated Wife'.

In less than a second her energy had dribbled almost entirely away. Her fingers, although not strictly clammy, stuck to each other in prickly dryness and her eyes watered. Ramrod stiff, she stared into the chest and raged against Lizzie. It was monstrous of her to have stored reminders of dire days. Monstrous, vulgar and disloyal. Lizzie did not pay Muriel to work in her shop, but regarded the dreary hours she spent there as a form of therapy, announcing, when Muriel was grumpy, 'Seriously, Muriel, it does you good.'

And this was the second time that the flipping shop had brought upon her a bout of startling grief.

The customer called to her in a foreign voice as the telephone rang once more. Hoping to hide her stiffness Muriel marched back to the front of the shop to see the man dump the lamp upon the table of his earlier interest and mince his way out into the street. Although tempted, in her hatred of the shop, to hurl the lamp to the floor she picked up the telephone and yearned to be sousing herself in a huge, hot bath.

'Has he gone?' It was Mambles again in commanding mood. 'Don't forget you've promised me Saturday night. It's only Thursday today so I've got a beastly wait. I've been having a horrid time with the nephews' wives, and frankly, Muriel, you haven't been much help.'

It had never been in Muriel's scheme of things to find herself pursued, especially by the sister of the reigning Monarch. No more had it been in her scheme of things to hit the headlines. The Mambles business was an inheritance from her parents. Both now dead. They had been friends of King George VI; had, when he and his wife were Duke and Duchess of York, remained close during the abdication crisis and had each been appointed godparents to the royal couple's afterthought when she came along. Muriel's association with Princess Matilda was a pre-arranged and well-seasoned one.

'It may be hard,' Muriel considered, 'to get into Mamble's good books but it's nothing short of impossible to get out of them again.'

In her time she had been downright rude to Princess Matilda; had once hung up on her when her demands became incessant. On that occasion she had been windy for a while. Laise majesté? Either through loneliness, loyalty or thick skin Mambles had continued to persecute her. Marco, Muriel's son, once said to his mother, 'Me and Flavia think she's in love with you. It's the only explanation.'

Oddly enough this suggestion had set up in Muriel a sense of agitated well-being in spite of which, since childhood, she had dedicated much energy to the avoidance of being swallowed up by royal demands.

The headline business had been Hugh's fault although, she had to admit, she had not handled the affair with common sense.

'I'm sorry Mambles. Of course I'm coming on Saturday. It's all been hopeless. A peculiar woman keeps ringing to say she's married to a vicar and that I've got an uncle. I just fob her off.'

'Why?'

'Why? Well, I don't know exactly.'

'It might be exciting. If she rings again make sure to find out what she's after. Don't be wet.'

'I suppose one should try not to be wet but, Mambles, the papers. The awful ones when Hugh had that affair and I flipped. Lizzie kept them all. They're in a box at the back of the shop. I tumbled into them. I do think it was mean of her to hoard them away like that.'

She was livid with Lizzie; hated her, even, for the loan of the Chanel suit. Hated everyone who had played any part, mean or generous, in that horrifying episode. Lizzie deserved to be strangled with bare hands for squirreling the press cuttings.

'Take them home and rip them to pieces. What do you think me and my family go through with the press? What about the abdication? It's over Muriel. Over and done with.'

Of course Mambles was right but the grievance had returned too suddenly and was too heavy to discard without rehearsal.

As she returned the lamp to its original position on the shelf, closed the shop and walked the short distance to her small white-painted house in a nearby street, lists of old betrayals and little snubs pierced their way into the present and brought tears to the surface.

There had been the business of the bra. Her buttoned-up mother had not thought fit to send her back to school with one, although during a long summer holiday her bust had developed and wobbled with her every step. Nor did she have the wherewithal to buy one for herself. She wouldn't have known where to begin. After weeks of mortification on the netball court, she ripped up a pillowcase, and with lengths of elastic and a packet of safety pins, cobbled one together. The following term she swallowed her pride and, with pocket money, bought an old one from a fat friend who had outgrown it. That had lasted until she was given an allowance. Insults and injuries pursued her, and on arriving at her front door she decided not to go in but to carry on walking. She lived alone now; alone with a dog she didn't love.

Her husband, Hugh, a radio journalist, had departed a year since for Johannesburg and continued to broadcast there. Jaw. Jaw. Jaw. Muriel, he had said, could accompany him but by no means had he been on bended knee; had in fact discouraged her, and she was having none of it. Of all places. He had, she decided, been fairly hopeless anyway, but perhaps one day he would miss her and return. Sometimes she missed him.

In earlier days Lizzie had indulged in brittle prattle on the topic of Hugh.

'I have to say, Muriel, although I chose to live alone, I do envy you your husband.' Muriel suspected that Lizzie had slept with him once or twice. Hugh had always been employable and extraordinarily handsome, but his looks, his back view in particular, showed conceit and determined right-mindedness. On holidays, particularly in Italy where they often travelled, he sought to display manly strength; to rootle out tiny forest fires and to extinguish them, single-handed, with improvised hosepipes. He would rescue underweight kittens from sewers and feed them with drips ingeniously constructed from corks and uncooked macaroni, while he spoke in authoritatively faulty Italian. As far as she remembered the kittens got left behind. Clearing his throat, Hugh often brought the car to a halt, however great the rush, to remove a wisp of paper from the road and to bag and bin it.

He slept with the wives of other men, overlooking the pain he caused his own, but was always conscientious with his condom.

Hugh had not always been a radio journalist. For most of their married life he had been a Member of Parliament, working for a constituency that bordered on Central London and which he was able to nurse from their small Chelsea house. They had been married for twenty years before he started to stray in earnest. Once he started he was unable to stop which tied in poorly with his goody-goody image, and there were times when he drove Muriel nearly insane – so many lies did he tell. Yet she believed herself and Hugh, in spite of his absurdities which bordered on bogusness, to be indissolubly united. There was no good reason why they should not totter on together for, up to a point, she loved him and they were both devoted to their only son, although Hugh took more notice of whichever dog happened to be in residence. This was not a feature to unite the couple for Muriel had no patience with dogs.

A year before the hurricane blew, Peter, Hugh's brother, a published poet and a bachelor, moved to a house three doors away from Hugh and Muriel. It was Muriel who had tipped off her brother-in-law when first she saw a notice on a board as she posted a letter. It was instantly obvious that Hugh was not inclined to spend time with Peter; propinquity or not.

'Shouldn't we invite him to supper?' Muriel had asked.

'No need. He's always been a loner. Come to think of it, I can't imagine what induced him to move in up the road. I always assumed he was up to no good in that dingy flat of his. Now I gather I was wrong and all he does is write bilge and smoke.'

At the start they saw only an average amount of their new neighbour, by occasional invitation or the odd chance meeting. Peter, although friendly, kept himself to himself and passed most of most days sitting at a window at the back of his house; writing, reading, smoking and fiddling with indistinguishable knobs on an unnervingly modern machine.

However, as Hugh spent less time with his wife, she took to popping in for chats with Peter, finding the arrangement comfortable, for the brothers, in outward aspect, resembled each other, and contact with Peter took her mind off the lack of it with Hugh.

During one night, without satisfactory explanation either at the time or at any later date, Peter lost his eyesight. Muriel remembered the event with curious clarity. Hugh had swallowed a handful of vitamin pills, swilling them down with a wholesome expression on his face, before leaving the house one working weekday. A Wednesday.

Ellen stood on tiptoe with a can of spray polish in one hand and a scrunched-up duster in the other when there came a loud banging upon the front door, causing both Ellen and Muriel to rush towards it.

Tessie, Peter's Filipino helper, stood there, her face full of fear and drained of colour.

6

'Mr. Cottle. My Mr. Cottle. Not your Mr. Cottle, Mum. He can't see, Mum.'

Although fearful of interfering, Muriel offered help; cried for Peter's loss and did all she could to assuage it; bringing Turkish cigarettes which he enjoyed and which were hard to come by. The involvement took her attention from her husband's wandering ways. When the crunch came, it was from the blue.

On that summer evening as she walked along the Fulham Road after closing the shop, the pain of the episode pricked and the memory of her own wild acts filled her with fresh horror.

It had been plain to her, one winter evening as Hugh returned and greeted his dog, Monopoly, in strained accents in the hall, that calamity was about to strike.

It was not Hugh's height or his gait or his features that had altered; it was his manner that was worrying. 'I say, old girl,' he said, as he made to kiss her cheek, 'I was just wondering. Do you…er…suffer from cramp? You seem to be walking rather stiffly. It worries me.'

'A blister.'

'I just wondered. Have you been taking those vitamin supplements I left out for you?'

'Stop wondering. I don't believe in vitamins. You know I don't.'

Having failed to kiss her, he presented her with a butterfly-shaped brooch and offered to make her a cup of tea. Then he asked, considerately, if she would mind sitting down. She sat as, from behind his back and with a swiftness that alarmed her, he whipped out an evening newspaper and tossed it to her.

The telephone rang but Hugh signalled her to ignore it as she scanned the headlines but noticed nothing to shock. 'Inside. Page three,' Hugh advised in a low voice. Again she scanned and saw (the letters M and P united always jumped out at her) a small insertion.

'An unnamed MP is about to be disgraced after the discovery of a two-year affair.'

She glowered at him.

Hugh, hangdog, mumbled, 'Peter. You spend half your life round at Peter's.'

'Are you accusing me? He's your brother. He's blind. You are hardly ever at home. When you are you blather on about vitamins and whether or not I've taken Monopoly to the park.'

They wrangled their way through the evening. By the next day Hugh had been named: his paramour, a Miss Ingrid Malone, had received money for her story.

Lizzie arrived with the Chanel suit, appropriate for press interviews, as Hugh offered his resignation by telephone and heard it accepted. Peter rang and asked Hugh if he would care to disappear; since the brothers looked alike, Peter was prepared to stand in for mug shots.

When the first reporter rang, it was Muriel who picked up the telephone. A female voice asked, 'Excuse me, but would you be Mr Cottle's cheated wife?'

She put down the receiver and looked at Hugh who patted Monopoly and whispered, 'So, old man. That's our goose cooked.' Had Monopoly been party to Hugh's plans?

The doorbell rang and Hugh, who had walked to the window, announced, 'Cameramen. Two. Three. No. Hang on. Seven. More than seven.' Then he ordered, 'Keep calm now, Muriel. Don't answer the door. Neither the door nor the telephone.'

Muriel's mind gave way to vagueness as she made cups of tea and, from time to time, peered out to where pressmen posted themselves on the doorstep and beyond, while Hugh continued to reassure Monopoly.

During this time Hugh initiated conversations with the party leader, the party chairman and the secretary of his constituency, each one tense and low-toned. In the midst of this their son, Marco, brushed his way through the gloating crowd outside, let himself in with his own latchkey and joined his parents in the sitting room. He, too, was tall and handsome, and clearly diverted to find his father in the thick of things. He kissed Muriel but then, to her fury and dismay, he turned to Hugh and winked. Hugh leered and winked back. Man to man. It was Hugh's leer and wink that did it. The doorbell rang mercilessly and Hugh informed Muriel that they must brave the reporters.

Muriel put on the Chanel suit. It was a trifle too large and a great deal too smart. She mouthed the words 'trifle too large' several times for she loved the word 'trifle'.

Hugh handed her a written statement. It had been prepared by someone or other and dictated to Hugh down the telephone. He grabbed her by the arm and warned, 'Now. Remember. That's all you have to say. Only what's on the paper. Not a word more. Stick close and smile. Don't cry - whatever else.'

She peeked at the paper and caught the gist of her instructions. She was to say that she respected Hugh's decision to retire from politics; that she loved him; that she stood by him. She looked at Hugh and remembered the leer and the wink. She remembered him ordering her not to cry, whatever else. *Whatever else.*

She scrunched the paper and faced her audience. 'I'd like to kick my fornicating husband in the balls.'

The crowd could barely believe in its collective good fortune. The whirring, the gasps, the flashing, illuminated and deafened the neighbourhood. Hugh croaked, 'Muriel. What the hell? Are you mad?'

Notebooks flapped and filled with words. Pressmen and women ran in all directions jabbering into mouthpieces.

The next day and for days to follow newspapers and television channels enjoyed the plight of Mr and Mrs Cottle.

Lizzie came round each morning with yards of proof. One headline read 'Revenge of Cheated Wife.' Another 'Hell knows no fury.'

Muriel was mortified; mortified, contrite and panic-stricken. Hugh was repentant and furious; furious, as was to be expected, with Miss Ingrid Malone for landing him in it; furious for he had loved his job, and baffled to stupefaction by his wife's outburst. He was repentant, for he was ashamed of his choice of mistress and sad, for hitherto he had liked Muriel well enough and had appreciated her connections. During these days of repentant fury, apart from offering Muriel cups of tea and talking to ex-colleagues who were too coy to refer to her solecism on the telephone, Hugh burdened her with lamentations and complained of his own worthlessness and of her grotesque lack of judgement.

The aftermath went on and on. Journalists were tickled by Muriel's flagrancy but, for the most part, chastised her in their columns. There were, of course, those who championed her. In the main though, they attacked her for having spoken to them at all and she was despondently amused. Their game was to bully and badger for a comment, but upon being dealt one, to round on their informant and to praise only 'the Dignity of Silence.'

Mambles was staunch. Lifelong experience had taught her to ignore the media and she refused to discuss the publicity surrounding the scandal; she simply offered views on the facts that lay behind the story.

'Imagine,' she said, not for the first time, 'what the King and Mummy went through when Uncle David abdicated.'

9

There were others; Marco and his girlfriend, Flavia, who were dumfounded by Muriel's eccentric behaviour and avoided her until the interest subsided. Marco appeared to side with Hugh and took to meeting him in bars and cafes. Winking, Muriel imagined. Monopoly adopted the same line and usually accompanied his master to the bars and cafes where, more often than not, he was tethered to an outside railing.

Lizzie's voice reached a crescendo as she released Muriel from shop duty. 'For your own sake. Seriously. I do love you, Muriel, I'll always be your friend but we do all wonder how you can have been so cruel to Hugh. After all…' Muriel knew that Lizzie sided with men.

Eventually interest waned and the pain began to settle. Muriel, smarting with shame and wondering what fresh degradation might yet be in store for her, managed to resuscitate affection for her husband during his period of self-pity. Peter listened and cajoled.

Less than a year after this episode Hugh landed a job at the BBC. Less than a year later he left for South Africa. Rather late in the day Muriel returned the Chanel suit to Lizzie who had forgiven her.

Now Muriel found herself back upon her front doorstep; a quiet and tranquil step, no longer of interest to the world of watchers. She entered to hear the telephone ringing. The owner of the animated voice introduced herself again. She spoke fast. 'Please, my dear, don't ring off. It's me. Delilah. The rector's wife at Bradstow. Bradstow. Where your uncle Jerome lives.'

Muriel shifted on her feet. 'Look. I'm sorry. I don't have an uncle Jerome. I don't have an uncle at all.'

'That's strange I must say. Muriel Cottle? You are Muriel Cottle aren't you? His secretary, Sonia, gave me your name and this number as well as the one where I rang you this afternoon. She got them from Jerome's solicitor who's a sweetie.'

Muriel, heeding Mambles's advice, tested her memory and mustered consecutive thoughts. There was a figure who, at a pinch, might be acknowledged as an uncle and his name was Jerome, she remembered.

'He's not my uncle. Not quite, but I do know who you might mean.'

'Good. So that's established. We all think you should put in an appearance down here. He wanders but, of course, you know all this. It's becoming awkward in the village. He drops in on everyone at all hours – night-time included.'

Muriel knew nothing, but continued to abide by Mambles's instinct that she might hear something of interest - and listened.

'Not that we mind. This is a Christian village. Lovely atmosphere in Bradstow. It's him we're thinking of, of course. Then he'll walk to the station, ten miles off, and catch a train. Any old train. He does have a keeper. Phyllis. But, and I hate to speak against any of God's creatures, we do all wonder if she's effective.'

Muriel said, 'I'm dreadfully sorry, really I am, but I've never met him. He was married to a cousin of my mother's I think. That is, if it's him. She died. My mother died. I assumed that he'd died too.'

'There's nobody else and we think you should come. You're to get the estate by all accounts. Gorgeous place. We're all dying to meet you. Dawson - my husband, he's considerably older than me, but you probably knew that - is retiring shortly and we're hoping to buy this rectory. The church will be selling it off. There isn't going to be another rector here you see. Bradstow is going in with Westrey, but more of that when we meet.'

Jerome and Alice Atkins. Muriel recalled her mother clearing her throat as she spoke of Aunt Alice. 'I'm afraid, dear, that my cousin Alice is not very satisfactory.'

Muriel, in her teens, pressing for details, asked, 'Why? What's wrong with her?' Her mother, close to royalty, drew back.

'You're old enough now, dear, I suppose. It has been hinted that she has always preferred ladies to gentlemen.'

'What about him? Her husband?'

'Oh dear. It's said that Jerome's as bad. Different, of course, but just as bad. Prefers, if one can believe it, the gentlemen to the ladies.'

After that she had recoiled into discretion and the unorthodox couple was not mentioned. Occasional barbed mumbles about a tantalising house in Lincolnshire had entered topographical conversation. Little more.

Muriel's interest was aroused and before ringing off she made a date to lunch with Dawson, Rector of Bradstow, and his wife Delilah, the very next day.

Delilah had promised to take her to meet the barmy old boy after lunch. Visit over, they were to return to the rectory to discuss his future and the complications to which his behaviour gave rise in the old-world village. The incomparable beauty spot, Delilah insisted, had once belonged to the neighbouring county - before the interference of a certain Mr

11

Walker. The shock at the time had been dreadful but, she underlined, 'It takes all sorts and I daresay he had his reasons.'

Monopoly nestled close; writhing and wriggling. She dialled Peter's number. 'Look. It's me. Can you keep an eye on Monopoly for me tomorrow?' No sooner had she spoken than she regretted her words. Peter understood and laughed. 'I'll certainly look after the brute if you like. Why? What's up?'

'Listen. I had a sort of lesbian aunt who married a poof and they lived – he still does, she's dead – somewhere in Lincolnshire.' She explained about Dawson and Delilah and Mr Walker and Jerome catching trains. He was much amused. 'And listen. Can you ring Lizzie for me? Say that I can't go to the shop tomorrow. Don't let on. She'd go berserk if she thought I was going to inherit anything – however foul.' Peter agreed to everything and said that he anticipated her return with eagerness.

Muriel wallowed in her bath; failed to answer the telephone when it rang and thought instead of what awaited her in Lincolnshire.

Chapter 2

 S he entered the village of Bradstow, 'No shop,' she said to herself as she looked from left to right. Slowing down with a jolt, Muriel peered through the spikes of an iron gateway and up an ilex-lined avenue to an Elizabethan house that made her heart ache with ignominious desire. But no. It was too far-fetched. She drove on past a pretty church and over a cattle grid that led to a row of ancient almshouses beyond which, she guessed, lay the rectory and beyond that the village school. She had seen a sign reading 'To the School', all but obscured by a chestnut tree that had earlier flowered, she was later to learn, in salmon-pink.

The gabled, red-brick rectory was easy to recognise. Delilah had provided her with impeccable instructions and stood with Dawson on the doorstep, both looking as though they had been rooted there all morning.

Without advance admonition it would have been clear to Muriel that Dawson was older by several decades than Delilah, who was not without a certain glamour. Curls and teeth; rather a coup for the dilapidated Dawson. Hands were clasped, then Delilah led her guest into the house which was very splendid. Muriel suspected Delilah of being an heiress (like herself?), what with hoping to buy the rectory upon Dawson's retirement. Dawson was dingy.

'We're glad to have got you here - aren't we Dawson?'

'Certainly are.' Dawson's yellow eyes swivelled as he planned to pull his weight. In he plunged. 'In church too. That's been one of the problems. Disrupts the services. Throws the hymnbooks around and so on. Then he makes full use of that stick of his. Of course, we're very broad-minded

13

people here. You could call him a law unto himself. We brew our own beer by the way. Would you care to sample it? We get the kit over at Blueton.'

Delilah held up a hand. 'Later dear. We're here, or rather Muriel is, to talk about Jerome. Christian names only by the way. It's a rule of the village.'

Christ. What a pickle, Muriel thought, but said, 'The trouble is that I don't know him. Actually, we're not even related.'

'Never mind that. You're here and we'll see what we can do.'

They lunched off silver, mahogany and sparkling glass as the conversation sped.

'He should be in a home but that's up to you. I believe that there are some arrangements already in the making, awaiting your sanction. There's a lovely one at Shifford. Gorgeous matron. Just beside the church. We're already booked to go there. Well. Dawson first. We have no desire to be a burden on our children. Two boys. Do you have a family?'

Delilah did not enquire precisely as to the existence of a husband so Muriel replied, 'Yup. One boy. He's gone, really. Married I mean.' Earlier that year Marco had, to an accompaniment of maternal anxiety, married Flavia. She dwelt for a painful moment on the image of her son and daughter-in-law and their lazy pub-crawling ways.

Marco had been a bright boy, pleasing teachers and passing examinations. Even at nursery school he had excelled himself and enjoyed popularity. Love inundated her as she remembered standing amongst other mothers waiting for their children to burst from the door. She swept Marco into her arms and into the car. She smelled the heat of his cheeks and the softness of his hair, now dusty and thin.

Delilah waved her arms, teeth glimmering, buttons popping. 'I'm sure your boy would never have you say he'd gone. One never loses them. You do have a sense of humour. Are you artistic? I said to Dawson after talking to you on the telephone that you would be a kindred spirit. Can I ask you this?' Leaning forward, 'Are you a churchgoer?'

'I enjoy it when I can.'

Muriel would have liked to have been warmer, kinder, to have given more pleasure to the rector's wife, but a lonely hopelessness held her back. That, tinged with apprehension too, for no matter how capable of broad-mindedness the inhabitants of Bradstow, it was unlikely that the elasticity of their minds would stretch to the extent of absorbing Hugh's philander with Miss Ingrid Malone or of condoning Muriel's public and wayward reaction to it. The past was certain to catch up with her for the place was unlikely to be devoid of inmates with a memory for scandal.

Delilah, although ignorant of Muriel's fears, filed away a thousand warnings with which to bombard her when, later, the two women walked through the village alongside a bulging wall that hid the mysterious property from view. Bradstow Manor was the only large house for miles around and commanded local awe - as, Muriel was later to find out, did the head teacher, the Member for Lincoln, and a tall folly that reigned high on the distant horizon.

The pair stood on a white-splattered porch where house martins nested in the spring and early summer. Delilah tugged at a brass hanging bell.

'I expect Sonia will let us in,' she whispered. 'She's a bit of a loner. Won't socialise in the village, which is a shame. Not even the Harvest Supper. We've done our best to include her.' The door was opened by a pixie-like person who could not have measured more than four foot high, although she was built to proportion. Her eyes were held widely open and her unseasonably thick clothes fitted snugly as she stared at Muriel but spoke not a word.

As the group reformed in a busily-furnished hall, Muriel was hit by a tinge of mustiness in the air that told of ancient wood and ancient occupants. At first glance it was an irresistibly irregular house with bountiful provision for extra passages, of even older rooms leading off them in unexpected places - each twist offering an impression of familiarity. In fact, this was not strictly true but it reminded her of something, something she had heard described, or maybe read about. She was reasonably sure that it was not from visual nostalgia that she suffered.

Persian rugs lay piled one upon another. Beams, angles, darkness and light caught Muriel's eye at every twist. A kaleidoscope of witch's balls, tapestries, portraits, plants, pots and piano legs jammed the hall; each object absurdly desirable. It was, indeed, the very house that she had seen when first arriving in the village.

At the back of the hall a dark oak Elizabethan staircase rose through two floors, as far as she could see. Its immense newel-posts strained towards each other. Maybe one day they would meet. The steps were broad and shallow; the whole construction sturdy beneath arcading and balustrade.

Delilah engaged the poor-spirited Sonia in conversation as Muriel stared out through a stone-mullioned window to a walnut tree where squirrels seethed and a number of longhaired cats watched from a tufty grass circle. At some recent time the walnut tree had been hacked very nearly to death and stubby branches protruded from the top of the trunk, telling of man's interference.

Sonia said, 'It's coming in a minute.'

'So soon?' Delilah smiled showing gum.

'It had to coincide with Mrs Cottle's visit.'

Muriel turned to face them, wishing to understand what unnerving part she played in the lives of these strangers as an arched door to the left of the staircase opened and a wheelbarrow, piled high with logs, appeared.

Strange to be burning logs, Muriel thought. It was the hottest day of a hot summer. A man was pushing the barrow; very bent with thin, grey, shoulder-length hair, his shirt open and his trousers baggy.

Delilah broke away from Sonia. 'Here's Dulcie. Dulcie, this is Muriel. You know. The one who is going to take charge.'

An appalling noise came from Dulcie's mouth. 'About time too.' She glinted through bifocals at the floor.

'He set his bed alight this morning - and another thing. I'm fed up with bringing in the blocks. He insists on a fire any time of year. Lost touch with the seasons.'

She simply cannot be a she, Muriel agitated, turning again to the walnut tree. Following Muriel's glance, Dulcie advised, 'Yes. You'd do well to cut it down and plant another. That tree was saved by the skin of its teeth, and I mean it. Dangerous. They did their best, but if you ask me, it's had its chips and if you don't get weaving on another you'll bring the whole lot of us bad luck.'

Muriel made up her mind to hack it down and plant another within the week as she attempted to understand the intricacies of ownership. Would she, should events run smoothly, verily possess that sorry object? Was every nut hidden in its stubby branches on the eve of becoming hers?

'Good job you've come,' continued Dulcie. 'We could do with more pet food. Him what used to fetch it has stopped coming - cheques or no cheques. Couldn't cope with his Lordship any longer.'

Delilah hastened to set things straight. 'Dulcie's little joke. Your uncle isn't really a lord but, of course, you knew that already.'

'I can't,' cried Muriel, half to herself.

Delilah was over-merciful. 'I'm sure you can. You look most capable.'

Dulcie began to hump logs into a basket that stood under an ornamental dinner gong that protruded from a wall at the foot of the staircase while Muriel, supported by the post, hoped for a lead. Breathing belligerence into every syllable, Dulcie spoke, 'Talking of his Lordship. Isn't it about time he produced that letter entrusted to him by his wife? I'd like to know what the hell he's done with that.'

Doubled up once more, Dulcie redirected the wheelbarrow.

Fear in the air warned, only seconds before Muriel looked up to see Jerome Atkins walk briskly down the stairs, that his appearance was imminent. Even at that first sighting she could tell that he was proud of his not-very-wrinkly skin. Winged eyebrows added a look of misleading amiability as he picked his way over the treads. All at once he was on the ground beside them - a colourless, parched turkey; feet and hands small and neat; eyes conker-brown and dead as lavatory windows.

It must be admitted, Muriel mused, that he has a full complement of grey-white hair. He looks younger than his years. She was unable to concentrate on anything but detail and continued to assess him thus until he opened his mouth. He clutched at Delilah's hand but stared at Muriel through the lavatory windows. 'Her. Who? Horrible face. Horrible.' Delilah smoothed the path. 'Your niece Jerome. The one you used to talk about. Muriel.'

As she wondered what he could have said about her, his face turned goofy and a thin smile travelled his lips; a smile that transformed into a leer (reminding her of Hugh) as he advanced upon Muriel. 'Good. Excellent. Come with you.'

Many eyes wheeled towards them. Delilah's twinkled. Dulcie's, glowered through her bifocals, and those (blue) of a sweetly-expressioned young lady who had crept upon the scene, filled with tears.

Delilah to the fore. 'That's right Jerome. Follow Muriel.' To Muriel she piped, 'Guide him to the front door. Take him by the hand. He'll follow you.' Muriel was her protégée. Tonight, the protégée decided, as she supported her uncle across the carpet, I will not write one of my reproachful letters to Hugh. I will not hark back to his imperturbable malice. Nor will I cringe under the weight of my own folly. I will not writhe in bed and work myself into a querulous state. Pray, Dawson, in

17

that church up the road, that it is true. She swayed to the rhythm of Jerome's step as he held fast to her arm. The tearful young lady followed on spindly heels as Jerome, jaunty, poured forth flattery. 'Good. Excellent. Wonderful woman. I always said so. Quite attractive, I think, don't you?' he asked of nobody in particular.

Muriel, cow-like, agreed as they reached the door and as Sonia, who had been absent when Jerome appeared, returned holding a piece of paper which she thrust into Muriel's face.

'I'm only the secretary,' her vocal organs quivered, 'but I've done the donkey work. This is what you need to show to the ambulance men and here's the name of the doctor. He's the one you have to register him with when you get him there.'

She pushed a paper into Muriel's spare hand and advised, 'Don't think this honeymoon is going to last. He takes to strangers. Then he turns on them like he does on the rest of us.'

Sonia affected triumph but Muriel's attention was taken by the arrival of an ambulance as it moved in low gear towards the front door. Her energy flagged as she realised that she was expected, by all who watched, to travel with the patient.

The ambulance stopped and two uniformed men jumped out, bulging with resolve and flashing statutory smiles at Jerome as he stood, in blistering sunlight, in his thick grey suit.

'He's worn that suit,' Delilah spoke low, 'year in year out,' For a second Muriel thought the rector's wife had said 'urine'. 'Weddings, church, fete, musical evenings, school manager's meetings, you name it, whatever the weather.'

Although neat, the suit was distressingly rank.

The attendants opened the door at the side of the great vehicle and out shot a metal ladder that clanked down upon the gravel. Jerome squeezed Muriel's hand and appealed to her in toothy intimacy. 'Up. Up.' He pointed with his stick at the ladder. A lad with a high colour and a healthy face joined the band in front of the house as Muriel, with the eyes of the nameless follower upon her, urged Jerome forward.

'What's this then?' the lad asked Delilah. 'Are they carting him off at last?'

'Yes. His relative's here. I got hold of her as a matter of fact. There she is, holding his arm. The tall lady. She's taking him to Shifford. There's a gorgeous matron there.'

18

Sonia, in piteous perplexity, was beside him, tears streaming down her fluffy cheeks, falling to her knees at Muriel's feet and clasping her hands as one in prayer.

'Spare him. Spare my master. I beg of you. I only ask one thing. Spare my master.'

Muriel said, 'I'm sorry. I never ordered the thing. I know nothing.'

Once again she wished she could have been kinder, but timidity and the feeling that she was being framed rioted within her and held her back. With his stick, Jerome lashed out at the beseeching creature.

'Horrible. Get away. I'm going with her,' he said, pointing at Muriel; wooing his 'niece'.

They climbed the metal ladder at the top of which the attendants stood at the ready to greet their patient and his companion, while Sonia, upon her knees, prayed to an elusive saviour.

Butterflies fussed in the sun and rooks raged in tall trees at the foot of the land that slipped away to the side of the house. Sunlight set dancing cross-gleams of spangled light where the uniformed men stretched out their hands to assist their guests.

Jerome quivered and Muriel clung to him as he tried to gain control of his stick. Suddenly he dug her hard on the hip. There was little room at the top of the steps, and had she not wound her fingers around a lever that jutted from the door she would have toppled over. He held his stick high in both hands before bringing it down on the shoulder of one of the men.

Once, years before, Muriel had failed to coax a donkey into a loose box. Her mother had complained that she had no way with dumb creatures. Would never be a 'proper country person'.

As Sonia continued to belt out 'Save him', Delilah ran forward, reached up and snatched the weapon. Jerome kicked out at her but, niftily, she dodged and muttered, 'Poor old dear. It will come to us all I daresay.'

He rounded on Muriel now, forcing her grip on the lever to loosen and she fell backwards, onto the gravel beside the supplicating Sonia. Delilah brushed away stones from Muriel's clothes and urged her to make haste. 'So long as you're not hurt of course. Your car. It's at the rectory. Run as fast as you can and bring it here. We'll have another go at getting him into the ambulance but we'd be better off with backup.'

At a startling pace Muriel retraced her steps to the rectory where she found Dawson on the doorstep. He tugged a pipe from his mouth and advanced, 'Where's Delilah? I thought you would be bound to come back together. Sure to be good pals, you two. How did it go?'

'It didn't. That's why I'm here. They need my car.' Both her legs ached.

'Since you are here, I wonder if I could have a word with you? There are one or two things which we ought to discuss. I think you would do well to join the Board of Governors. Church School.' He pointed to a low building beyond his garden boundary. 'Voluntary-aided. The only one of its kind for miles. Old Jerome used to be a governor. Well, we had to persuade him to stand down a while back. He couldn't catch the drift which caused all sorts of problems. Bad language too, in front of the head teacher.'

Muriel screeched, 'I must go. I'll be back.' She drove to the front of Jerome's house where her 'uncle' stood upon the ground, flanked by hot officials. The crowd around him had swelled.

A happy woman, on the tubby side, in a patterned frock and accompanied by a female child of five or six, stood excited as Delilah continued to offer advice.

'Here comes Muriel. Your niece.' Jerome lurched towards her as she extricated herself from the car. 'You. Like it. It's yours,' he said, pointing to it.

Delilah, quick on the uptake, snapped, 'Get him into it Muriel. The men can't take him against his will. Something to do with the law I gather. We'll send them on ahead and I'll pop in the back of your car to guide you to Shifford.'

Jerome, in a mellower mood, installed himself in the front passenger seat which Delilah held open as the sweet-faced lady, carrying a canvas holdall, ran forward and placed herself in the back of the car.

Thus Muriel drove, gingerly, to the psychiatric wing of the geriatric home at Shifford. By her side Jerome smiled while Delilah navigated, and her neighbour snivelled into a handkerchief. At one moment the car was overtaken by the ambulance; mission unaccomplished, returning to base.

They drove over tarmac to a long white building, the ground planted gaily with pansies and geraniums, and the surrounding grass a greyish-yellow. Sprinklers were banned in the unprecedented drought. The empty-handed ambulance men had issued a warning and an assembly of tidy nurses waited for Jerome at the door of the institution. The car stopped and he sat, implacable, during which pause his three female chaperones rushed to his door.

Delilah drew away and engaged herself in explanation to the waiting committee, whereupon they, with bland faces, wreathed around the passenger who, brows furrowed and parched skin drawn in anger at his loss of authority, refused to budge.

Muriel spoke to the lady with the handkerchief. 'Should we introduce ourselves? My name is Muriel Cottle.'

'I think we all know that. Mine is Phyllis. I've looked after the old gentleman for five years now. Ever since his wife died. Nursed him through that and his illness. I can manage him, I assure you. This might be the moment to mention that he always promised that I should be cared for.'

Silently Muriel queried Phyllis's conscientiousness in relation to the rankness of Jerome's suit, and thought back to Delilah's reluctant criticism of her during their first and only telephone conversation.

'Perhaps they should keep him here for a little. He may need different pills or something.'

'His pills are adequate. First time you've met him isn't it? He used to go on about you poor soul. We did all wonder why you never spared him the time of day. Fortunate,' she added, with justification, 'that I thought to pop his things into an overnight bag. Disappointed, he was, when you never showed up.'

'I never knew.'

Nurses meddled with Jerome through the car door, speaking in soppy voices; prompting and lobbying. Once again he turned to Muriel. 'She like it. Take me.' Encouraged by the nurses and Delilah she walked to Jerome's side as he, with no help from his stick, disentangled himself from the car seat. Hospital doors flew open and Muriel and Jerome, face serene, entered the building.

Delilah, the furious Phyllis and the nurses followed them into the hall and one nurse ran away down a passage to return with a huge, clanking wheelchair.

Muriel gibbered in awkwardness and wondered how it had come about that she should be the only member of the cast able to befool him. Where was the gorgeous matron that Delilah had recommended?

'Let it be true.' She thought of the words that she might write to Hugh. Only might. 'Let it be true that I am about to inherit a turbulent kingdom. I will become a proper country person.'

Marco and Flavia. Would they sober up in awe? Would the enervating effects of their dissipation evaporate? Had Marco gone downhill since his parents disgraced themselves? And what was Peter to do without her if she abandoned her London life? She would have to break the news to Lizzie and explain about ditching her duties at the shop. Perhaps she could go to London once a week.

At her bidding Jerome sat in the monstrous chair and searched for reassurance. 'Not here. Go with you. Horrible people. Horrible faces.'

He pointed to an ill-favoured nurse with a swollen upper lip, who said, 'There dear. We'll make you a cup of tea and show you to your room.' Then, to Muriel, 'No need to worry. The doctor will be along to sedate your daddy shortly. He'll soon settle.' With that she seized the bar behind the seat, made a dramatic half-turn, and wheeled him away out of sight down a long, thin corridor. The three women could do no more than hang about. Phyllis mopped her eyes and said, 'That's me out of a job. Will you be moving in at once?'

Muriel appealed to Delilah. 'Where do I stand? It seems to me that already I am expected to chop down trees and buy crates of pet food. Is there a dog?'

'Heavens, no! Dogs at Bradstow Manor? I'd like to see Dulcie's face. Sonia's too, come to that. You don't have one do you?' Delilah looked alarmed. 'I'm afraid that's not allowed.'

The words 'Who by?' ran through Muriel's head.

Delilah said, 'We'll ring Arthur when we get back to the rectory. He's a sweetie. He's Jerome's solicitor. Does work for the church as well. He'll be able to put you in the picture.'

Arthur. The secrets lay with Arthur. Within an hour or two she would know where they lay. It was too thrilling. She imagined a doctor rendering Jerome unconscious as Phyllis asked, 'May I keep my room for the present? I have no plans.' She must have clocked up forty years. Walled in behind her sweet prettiness, scars of betrayal putrefied. 'What about Sonia and Dulcie? Are they for the high jump too? I don't see Dulcie taking this lying down.' Saddened by the anxieties of these uncertain women, Muriel answered that she knew nothing.

Delilah came to the rescue. 'But you will as soon as you've had a powwow with Arthur.'

Towards them marched an unusually tall man who lowered his eyes to look at the group. 'Which is the relative?'

Delilah promoted Muriel. 'Mrs Cottle. She's his next of kin.'

The tall doctor addressed her. 'I'm afraid there's little chance of improvement. I'm sorry to have to tell you this.'

Feel free, I'd never heard of him, or barely, until yesterday, Muriel thought, but said, 'Please go on.' Since her wild exposure to the press on the day of Hugh's debacle she had learnt to keep contentious thoughts to herself.

'We can sedate him so there will be no recurrence of violence. I have spoken to his GP who has put me in the picture.'

'Lucky you,' she said to herself, biting her lip. It would not do to chuckle.

'Of course there's no reason to suppose he won't go on like this for many years. His heart is unusually strong.'

Muriel said, 'My position is not very clear. May I ring you tomorrow for news of him?'

The tall doctor agreed before shaking their hands.

In the back of the car Phyllis resumed her snivelling. When they left her under the porch Delilah consoled her with a bright, 'Worry not Phyllis. Muriel will see to it that you're all right.' Phyllis, unconvinced, turned her own key in the magnificent lock.

At the rectory, Dawson was agog as Delilah filled him in on the afternoon's activities and as Muriel acknowledged herself staggered to realise how little time had been consumed by momentous events. She had not only become acquainted with her uncle and with members of his household, but Jerome had been incarcerated all in the space of a few hours.

It was four-thirty when they sat down in the spotless sitting room. Dawson spread his legs, puffed on his pipe and said, 'It's a rum do. Will you be staying on now? The place could do with a bit of pulling together.'

Delilah insisted that Arthur be approached. 'Don't worry. He's a sweetie,' she persisted, then dialled a number and launched without preamble, 'I have Muriel here. Muriel Cottle. I got hold of her as a matter of fact. I'm handing her over to you. We have just managed to pop Jerome into that gorgeous place at Shifford. By the way, Arthur, drinks here when she takes over. She'll need to socialise. It's going to be lonely for her.'

Muriel took the receiver, and for fifteen minutes or more learnt of her fate from Arthur Stiller, solicitor to Jerome Atkins.

'You are his sole heir. I am at liberty to tell you this. There's been a bit of chatter about a letter intended for Dulcie. Hints about Phyllis too, but no need to pay any attention to such claims. No way of changing his will now - not since, if I heard right, he has been committed. Upon the death of my client, however, there will be considerable duty payable. Of course we might be able to think up some way whereby he could hand it all over to you now. There's oodles of money there, but what with keeping the place going - far too many on the payroll - and now the additional cost of the nursing home...' At this stage Muriel failed to pay attention. Her heart sprang up more elastic than ever before and her body thrilled, for if Arthur was to be believed, she was indeed in line for Bradstow Manor.

Re-engaging, she listened to Arthur's flow of words. 'Whether or not you want to take the place over now, of course, I don't know. I imagine there could be some resentment. Too much of a free hand down there. Might you be moving in? If so we will have to apply to the court to get you power of attorney. Sonia, the secretary, is entitled to sign cheques as it is; wages, household goods and so on. She doesn't hold full power. For major items, roof or what you will, we would always be called in to advise and to get Jerome's signature out of him. It's really going to be up to you. How do you view it?'

'I need to think things over.'

It was decided that Dawson and Delilah should put her up for the night and that, in the morning, she pay a visit to Arthur's office in the local town.

'You can sleep in Sebastian's room.' Delilah, beside herself with excitement. 'He's our first-born. In the army. As a matter of fact neither of our boys is at home at present. Alastair, our baby, is normally with us but this week, as ill luck would have it, he's over at his aunt and uncle's. He will be sorry to have missed you. I'm afraid all the rooms are piled high with jumble for the fete in three weeks time. It's always held in Jerome's grounds. Will you be willing to lend them? I'm sure you will.' Delilah whipped clean bedlinen from a cupboard. As she struggled with a pillowcase she brightened. 'I've just had a lovely idea. As a newcomer you could tell fortunes for us. We're all too well known down here to get away with it any longer. In fact we haven't done it for several years. There's a gorgeous thatched summerhouse in the sunken garden that we could fill with atmosphere. All you'll have to do is get hold of a pack of cards - crystal balls have had their day.' Nothing, now, was to stop the flow. 'We'll tie your gorgeous hair up in a gypsy scarf and blacken your face with walnut juice. Alastair will make a sign for you. He's clever with his hands. 'Gypsy Rosalee.' She turned her attention back to the bedroom. 'We can soon clear a space in here and, by the by, we don't have much more than a snack in the evening - other than when we're socialising. As you can see, Dawson isn't young and he needs his sleep. In fact, and you may find this shocking, we usually treat ourselves to a little something in front of the television and, occasionally, we indulge in a bottle of plonk – that, or some of Dawson's home-brewed beer. He gets the kit over at Blueton but, of course, he's told you that already.'

The rectory party watched *Treasures of the Deep*, ate sardines on toast and drank both hot chocolate and plonk. The combination made Muriel queasy.

She thought of Peter and Hugh; of Marco and Flavia. She thought of HRH Princess Matilda. There were others; Lizzie, and more besides.

Chapter 3

After breakfast Muriel visited Arthur. He wagged a dumpling finger at her and she wondered why Delilah labelled him a 'sweetie'. She listened intermittently as he outlined a series of confusing alternatives. 'I think it would be advisable for you to move in there as soon as possible. We'll get this power of attorney thing going. Of course a lot depends on the old boy's life span. Dulcie will continue to search high and low for some letter that she has a bee in her bonnet about but – worry not! Jerome never actually denied having been given one but refused to be forthcoming. Meanwhile the years have slipped by.'

That day Muriel did not call in at the house. Nor did she visit Jerome. Instead, and guiltily, she rang the doctor from the lawyer's office and learnt that her uncle was calm. As she drove to London some of Arthur's words revisited her. 'Hope he lives for seven years. Have to see exactly how much land there is. Some could be sold off if necessary.' There had been talk of farmland and property in the town. Perhaps she owned the nursing home.

As she drew up outside her front door she said to herself, 'By hook or by crook I'll do it.' She had needed to hold a card or two in her hands. This palaver amounted to a pack.

Within an hour Peter had returned the dog. She could have done without Monopoly who, as usual, acted as though hell-bent on tormenting her but was delighted to see Peter.

'How was it?' he asked. Muriel was stretched out in an armchair, smoking. She cracked her knuckles, then ran through the encounters, pausing to answer questions.

When the whole had been fully recounted, when Peter had shown sympathy and interest, their colloquy converted into familiar silence before he left her

Later, as she missed the peace of Peter's company, the telephone rang but she didn't answer it. Her head was full and she guessed it was Marco; either him or Princess Matilda. She wondered when and how to break the news to her son. After Hugh's departure he had swung back towards his mother. He tugged at her love. Her tidiness soothed his restlessness and Ellen washed his clothes without complaint. Flavia had no knack for domesticity. Their council flat, underground and further down the King's Road than Muriel and Peter's houses, was disorderly. Flavia, somehow, had wangled a lease on it some years before Marco moved in with her. She exploited Muriel's girlishness and borrowed brooches and outfits. In short, the pair had come to depend on her and the sporadic use of her purse. The arrangement suited Muriel and filled gaps.

She wondered whether to tell Hugh; worried, too, about what to say to Princess Matilda. Things were not yet definite enough for celebration. Suffering an urge to telephone Hugh in Johannesburg, Muriel dithered. The challenges and confusions ahead were formidable but, on the whole, she decided that she preferred to meet them alone. Although, she predicted crossly, Flavia was certain to be full of suggestions as to how to tart the place up before allowing her to glory in the pride of ownership. Again the telephone rang. She answered and Marco spoke quickly,

'Where the hell have you been?'

Muriel did not touch upon events; merely mentioned that she was tired and that she would ring him in the morning. As she flopped, she pictured her son saying to his wife, 'Poor old bag.'

The house seemed dreadfully cramped as she searched for a pen and planned to draft a letter to Hugh thinking, as she fretted, of the Bradstow garden; glimpses of a ruin and a stream beyond. Magic that she had not had the time or the nerve to investigate.

'Dear Hugh. I wonder how you are. She didn't. Not at present. Sorry not to have written sooner but things have taken an unexpected turn. You may remember (not that I did - or barely) my mother hinting at an Aunt Alice. Alice and Jerome Atkins. Well. It turns out that I am his heir. Alice is dead and Jerome has gone barmy. He's in a bin. The house, Bradstow Manor, is of archetypal beauty. It's idyllic; stuffed with goodies. Oh Hugh'... She stopped writing and scrunched the page, as she had done on the day of the crisis, then threw it into the waste-paper basket under her writing table. 'Can't be fished,' she said to herself as she prepared for bed.

She didn't sleep - for thoughts of Hugh annoyed her. After hunting for a pen and pad she began to write and continued to do so for most of the night. In the morning, before throwing her scrawls away, she read some parts of them.

'I hear from Hugh so seldom. His first letter had an impact but, since that, I've barely bothered to read any others. Still. I've kept them. I can't sleep. I'll read that first one - just to remind myself. Hugh writes in bold italics. He learnt to do it at school and the very sight of those spiky letters bugs me. I propped myself up and let my eyes run over the whole before tackling the letter in detail. It arrived soon after he left for Johannesburg. The paper bears the heading of a smart hotel. He didn't say that he stayed there but gave a PO address. Perhaps he pinched the paper.

"My dear Muriel. As you see I haven't yet found suitable accommodation but work goes well and colleagues are congenial. I can't help wondering how you and Monopoly are. Marco, too, of course. I sincerely believe that it's better, at this stage, for you to stay in London to keep an eye on both of them. Monopoly needs love and exercise." My blood boiled. I remembered first reading this at a point when I actually loathed Monopoly. The letter went on.

"Marco, too, needs both but, I fear, takes little of the latter. Apropos of which I have joined a surfing club out here. That and a gym. The climate is excellent and, all in all, Johannesburg is a good place to live in. For a man, that is. I'm not sure that women get too much of an innings out here. Money is tight. I'm sorry, Muriel, that I've been unable to do anything in that line for you or for Marco. I know how you treasure your little bit of independence and I know how you enjoy a challenge."

How dare he? Enjoy my own bit of money? Where the hell would I be without it?

Enjoy a challenge? Does he suggest that I actually enjoy taking his dog for walks? That I enjoy keeping an eye on his feckless son? Hugh is dreadful. Deceitful and mingy to boot. I didn't read any more but turned out the light and brooded. Try though I did to concentrate on Hugh, on his faults and, where possible, on his better points, his image transformed meekly into that of Peter. Peter, whom I daren't admit I love.'

In the morning Muriel deemed it too early to ring Marco, and occupied herself with other trifles. As we know, she adored the word 'trifle'.

It was after eleven when a rattled Marco shouted down the line, 'What happened to you? Me and Flavia can't make out what's going on. What about tonight?'

'Tonight. Oh dear. I've promised it to Mambles.'

Marco, normally gratified by his mother's link with royalty, on this occasion, became belligerent. 'OK then. When do we meet?'

'Monday. I'll ring you this evening before I go out.'

Marco said to Flavia, 'What's going on? Not one single whinge about father. No hurry to see us either. She's got HRH tonight but what about tomorrow?'

Flavia pouted. 'Trying to be interesting. Smothering your Uncle Peter. Tormenting that poor dog. I don't know.'

There was no doubt that the change of circumstances had knitted around her a layer of protection. She left Chelsea in her black Fiat Panda and headed for the grace and favour complex where her lifelong spinster friend resided, alone but for her Corgi, Jubilee, and a handful of crabbed servants no longer considered brisk enough for Buckingham Palace. Secretaries, detectives and chauffeurs came and went during day hours, but Mambles was only allocated spare ladies-in-waiting for formal occasions.

Muriel was known at the kiosk. 'Good evening Mrs Cottle. Through you go.' A charming man smiled as he waved her past the barrier. She was on a strip of private road driving along an avenue of limes.

'Miraculous for the heart of London,' she said to herself for the umpteenth time. There came a bend where she rounded to the right and stopped in a cobbled courtyard where the Queen Mother's minibus stood parked outside the front door of Princess Margaret's special apartment. Muriel couldn't remember how she had come by the information that the shiny new minibus was the property of her friend's mother, but the fact lay lodged in her head as she parked beside it and then wobbled over the cobbles to Mambles's front door.

She rang the bell.

Upon the instant both a relegated maid and Mambles opened the door. To be accurate, the maid saw to the actual opening but Mambles stood as close as space allowed. Although encouraged by the warmth of the welcome, Muriel felt giddy for she knew that, during the evening, she would have to tell Princess Matilda of the changes looming in her life. And how, she screamed in silence, would Mambles cope with such tidings? Mambles revelled in being the giver of gifts although these offerings were, by and large, disappointing. Neither did she care for the turning of tables, any more than did Lizzie or others among Muriel's friends. Peter was different.

Dodging the maid, the two women walked through the hall; Muriel having dropped a curtsey. Notwithstanding the countless times she had performed this ritual Muriel always experienced consternation beforehand. The golden rule, she knew, was to move one leg a pace backwards in preparation. This had to be achieved simultaneously with a forward lean and the planting of a kiss on the royal cheek. She was always tempted by the same urge; to put one foot in front of the other – causing a collision - particularly when greeting Mambles's mother. However, today all went well.

Princess Matilda had a tendency to walk lackadaisically with her feet turned in, but that evening she moved quite normally. When she was lit up or excited her gait posed no problem. She had inherited many of the characteristics of her Scandinavian ancestors.

Considerably taller than either of her sisters, Mambles was thickset, with legs like columns, and she wore her silvery hair loose and straight; always shining. Her eyes were brown and hard; her lips thin and cracked.

She spoke petulantly and with waspishness. 'Did you see Mummy's minibus? It's been lent to Princess Margaret for the evening to take a group to the music hall. You know how she still loves the bright lights.'

Heralded by the maid they walked through the marbled hall to a large square room. It was comfortably furnished and looked onto well-watered gardens. The maid drifted away, and before they sat down side by side Princess Matilda poured strong drinks.

Jubilee took his place at the feet of his mistress, slobbering through a clamped mouth, whilst Monopoly, as was his custom, remained in Muriel's car.

Muriel abhorred this side-by-side arrangement; the proximity caused her to fidget and she preferred to converse face to face. Ice swam in neat vodka as each woman raised a heavy glass. The Princess complained, 'I rang you, well, one of my helpers did, at least twenty times. Why didn't you leave a message?'

Muriel noticed that her friend was running to fat and that her body creaked, whalebone giving in rhythm with sipping. She was about to reply when she looked across to the piano upon which, in prominent display, stood a silver-framed, up-to-the-minute photograph of Queen Elizabeth, the Queen Mother.

'Lovely photograph of Queen Elizabeth.'

'Yes. Mummy.' Princess Matilda unswervingly referred to her elder sisters as the Queen and Princess Margaret but when it came to Queen Elizabeth her voice uttered the one word 'Mummy'.

'Poor Mummy. It was taken for her ninetieth. They've been organising a rehearsal for her funeral. I think it's horrid. Had you heard? I've had a row with the Queen and Princess Margaret refuses to talk about it. Knows which side her bread is buttered.'

She smiled as Muriel turned to face her. 'Both the Queen and John Major said it had to be done, and I daresay Norma had a hand in it - so there we go.'

She smoked as her glass emptied. 'A little top up?' Muriel put her hand over the glass and said, 'Sorry. I'm being slow.' She intended to avoid the breathalyser at all costs. Lady of the Manor.

Soon she would take the bull, this ageing biped of royal blood, by the horns. Dinner was announced and they took their spindly seats at the dining table.

'Mambles. My disappearing act. I must explain.'

She reported on the drama of the last two days. Mambles sighed and her hand descended to Jubilee. 'So. Jubilee. We're going to be deserted. Who are we going to talk to if horrid Muriel goes to live in the boring old country?'

Jubilee wriggled.

Muriel let slip rash words. 'Won't you come and stay with me there? That is if things work out.'

Weekends posed a problem for Mambles. Few were equipped to entertain her in necessary style (lady-in-waiting, Jubilee and detectives, although the latter, these scruffy days, were more often than not billeted at a nearby pub). The Queen did not press her youngest sister to visit regularly at Sandringham, Windsor or Balmoral, (referred to *sotto voce* as S, W and B by royal groupies) for she was troubled enough by her descendants and the situation often led to terrible loose ends for Mambles.

'House parties?' Mambles extracted a drop-earring from each ear and placed the pair beside a piece of fairy toast upon a glass side plate. 'Killing me,' she explained. 'Is it grand enough for house parties?' Mambles still thrilled to the chance of young men.

Marco must rally, decided his distracted mother, and garner some blades together; enough to fill each seat on Queen Elizabeth's minibus. She imagined the vehicle chock-a-block with reprobates swaying up the ilex avenue to be greeted by Dulcie, Sonia and Phyllis, with Dawson and Delilah peeping from the bushes. The cellar would be raided and the plumbing put to terrifying tests. She assumed there must be a cellar and some plumbing.

'I'm not sure. I expect so. Perhaps not to start with. You must come alone the first time and help me to decide.'

'When?'

'Not yet Mambles. I'll keep you posted.'

'What about Christmas?'

Muriel said, 'Gosh.' It was only the eleventh of July.

'I can't face another one at S, even if I'm asked. The new lot get on my nerves, always sucking up to the Queen and taking Mummy in.'

She wrinkled her nose and her brown eyes caught those of her guest as she spoke. 'I'll bring Jubilee and stay a lovely long time.' Her smile smacked of flimsiness as the butler came and went.

After dinner they sat, again side by side, on the sofa and Mambles rang a hand bell. A maid flew forward. 'Your Royal Highness.'

'The video Hedges. *The Sound of Music*. Can you put it on?'

Muriel ached for bed but Mambles's voice was triumphant. 'I know it's soppy but Christopher Plummer is so dishy.'

For an hour and a half they smoked and drank, Muriel forgetting about the breathalyser, and raised their ageing voices to the strain of 'Eidelweiss'. Mambles yodelled throughout a puppet show involving a goat.

Muriel kissed and curtseyed in the wrong order and sped to her Chelsea house with much to mull over. She was lucky not to be stopped and rued her weakness in issuing unfulfillable promises and allowing herself to be bossed by a dog she really could not bear.

She didn't like dogs at all but in her depths she knew that it was, almost always, their owners who caused the antipathy. Monopoly, of course, belonged to Hugh and nothing but his betrayal of them both held the two together.

To begin with they had complained jointly of Hugh's bunk as they looked at each other through mists of tears. Later, however, she began to allow the dog some sympathy. Muriel wondered if life was not worse for Monopoly than it was for her. After all she had found Hugh hindering in recent years whereas Monopoly had shown no restraint in his adoration of him. Nonetheless, Muriel had, with gaps, pined and railed against her husband's behaviour for she had been fooled. The affair of Miss Ingrid Malone no longer bugged her although thoughts of her own public denouncement regularly smarted, but it was the effort she had put into their rapprochement and the triumph she had inwardly boasted when she and Hugh had shaken down together, or so she believed at the time, that jarred and jangled on her nervous system.

She let Monopoly out into the yard at the back of the kitchen and waited crossly to let him in again, then made her way shakily to bed. By the time she settled down she had disintegrated into misery. She turned off her bedside light and tried to shut her eyes, ears and mind to any suggestion of the world, but images arose of Bradstow and the mad old man who lay sedated in a hospital bed on the eve of signing away his estate to a stranger. Her.

Her imagination recoiled from havoc, past and future, as she slipped from time and torment into that glassy state in which pain no longer exists, before sleep took control.

In the morning she heard Monopoly snarl in the kitchen - asking to be let out. He probably thought he had heard Hugh on the area step. Muriel pulled a dressing gown around her, a Japanese contraption handed on to her from Mambles. ('A present from those Nips that the Queen had to her beastly banquet. She has cupboards full of them and graciously allowed me to take my pick for once.')

Muriel went to free the dog. It was in her interest that the dog be fastidious and she appreciated his punctiliousness. She was fluttering in the Queen's kimono when he yelped again and scratched at the door. 'Ok,' she called, 'I'll be with you in a jiffy.'

When she was dressed she intended to pop in on Peter.

Chapter 4

Before Muriel had time to pop out Mambles rang from her feather bed. 'Anything further on your horrid inheritance? By the way, who is that poor old man you shut up? Mummy wants to know.' Muriel fobbed her friend off with a date that she would sooner not have made for her thoughts were focused on Marco. There had been good times when he was young. Peter had no children and had made a pet of him but, to Muriel's unease, Marco had never repaid these attentions. He was nettled by his mother's understanding with his uncle and suspected that his own weaknesses might be hinted at between the pair. He was stung, too, that Peter provided a sturdy sanctuary for Muriel with which he was ill equipped to compete.

Tessie opened the front door. Since the shutting down of Peter's eyes and thanks to a small private income and various disability allowances, he was able to employ Tessie for most of every day.

'Morning Mum. Mr Cottle pleased to see you Mum.'

Peter was smoking on the sofa and counting aloud in high numbers.

'Planning my future,' he explained as Muriel touched his hand. The smell of tobacco and ink (for Peter wrote with pen and ink, dripping and spilling) pleased her. It contrasted happily with Hugh's squeaky aura of vitamins and mouthwash.

'How was last night?' he asked. Peter could not abide Mambles.

'I told her about Bradstow. Not best pleased until she began to bargain on house parties.'

'I'd love to have seen you - well, heard you if you prefer it.'

She sat beside him and asked about the high numbers. 'Mental exercise. Money in verse. Will you take Monopoly if you go to the country? I'm not sure if I can face him as a fixture.'

'I'm sorry. I shouldn't dump him on you.'

'Don't be absurd. I enjoy sharing him. He keeps us in daily contact. It just wouldn't be so much fun without you around.'

Muriel started. It thrilled her when Peter became personal. At the same time it made her awkward and unsure. She fished about to change the subject. Not ready.

She went out, shopped and on returning unwrapped cheese and olives and potted shrimps in Peter's sitting room. They ate, and later, walked together in Kensington Gardens, allowing Monopoly off his lead and complaining of his shortcomings. During the evening, which they spent smoking and listening to taped songs, they kept away from topics that might confuse either.

Back at her own house, the telephone waxed fiery; frenzied in the frustration of unanswered jangling. As she lay down ready to sleep her friendship with Peter presented itself with indefinite boundaries; with a vagueness that allowed itself to evaporate. It never inched on or allowed for raw confidences. It was not, she concluded as she started to doze, an object she could call her own.

In the morning she rang the Royal Opera House and tried, with success, for tickets. It was arranged that Marco, Flavia and she would sit in the stalls that very evening to watch a performance of *Simon Boccanegra*.

As they took to their seats each of them held a programme. Before the lights dimmed they endeavoured to master threads of the plot; more complicated than any hiding in Muriel's heart. The production was velvety, exhibiting a background of Genoese water and a vocal foreground of poison and surprise paternity. Muriel concentrated on the moment, for she sat beside her son. Their arms touched while lights were low and singers screamed. She knew that he was losing his hair and that he drank far too much, but that nothing could part them, no matter where their thoughts lay or how strongly he despised her for her failure with Hugh, or for her lack of resilience in other matters. Other matters.

Emilia, on stage, yelped in musical joy as she recognised and became reconciled with her long-lost progenitor.

Is one's father one's father whatever the weather? Muriel wanted to know. And should I have experienced fresh surges upon each encounter with my own? And what was Marco cooking up in his head concerning Hugh? Was siring of superabundant importance? Should the fact of it invade every particle of the central nervous system?

Flavia, dazzling in her prettiness, sat on the other side of Marco. In near darkness Muriel watched her as the operatic heat swelled to its height. Flavia, who had known neither of her parents, became, in the vagaries of her mother-in-law, a wandering waif on the centre of the stage.

Muriel left her there and drifted back to one of Marco's sports days during his boarding school years. They had laid out their lunch on grass above a cricket pavilion although neither of them had any inclination to pay attention to the game. Hugh had been absent. 'Pressure of work.' They wanted to talk and pop corks off champagne bottles. Marco had ordered the picnic down to the last grain of coffee, even urging his mother to produce damask napkins. He had insisted on tapestry cushions.

Plenty of them in Lincolnshire.

They had spread out strawberries and cream and chocolate Bath Olivers that had melted in the sun. Nothing but the best as they ate off ironstone plates and drank from fragile glasses - long since fragmented.

She had spoiled him to death. Soon she might be in a position to continue the good work.

Afterwards, in a restaurant, Muriel considered, 'What shall I say to them?'

Her thoughts took precedence over conversation and very nearly chased away the hour. She loved and pitied them both and it was only fair that she should come clean and tell them of her good fortune; excite them with a promise of a brighter future than expected. (The small Chelsea house and possibly a pittance from Uncle Peter were their only hope for long-term betterment.) Marco would never be a breadwinner any more than Hugh would ever put anything by.

To the surprise of her companions she had chosen an expensive restaurant. Was she not on the eve of becoming a wealthy woman? The owner of a house stuffed with what Mambles would call 'nice things'.

When dinner was over, Muriel asked Marco to order liqueurs. He ogled the waitress as he ordered another bottle of red wine to boot. The three resettled, more intimate than before, not knowing that a storm had blown up outside.

Marco, cavernous for wine, gulped and looked cheerfully alert. 'So. What's going on? Why the expensive outing? What's the mystery for fuck's sake?'

As he spoke certain lines of his countenance descended to malevolent grimness. 'What the hell are you playing at?'

Flavia, a geisha girl in bright white, was attentive; rapacious for news that might tell to her advantage. She was fed up with the squalor of pub-crawling and desultory dabbles with drugs. Although slave to Marco's charm, the life he provided sickened her to the quick and tempted her to stray.

Muriel's senses were pinched and she loosened them with wine. Her head rattled as she leaned towards Marco, thrilling to the response she knew her information would produce and to the complicity; the conspiratorial closeness that would follow her disclosures - for Hugh was out of it. The three present were to be in possession of cataclysmic knowledge denied the errant one in Johannesburg. Earlier she had determined to hug her secret until the bird was in the hand for fear that Marco and Flavia would begin manipulations before she had had time to gloat or act, for the first time, with independence of spirit. The knowledge that her resolve was shattered saddened her while the young ones urged her for information; dates, measurements, assets, river-frontage. Again she was alone.

Her companions were uninterested in the hassles that lay ahead; the intricacies to be unravelled and lived through. Uninterested, too, in the decrepit old geyser in his rank suit, foul-mouthing his way along corridors.

Flavia's eyes flickered, 'I say, Chick.' She sometimes called her mother-in-law 'Chick'. 'When can we have a squizz at it?'

Muriel clamped. There were limits. She wasn't going to have the pair put their feet in it; not before she had come to some heavenly recognition of the hierarchy of inheritance.

'Some time soon, of course.' She smiled and drew away.

'For Christ's sake Ma.' Marco tipped ash onto his free hand. 'Don't come over the mysterious heiress. We're in it together. You'll be needing all the help you can get.' This was true but her thoughts stuck as she said, 'We'll play it by ear.' An expression that had exasperated her for years. Marco used it at every turn when he avoided being pinned down to a date.

Muriel paid the bill and the three walked out into the stormy night. Dirty water splashed the whiteness of Flavia's outfit, and billowed the drunken group towards Muriel's car.

Chapter 5

Muriel woke to a hangover, Monopoly's yelps and a sensation of despair. She had blown it. In spite of her resolutions she had exposed herself, and on the very path where she had planned to be wary. For all she knew Marco kept in touch with his father; might have laid bare his mothers' frailties and complained of her complaints - fortifying Hugh in his wish to steer clear of her and justifying his bunk to freedom. Now, surely, he was capable of telling Hugh of the reversal in her fortune. Together they might plot to overthrow her; Hugh persuading himself that he was needed, a man about the place, and deciding to return - a knight in shining armour; unselfishly and against his will, to take charge. If she asked Marco not to spill the beans then he might hasten to do so, as well as telling Hugh of her request. She would be open to charges of deviousness, stinginess, unwillingness to share good fortune. There was a possibility, though, that Marco in his fathers' absence, might welcome the opportunity of stepping into his shoes.

Muriel clambered out of bed and made up her mind to ring Arthur, the sweetie, and push some pattern into things. The sooner she dialled his number the sooner would her own be blocked - making it impossible for Marco or Mambles (or Hugh from Johannesburg armed with her news) to combat her.

Arthur advised - ordained even - that Muriel sleep at Bradstow within a few days and for an unspecified length of time. He told her that he planned to alert the household; to see that a room be prepared for her and her needs attended to. In fact the sweetie proposed to meet her there himself. She did not warn that she was to be accompanied by Monopoly.

In spite of the storm the heat had returned and she left London as soon as she had packed, cancelled, left a letter for Ellen, locked and tidied. She hoped and believed that, during her reckless outpourings, she had forborne to tell Marco the name or the exact whereabouts of the house. Muriel and Monopoly picnicked in a damp cornfield somewhere between London and Bradstow as she fumed about her husband. She felt in all her bones that Monopoly was on the eve of sabotaging her future. Delilah had warned on the subject of dogs. It was going to be hard; catching the blame for a dog that wasn't hers and that she could not abide. It crossed her mind to leave him in the soggy cornfield to forage for himself. Serve him right. Egotistical beast.

Nonetheless she bundled Monopoly into the back of the car which was densely patterned with his gingery hair. He moulted all the year round. Muriel could never understand where all the hair came from or how his body continued to replace the ones that had dropped away. His wicker basket was in the boot and she was unhappy as to how to handle it on arrival. She would start by putting it in her bedroom but she was blowed if she was going to share her quarters with the dog for the rest of his natural life.

It was all dreadfully peculiar. She was on her way to stay with strangers in a house of which she was the proxy owner; a hostess to be shown to her own bedroom and introduced to her hostile staff.

Were flowers to be placed on her dressing table?

Were her meals to be prepared? Served to her?

Was her suitcase to be unpacked? Did she live in style?

It was only sensible to stop short of her destination and allow Monopoly to scamper. The chances were that, on arrival, she would be savaged by members of the household who would observe the dog with equal hostility. Simpler to leave him in the car to moult and for her to spring out, fair and square, alone. Eventually, of course, she would release him - but one thing at a time.

At a loop in the road, beside a wide, tufty verge, Muriel pulled up, got out, and turning to Monopoly, said, 'Come on. Walkies. Clean dog.' She went on, 'Out. Walkies then,' and pulled a lever under her seat that triggered it forward. Monopoly gave her a funny look; half smile; half leer. It reminded her of Jerome as he walked the plank towards the open ambulance doors.

He was a mongrel. Half Jerome and half Hugh. As he moulted his way round the grassy space she realised she had forgotten to bring tinned food for him and wondered to whom she could apply for help. Surely, among that crew of dependants, there would be a dog freak. Delilah must advise.

Having done his duty, Monopoly climbed back into the car and they journeyed together at snail's pace.

The ilex avenue shimmered as they drove towards the house of unremitting beauty. On stopping she jumped out and shut the car door behind her with a sharp snap. Walking away, both from the car and the front door, her eye lit upon a quiver of water. She knew nothing of gardens.

No other car stood parked at the front of the house and she looked at her watch. She was early. It was twenty minutes before the time she had arranged to meet Arthur. It had not been easy to dawdle, with Monopoly twitching and harassing her. She wished she had dallied longer at that verge where Monopoly had relieved himself. But there was to be no going back. Soon somebody would spot her and she wished to appear capable.

Dulcie, tall in army trousers, glowering through bifocals, smoothing back grey hair, was the first to take up the alert.

'They never told me you was bringing a dog. That'll cause problems. How long do you intend leaving it in the car without a window open?' Muriel had forgotten about the window.

'Dogs may not be too popular around here but there's not many as will put up with witnessing their discomfort. Downright cruelty. As it so happens I have one honey-flavoured chew in my pocket. She can have it this once and I'm calling her Josephine.'

Muriel did not mind a scrap if Dulcie called her male dog Josephine and agreed to his accepting a honey-flavoured chew, although she wished with all her force that Monopoly be left to his own devices. Having to consider him was awful. She turned away. Dulcie and Josephine were entitled to assess each other.

Arthur was early and appeared from under the ilexes in a glistening white Rover - bought with the pickings, perhaps, of her putative fortune. They shook hands. He was affable in summer suiting and tidy tie. 'Delighted to see you. I think the team will have made all the necessary preparations. Being a Saturday Sonia won't be in. Good thing in many ways. She can be difficult. I see that you've already said hello to Dulcie.'

Dulcie turned towards them. Monopoly, now Josephine, was still imprisoned in the car but a window had been left a few inches open.

She rounded on Arthur. 'Why weren't we told she was bringing a dog? Good job Sonia's not in today. There'll be trouble on Monday. We don't know if she's a cat-chaser. If she is she'll have to go.'

Poor Josephine. Hugh's fault. Marco should have taken Monopoly on but couldn't. Something to do with opening hours.

'So,' said Arthur, 'shall we cross the threshold?'

Muriel followed him into the hall. It was dark in there amongst towering plants and carved wooden saints, picked out in faded pink.

It smelled of wood and polish and ancient dust; bliss beyond belief. Delirium flooded her as she gazed again at the wonders of the trove. Hugh would be beside himself, were he to pursue her. Joint ownership? They were not divorced; had made no plans in that direction. Presumably he was entitled to half of her estate; lowly or otherwise.

She picked out features of chairs and tables as Arthur spoke to Dulcie who had followed them.

'Is Phyllis in charge of the rooms? Do you know where Mrs Cottle is to sleep? We were to have rung the doorbell to warn her of our arrival but found it open.'

Muriel jumped. Security? Was everything going to get pinched before she had time to wallow? No dogs. That was clear; the only thing that was.

Dulcie abounded in spleen. 'She should be around. That's one of the problems with Phyllis. In and out like a fiddler's elbow - and another thing,' she turned to Muriel, 'I'll be thanking you to put that filthy cigarette out. This is a no-smoking zone. Sonia's allergic and my Burmese, Plod, commonly known as Fourpence-Halfpenny, is asthmatic.' Muriel stubbed out her cigarette on a priceless plate and marvelled that this cascade of verbiage flowed from but one whiskery mouth.

Is this, thought the owner of Bradstow Manor, the end of my carefree life?

She knew full well that her life had not been carefree, that it had constituted one long pitfall interrupted by spasms of intense pleasure. There had been long dead days when she had barely managed to lug her carcass about with her even though, by many standards, she owned a charming one. Circumstances, however, into which she had been pressed, prompted her to pretend that her days had hitherto been devoid of anxiety. She had to concoct a contrast.

Never, outwardly or in private, had Muriel been grasping. Never had she hankered for riches or envied those who spent recklessly. She was not impressed by excess unlike her son but, as Arthur and Dulcie discussed her needs, a sparkle of rapacity stirred in her. An Elizabethan portrait of a Gothic-faced female in a carved wooden frame hung above a Puginesque table of ineffable charm. She loved the word 'ineffable'. Might the one picture, alone, be worth a fortune? Interiors painted in oils, framed in gold, stacked one above the other, smothered dark recesses. She began to add. Clicketty-click. Thousand to thousand. Her head a calculator. Poetry in numbers.

Phyllis joined them.

'There you are. We wondered what you were up to.' Dulcie in command, 'She's brought a dog with her. Josephine. I've told her it's just as well it's a Saturday and Sonia's not about.' Muriel lit a cigarette and held it, between puffs, behind her back. Phyllis had perked up since their last meeting and shone bright as a button.

'We've prepared the four-poster bed for you. That's what Mr Atkins would have wished, not that he had any say - poor dear. What about your luggage?'

Muriel hoped that Monopoly, now Josephine, fared well in her car. Her own luggage rested with his basket in the boot. Arthur went for the case and Muriel told Phyllis that she was pleased to be where she was. She asked after her uncle.

Phyllis said it was a shame. He knew nobody - not even yours truly, in spite of his promises. She had been to see him most days. He was slipping, she thought. 'He hasn't mentioned you Mrs Cottle but then, of course, you weren't acquainted.'

Arthur returned with the case and together they ascended the powerful staircase. On the landing Muriel nearly bellowed with joy as she gloated over needlework hangings and Gothic chairs. Rugs from the ancient East piled one upon the other in dark and peaceful gloom, and shadow gave the impression of winter in spite of the heat that dried the earth outside.

Phyllis led her to the four-poster room where Arthur laid her case upon a stand at the end of the bed.

Never, Muriel thought, unless I absolutely have to, will I spend a night in any room other than this. What is more the bed is single and has no space in it for Hugh.

Wax figures under glass domes stood on Chinese cabinets; tapestry curtains, held back by fat tassels, fell in heavy coils to the floor. An ironstone ewer, set in a bowl, was beside her bed. Flavia was certain to freak.

As for Mambles. There might be problems with Jubilee, but she would be hard to discourage in the face of beauty and comfort; square pillows and fine linen.

Phyllis explained, 'Mavis prepared the room. I don't do housework. I was here to look after Mr Atkins and I shall need to know where I stand. Will he be returning here? I gather it's up to you. Did he get the opportunity to mention anything about me?'

Arthur weighed in. 'Plenty of time for all that, Phyllis. We have a round-table conference here on Monday. You are not to trouble Mrs Cottle for the present.' Phyllis elected to withdraw.

Arthur accompanied his new client into the drawing room where, Phyllis had said, tea awaited them and where no fire burned in the vast grate. With the incarceration of Jerome, Dulcie had let herself off the task of humping logs during the heatwave.

Muriel and Arthur sat down to sandwiches and cake, prepared by God knew who, as Phyllis returned to summon Muriel to the telephone. She jumped, very nearly, out of her thin skin. Who had tracked her down to this forsaken world? She followed Phyllis down a passage to a telephone, picked it up and listened. It was Delilah.

'Welcome. We heard you were here. Dawson and I wondered whether you were up to socialising. I gather you have Arthur with you. Isn't he a sweetie?'

Muriel said that she considered Arthur to be a real sweetie and that, alas, she wasn't up to socialising. Possibly tomorrow.

'That's Sunday of course. Will you be in church? Dawson's preaching. I probably shouldn't say this but his sermons are very brilliant. He's an academic, you see. Not like me. I'm just the rector's wife.'

Muriel promised that she would try to get to church; would keep in touch, loved the place, needed time, needed sleep, was grateful for the attention.

Back in the drawing room, Arthur warned that things would not be easy. 'Monday morning. How does that suit you? I'll get up here at about ten o'clock. I'll bring a list of everyone on the payroll and we'll set about defining their duties and so forth.'

He took his leave and Muriel reached for a sandwich filled with chopped egg. Did she keep chickens?

The time had come for her to turn her attention to Monopoly. He and his basket were still in the car and it was plain that this situation could not continue. Phyllis reappeared, smothering a sigh and wearing a knowing look that said 'Is there going to be no peace from now on?'

'Telephone again.'

It was Marco who wailed dementedly 'I've tracked you down.'

'Why?' his mother answered. Her voice was silvery and light; wispy. Marco didn't catch her single word.

'Answer for Christ's sake.' Her son was drunk.

'Sorry Marco. It's difficult. Things to sort out. Nothing straightforward.'

'We'll come and help. We'll leave now. Flave's found it on the map. See you in an hour or two.'

To whom did she apply? Where were they to sleep? What about supper? Resentment overtook her. Whatever unexpected new dawns broke for her she carried her incubi. Marco and Monopoly. Nothing to choose between them. Phyllis hovered, putting two and two together – not that she spoke. She was pleased to note that the disadvantages under which the interloper struggled were busily multiplying.

'My dog.' Muriel intended to tackle one hurdle at a time. She stood straight and made up her mind, in a flash, to take command. 'As you know, I have a dog with me. I am going to take him for a run. Will somebody please carry his basket to my bedroom? For the time being he will sleep there with me. When I come in I will have to find something for him to eat. He isn't fussy. Will you stand by? I'll need to be shown to the kitchen. Later we can discuss plans for the evening.'

Monopoly, plaintive and resembling Flavia, was barking in the car. Dulcie stood nearby. 'I was wondering when you were going to let Josephine out. You'll have to keep her on a lead. Some of our cats are elderly.'

A stretch lead, a conjuror's rope, lay in a car pocket. Muriel attached it to Monopoly's collar as he pulled. 'How many cats?'

'Well. I have seven. There's two belonging to the house. Phyllis has one and there's the other that Sonia fostered. She lives here and Sonia feeds her weekdays. During weekends she muddles in with mine. Sonia

45

normally pops over in the evenings. That's to say in summer. She brings a picnic for Tabby, who I call Corin, and they eat it together down by the stream. Won't take Corin home with her since she lives on a busy road.'

Eleven cats.

'There's never been a dog here and we've sworn there never would be.' She fermented against Muriel as one about to strike. 'So long as you can keep Josephine on a lead until matters are resolved.'

The knacker's yard?

Dulcie snorted and shuffled off; rounding a bend and disappearing. At a run, Monopoly took the entire length of the lead and made for a clump of shrubs that grew, dense and dark, beyond the gravel sweep.

It was a warm evening and the lawn that spread away from the clump was green and fresh; well cut and sprinkled. It contrasted with the hard, burnt surface that surrounded the nursing home at Shifford. Was Muriel, on her estate, breaking the water laws? Was she eligible for arrest? She felt dejected and guided Monopoly away from the house and down the drive under the ilex trees.

As they exercised, Monopoly wrestling for freedom, Muriel tried to stifle her rage. Marco had no right to thwart her. Phyllis, who appeared, in the absence of Jerome, to have become her housekeeper, had no right, whatever the grievance, to greet her with ire. She dreaded learning on her return that Mambles, Jubilee, Lizzie and Hugh were also on the rampage; eager for their slices.

A word with Peter would help.

A car approached head-on. It was too soon for Marco even if, inebriated, he had driven at a rattling pace. It slowed and Muriel was scrutinised by the smiling lady of the apron and patterned frock who had witnessed Jerome's departure.

She spoke in a wonderful way. 'I'm Kitty. I cook here. We live in the village and I do lunch and dinner. Well, I have done up to now. Phyllis is to see to the breakfast now you're here - like she did for Mr Atkins. How many will you be? You tell me. Plenty to eat up there - especially at this time of year.'

With no qualms, Muriel told Kitty that her son and daughter-in-law were on their way and that there were to be three for dinner. 'Is that all right?'

'Of course it's all right.' She laughed. 'That's lovely for you. It's your home now. You must do as you please. Do they know up there or should

I get Phyllis to help me with the double room? She'll grumble but don't take any notice.'

Kitty left Muriel standing at the end of Monopoly's lead. Thanks be to heaven for Kitty.

Nearly six o'clock. Muriel and her husband's hound walked into the house where Phyllis, disdain pressed into every pleat of her skirt, scowled before them.

'You never told me there were to be two more. Kitty always has to be first with the news. She's only cook here. I'm housekeeper, having previously been companion and nurse.'

'I didn't know until an hour ago. I was going to discuss arrangements, as I told you, when I came in from my walk. It happened that I met Kitty on the drive and she asked me, very properly, how many we were to be for dinner.'

In the dimness, Phyllis's breath upon her and Phyllis's gesticulations fanning the air, Muriel craved a biscuit. A Mars bar or a chocolate ice cream would be ideal. Her body hung lumpy and lifeless, in spite of the brief burst of exercise. Her eyes wheeled to a possible perching place.

A purple and blue armchair, smothered in stitch-work, stood at an angle to the stone fireplace, its skirt touching a long beaded stool.

'Sorry Phyllis. I need to sit down.' A mighty pain in her stomach warned Muriel that she must ask Phyllis to direct her to a lavatory. She had not noticed a single one since her first appearance at Bradstow. It was remarkable that she had not even been shown a bathroom when ushered to the four-poster bedroom of her dreams; remarkable, considering her bathing habits, that she had not asked for one. Time ran short. 'Before discussing anything further,' she began, 'can you show me to a lavatory?'

Phyllis waved her arms about; enraging Muriel. They ought to be pinned, by law, against her back - those arms, she thought. As she followed the woman, Muriel wondered if she walked deliberately slowly. The matter was urgent but she didn't admit it as she strode with tightened buttocks, the pain in her middle gathering momentum. They were in a passage again, the one that followed curves and wiggles to the telephone and off which lay cottagey rooms with latticed windows.

Muriel was in crisis.

'Hurry. It's urgent.' Nothing to be ashamed of. The Queen, in all probability, had the squitters from time to time. Princess Matilda certainly did, as Muriel knew to her cost, for on occasions she had had to cope with the aftermath. Not actually with buckets and cloths but with Mambles's laments. They ran the last lap and Phyllis pushed past her to open a china-handled panelled door. A mahogany lavatory was revealed and Muriel hurled off the wooden lid which spun and clanked upon the flagged flooring. The whole contraption was a work of art; the china, the chain, the warmth of the wood.

Phyllis waited outside and Muriel heard her fidgeting as she ran the basin tap to muffle her sounds. Never, normally, did she suffer in this way. She flushed away the confusions of the last week, stood tall once again and inspected her face in the mirror; flicking at her hair with both hands. Her inside subsided and she stalked out into the passage; keen to show poise. Making no mention of discomfort, she suggested to Phyllis that they return to the hall to resume their administrative talk. 'As you know, I am in ignorance of everything here. I am relying on all of you and on Mr Stiller, who will be here on Monday morning, to explain things to me and to the household. Meanwhile I have to take charge. That is the way it is.'

Was Dawson deep in prayer as he brewed his own beer and as Delilah planned her socialising calendar?

Phyllis replied, 'Very well. What are the orders?'

'I want a room prepared for my son and daughter-in-law who will,' she glared at her watch, 'be here in an hour or so. Dinner for three - no matter how simple - at about eight-fifteen, if that suits Kitty. Drinks before that. Where are the drinks normally set out?'

'Never. Mr Atkins didn't indulge and he'd sooner others didn't when they came.' She was not to be humbled or crushed.

'Perhaps there are no drinks, then, in the house?'

'There's the cellar. That's stacked. Has been since the start of time.'

Whew.

Muriel asked to be taken to the kitchen. A word with Kitty would cheer her up. The kitchen was unappealing; grey and white and smelling fridgey. The floor was covered in ice-cold linoleum and the surfaces with chipped Formica.

Aunt Alice, she supposed, had done it over when the war ended and servants came flooding back.

She resolved not to involve herself with the history of the house or the habits of its previous owners or to fall into traps. She did not wish to transform into a dyke in grateful memory of Aunt Alice. Anything was possible.

In the kitchen Kitty rolled a pin upon the table, extolling the delights of having someone to cook for once again. Mr Atkins had done no more than pick.

Muriel, with her stomach in a shaky state, did not attend to the details of the meal that Kitty was about to cook. She explained to the women present that she hoped they would all be able to muddle through until Monday, and wished to heaven that Phyllis would disappear. When she did no such thing, Muriel gave her the slip and went to her bedroom. On the bed she lay, aching in the middle, wishing that Monopoly didn't occupy a corner of the room and that Marco and Flavia were not on their way and hoping that they had not alerted Hugh. In the morning she must ring Mambles and Lizzie, if ever she could retrace her steps to the telephone.

She decided to tell them how foul it was; antiquated, de-alcoholised, haunted.....

Mind indistinct and mingled, she fell asleep, her head on a square pillow.

Chapter 6

Marco in merry mood, stood at the foot of the four-poster bed. 'Wake up. Flave's in the bath. What a bath. Animal feet and all. Everything's in control. I found an old hermaphrodite who showed me to the cellar. Full of it. Amazing stuff. This place really is the answer. Flave's speechless. I've arranged drinks with the help of the hermaphrodite. I think she's quite enjoying herself – says nobody's been down there for at least fifteen years.'

'Marco!'

Muriel sprang up and slipped on skirt and shoes and more besides. Then and there she decided not to admonish her boy, for was he not just what she needed? It would have taken another fifteen years to summon the courage to order Dulcie.

Marco was beside himself; wild in appreciation of the wonders of Bradstow. Wondering, his mother surmised, when she planned to expire. To drop off her perch. Whatever else, he had taste, style or whatnot. And panache too; wit, charm and mastery. She must carry him along with her.

Jerome, at least, lay in ignorance of the upheavals that were taking place under his vacated Elizabethan eaves.

'Hi Monopoly. How does this suit you? Not bad eh? Ma. I'm going for a bath after Flave. Downstairs in half an hour for treats from the cellar.'

Muriel, too, intended to take a bath. What about hot water? Her passion. Was it in superabundance?

They met in the drawing room. Flavia cooed, 'Hi Chick. What a place.'

Marco stood, a lively conductor, behind a tray of drinks and glasses, picking up bottle after bottle and reading from foxed labels. Holding one up, he whistled, 'Look at this. Château Laville Haut-Brion. Phew!'

51

He rolled his eyes and danced upon his feet. 'I'm saving the champagne until tomorrow. Veuve Clicquot. Ancient, flat and brown. Any Yanks in the neighbourhood? We could make a real scene with it. Dulcie has stacked some in the fridge. Time you got a new one by the way.'

Flavia battled with a French window as Muriel accepted a glass of red Bordeaux from her son who went for whisky; contents of a bottle he had brought with him from London. Just in case.

Glass in hand he followed Flavia through the French window, calling back that they planned to explore. Muriel was alone with her distinctly sweet and fruity wine, hoping that, in its antiquity, it would not disturb her stomach further. At least she knew where to find a lavatory.

As she sat the door flew open and Dulcie, an abomination, advanced holding a Stanley knife; a short, blunt, squat object that she shoved into Muriel's hand. With that she sat beside her on the sofa and wheezed, 'I've got a blood blister in my mouth. Pierce it,' and opened her mouth inordinately wide.

'I can't.'

'Stupid woman. Go on. Pierce it.'

'I might cut an artery.' She looked into the darkness of Dulcie's mouth and saw a huge red lump, larger than a ping-pong ball, encased in papery skin. It took up all available space and Dulcie's voice dwindled as she ordered, for the third time, 'Pierce it.'

Having set her glass down on a table, Muriel stabbed at the balloon. Blood spattered out upon her, covering hands and arms, shirt, skirt and shoes. It also flew in blobs onto the sofa in its priceless casing as Muriel seized upon a crewelwork cushion and clamped it over the source of the flood, obscuring Dulcie's face and knocking askew her bifocals.

Manslaughter? Hangdog, she presented herself in the dock. 'Do you mean to say, Mrs Cottle, that you, totally inexperienced in medical matters, plunged this knife into the mouth of one of your domestic staff?'

Inexperienced? She had taken a first-aid course.

But Dulcie was alive, holding the crewelwork cushion to her mouth and blundering out of the room. Muriel held the damp knife and looked down upon the dripping redness of her clothing. Up she went to change. God knew what the gyrating Phyllis was to suspect. First diarrhoea. Now haemorrhage.

As she peeled off her clothing she noticed that somebody had unpacked her things, and that Monopoly, curled up in his basket, cared not a whit for her bloody appearance. Were dogs the answer? Was it not an asset to share a room with one so infinitely more helpless, and idiotic even, than oneself?

Monopoly's head drooped over the wicker lip of his basket.

The door opened and in came Dulcie. 'Have you still got that knife I lent you?'

Until a moment earlier Muriel had been clasping it. Only as she changed her clothes had she put it down on the table by her bed. She picked it up and showed it off; proving reliability.

'Pierce it. It's come up again.' Her voice was steady, if muffled, and told that the need was immediate. She sat on a curving, carved stool and commanded, 'Go on. Pierce it.'

This time Muriel acted fast. The habit of piercing blood blisters in mouths had formed and caused her no further bother. In went the knife and out poured blood, re-sousing Muriel's clothes and a hand-stitched rug with a pattern of roses on a grey-pink background.

After the second piercing, Dulcie snatched a hand towel from a wooden horse standing in the corner of the bedroom alongside a painted wardrobe. She clapped it to her face and tripped, almost youthfully, from the room without making any signal to her new employer, if that, indeed, was Muriel's role in her life.

Was Dulcie a member of staff?

One of Muriel's myrmidons?

For the second time the lady of the manor dressed for dinner and fussed about the rug. She fussed, too, about her stained garments. No washing basket in evidence.

Leaving the bloody bundle behind a free-standing looking glass, she warned Monopoly not to nose, then found her way back to the drawing room.

Marco and Flavia had cut short their exploratory trip from the need to refill their glasses, and Muriel told them of her piercing sessions. Flavia squealed, 'What an absolute scream.'

Up to a point, thought Muriel, pleased to entertain.

The dining room, in Muriel's eye, took the cake for sparkling wonder.

Paintings of the early seventeenth century trapped in coarse wooden frames covered walls already half-hidden by discoloured Voiseyesque paper.

Candles, branching from neglected silver, filtered light across the table as Marco suggested, 'We can get one of your nutters to shine these up for your first major gala.' His mother hid a heave. Galas. Shimmering silver, fine wines with faded dates upon the bottles. As ever, Marco was running before he could walk and, as ever, with the use of Muriel's legs.

Flavia said, 'They'd give their eyes to photograph this for *Interiors*.'

Marco, behind her, 'Why not Ma? Rather fun. We could spill the beans to father that way. Airmail him a copy. Muriel Cottle, owner of Bradstow Manor. Bet it's Grade 1 and all that.'

Muriel wanted to enjoy herself, but in her queasy stomach, a knot formed.

She wanted no help: no advice, no stamping, no pressures upon her. She wanted the waves of pleasure to spread over her one by one. She wished to be the sole owner of her stately home, to exercise the authority it demanded. She wanted to boss her son and his wife about; to tell them that breakfast was to be served at nine o'clock the following morning and that they were expected to partake, fully dressed, at that hour. She had no power to do this. She knew nothing of breakfast.

An uncompromising hatch, possibly another of Aunt Alice's innovations, connected the dining room with the kitchen. Kitty maintained jolly contact through the opening - despatching full and excellent dishes and scooping away empty ones as soon as fielded by Marco who, unsteadily, proclaimed, 'We'll have to block in that awful thingumajig and slap some of your slaves into uniform. I'd like to see that Dulcie creature in livery.'

Flavia shone and giggled as Muriel's energy dribbled away.

'Kitty is the answer though. Nothing the matter with this fodder or, that's to say, nothing that a bit of whipping into shape won't remedy.'

Muriel knew that her boy was drunk and that Flavia had entered a private heaven in anticipation of inheritance. She, who had not long before called her 'Chick' and offered her the use of an eyebrow pencil, thought to a future in which Muriel's remains lay gnarled in a buried box.

Kitty's head appeared mid-hatch. 'Coffee in the dining room or next door, Mrs Cottle?' It was deliberate, Muriel knew, that Kitty addressed her and not her son.

Marco replied, 'Drawing room, Kitty, and what about liqueurs? I found a bottle of something celestial in the cellar. Vintage port - but are there any proper glasses?'

'I'm sorry. I wouldn't know.'

Muriel took to her feet and, staring sternly at Marco, said, 'Enough for tonight. I'll leave you two to drink your coffee and whatever else. Please, though, don't make any more discoveries or issue any orders.' Her voice was sharp and came as though from another corner of the room, from the clock or from the chandelier. 'Tomorrow,' she continued, 'I will try to get to the bottom of things. You two are jumping the gun. I may not even be able to keep this place. For all I know it belongs to The National Trust, Heritage or something.' She belted out each word at concert pitch. Marco, in his cups, whitened. 'OK Ma. We'll go quietly.'

As she prepared for the night she knew that, whatever else, the morning was hers to play with. The young ones were certain to sit late over port, with or without the appropriate glasses, and were sure to sleep until midday at the earliest. She would be up betimes to keep ahead of them; to plot for their departure, to convince them that the hurdles ahead were insurmountable. As she fell into sleep she believed she heard distant voices and the ping of a telephone bell and suspected Marco of ringing Hugh. Or friends perhaps; fellow idlers invited to celebrate.

Dulcie must turn on them wielding a Stanley knife. She would plant Sonia on the carpet before Marco and order her to beseech him to spare her mistress. Phyllis would put them in their places.

It was seven o'clock and another stupefying day promised through mist. 'Come along Josephine. She bent to rouse Monopoly who slept in his basket and who had, up to the present, behaved in exemplary fashion given the unexpectedness of events.

Wearing the Queen's dressing gown, Monopoly's flexible lead in her pocket, Muriel encouraged the dog to follow her onto the murky landing. Down the stairs they trod, enemies at heart but accomplices now since Monopoly had conducted himself far more conveniently than had her son. He had not disgraced her nor, in these new surroundings, had he hunted for Hugh.

Hugh. That ping she had heard in the night.

In the hall Muriel was nonplussed. It was dark and shuttered and she had no knowledge as to where she might find a light switch. The dog was beside her and, to her amazement, she heard herself addressing him tenderly. 'Oh Monopoly. What shall we do? I know you want to go out.'

It was not completely dark and the form of a window appeared before her eyes. She pulled aside a curtain and prised open a shutter, and then, in a state of euphoria, went on to draw back more curtains and unlatch more shutters in all of the windows.

But how were they going to get out? The solid door was locked and no key showed itself. Nothing stirred in the house and Muriel, pained to accept herself imprisoned with Marco, Flavia and God knew who else besides, bent to touch Monopoly; plucking at the flesh on his neck before pinching it into a hard, furry, tube-like band which she fondled between her fingers. She suggested to him that they search for a back door.

It was nearly seven-thirty when they found Phyllis waiting for them on the chill of the linoleum. Her eyes were hard and Muriel was close to fainting as she read the woman's mind. 'Phyllis. I must go out. Monopoly needs a run.'

Phyllis's face was taut and merciless, her expression pained. 'I daresay he does. It's normally me, by the way, who opens the shutters.' She led them to a door beyond the kitchen which ran out onto a flight of stairs that descended to a utility room. A clothes rack supporting damp towels and the odd thick sock, property of Jerome Atkins, was wound high to touch the ceiling and a barrow piled with logs stood alongside an antiquated refrigerator.

Muriel and her dog paused before pushing open yet another door that led into a barn-like space, cobwebbed and dark, sheltering a wondrous supply of fire wood; kindling, branches, trunks and twigs. House martins nested on beams and dropped their waste any old where.

Phyllis had left them to fend for themselves knowing full well that the room was unlit and the outer door hard to reach.

Muriel pulled Monopoly to her and clipped on his lead. It would not do to risk a solecism in the cat kingdom and complicate a day that already promised badly. She was not to know that Dulcie and her cats were slugabeds, and at that early hour Monopoly's whims would pass unnoticed.

As the sun rose and the mist cleared, Muriel, slippers dampening in the dew, led the dog past the maimed walnut tree. From there she walked northwards in line with a high hedge that preluded a dip beyond, approachable by a flight of stone steps. Down these steps her slippers flapped, Monopoly tugging as he nosed not far ahead. She found herself in an enclosure of flower beds. It had not occurred to her that she might, at the age of fifty-four, inherit a flower garden.

Red, pink and white roses, some as chunky as cabbages, grew amongst phlox, tall hollyhocks, tobacco plants and snapdragons. Climbers in silvery suits tussled in apple trees, intertwining themselves with small fruits showing bright in yellow, green and red.

Muriel returned to the steps and sat down, deciding to explore no further for the present but to ponder, among the roses, and try to decide how the hell to conduct herself in her new milieu. Monopoly lolloped to the end of his allowance of lead. Perhaps, she mused, to skin a cat. Can't be helped. Then, with a ghastly jerk of her brain, she recognised that Mambles was on her mind. They had agreed to a meeting but Muriel had forgotten when or where it was supposed to take place. She was eligible for a rocket and knew that wisdom lay in telephoning Kensington Palace. Not that she wanted to. Far from it.

She must curb Marco and Flavia. Nose in a rose, she moaned, 'How do I play it with Hugh? Do I or do I not wish for his return? Again she remembered the late-night ping. What was more, she knew that she must visit Jerome. It would not look good were she to neglect him now that her son had dipped into his cellar. She asked herself, as she shook her head, why it had to be populated with people. Surely they would disperse, these people on her mind, in the midst of beauty but no sooner did she rid herself of one than another forced its way in to gain supremacy.

The ghost of Aunt Alice, (possibly a dyke. That was where Dulcie fitted in: her Aunt Alice had once had fancies for the blood-blistered beast) waited in the long grass. Monopoly tugged at his lead and she was alone with hollyhocks and roses; looking down to water and ducks, to sunshine and vast clumps of borage that bordered the stream. But people flooded in and spoiled the fun. Dawson and Delilah, Arthur the sweetie and other friends from the outer world, if friends they were. People she knew at any rate.

'Oh, fancies flee away,' she bellowed to the surprise of a rook that hovered nearby while she made an effort to concentrate on the business in hand.

'Keep calm,' she ordered herself. 'Today is Sunday and I shall make the most of it.'

She listed her duties; tried to fit them in to a consecutive pattern and fussed as to where priorities lay. For a start she would have to talk to

Phyllis and explain that her son and daughter-in-law were unlikely to need breakfast. What about lunch? Then there was the question of church and Dawson's erudite sermon; the visit to her uncle; the ousting of Marco and Flavia; the telephoning to Mambles; the listing of thoughts and queries to be brought up at the Monday morning meeting with Arthur and the household; the reappearance of Sonia, and the confession of Monopoly's existence.

She began to rein in the dog. Time was up and she was wet all over – from her feet upwards. Matins must be scrapped. Pity. Had Hugh been around he could have read the lesson loud and strong, clearing his throat from time to time whilst throwing a knowing glance at the interruption of a toddler, a 'we-know-a-thing-or-two-don't we-old-chap' glance.

Churchwarden. Hugh must be sent for. Bonfires in the autumn and badinage with garden boys. There were probably many to have thus coaxed the roses.

What a feeble pair she and Hugh had been. They should have afforded their son unflinching discipline so that he might have been beside her now in the multitude of conundrums that teased her, rather than lying in bed wearing an alcoholic grin in anticipation of riches easily won.

It was time to go in.

She neared the back door, Monopoly now at her side, and they entered the house the way they had left it, to find Dulcie, unnaturally alert for the time of day, beside the cooker. She stared at the drenched, dressing-gowned figure of her employer; patron, landlady, owner or whatever.

'You'll catch your death and I'm giving you one piece of advice.' Her tummy stuck out, girder-like; shoulders back and head forward. 'Don't go to that Dr Maddock from Ranton. That time when I couldn't empty my bladder he was useless. Absolutely useless.'

'Help,' Muriel shivered, 'Am I going to have to pierce that too?'

'And what's more, I'm letting the cats out in precisely five minutes time so you'd better watch it with that dog of yours.'

Muriel ran to her room where she dried and dressed and, as she did so, blood rushed to her head and dispelled whatever caution that had hitherto held her back. She loathed herself when it came to the matter of vacillations with her son.

She left her room and stormed down the passage to the spare room. In she went and standing in near darkness at the foot of the vast bed, railed against the two who lay, knotted together, half across it - any old how. She ranted as she told them that they should be up and helping her in her strenuous role. If they wished to benefit from her fortune, they were to behave as adults and provide her with practical aid.

Marco, pyjamaless, features creased, forced himself to face her. 'Hang on old girl. It's only nine o'clock. We're not feeling exactly our best this morning. Touch of 'flu. I'll give you something. A calmer. Flave's got stacks in her sponge bag.' No sooner had he spoken than his mother charged towards the window. In a trice he was up with a towel about his middle while his wife hid herself in bedding and Muriel continued her remorseless harangue.

'What am I to do about breakfast? How can I get on top of things with you two raiding the cellar and ogling the silver in front of servants I hardly know by sight? You'll have to leave as soon as you've had a cup of coffee if I'm to get anywhere in this terrifying set-up.'

'Cool it old girl. You've flipped. Go back to bed and me and Flave'll take over. Roger's coming for lunch so it's just as well you woke us. We'll have to meet him at the nearest station - wherever that may be - as he's broken his leg and can't drive. Plaster of Paris and all that. Come to think of it, instead of going back to bed, can you find out about trains while we get dressed?'

'Roger? He's the last person I want to touch with a barge-pole.'

Roger wrote for the papers.

'We rang him last night. After you'd gone to bed.'

So, unless they had made more than one call, there was a chance that she was still safe from Hugh. But did she want to be? Muriel was spent. 'OK, then, lunch, if there's anything to eat. And I mean just lunch. You must drive him back to London in the early afternoon.'

'Steady on old thing. I told him about the cellar. He wants to go through it. He's doing a piece on undiscovered booze in forgotten country houses. Surely this is just the ticket. He foamed at the mouth when I told him about the Château d'Yquem. He'll have to have a day or two here if he's to do the job properly. Useful for us to know exactly what is down there. Might be worth a fortune. God knows how he'll tackle the steps with his leg in plaster.'

'Very well for now but, both of you, get dressed and come downstairs.' She left them.

Flavia, face lined from the stillness of her sleep, rooted to isolate recollections. Marco fell back beside her. 'Christ! What got into her? The whole thing's turned her head. I'm going for a bit more shut-eye.'

Flavia fumed. Her hangover was horrible. She had smoked too many cigarettes. She knew she was slack and knew Marco to own a dormant brain. She considered leaving him, joining Alcoholics Anonymous then, illogically, of joining Roger and his animal appeal. She wasn't well. Not far from vomiting. Every morning now, notwithstanding the amount she had or hadn't drunk the night before. Marco's drinking left him with little leaning to romance whereas Roger, however inebriated, seldom faltered in this respect. All the same, of the two, she favoured Marco, in particular with this promise of property.

But Roger had his points. Even when the worse for wear, he wrote his columns and breakfasted at a reasonable hour. For Flavia, nosy by nature, it was Roger's past involvement with her mother-in-law that intrigued her and carried her one stage further in her dealings with him than instinct willed. The ping that Muriel heard in the night had been Flavia urging Roger to join them. Marco had stood beside her, egging her on. With Flavia feeling seedy he needed Roger to help him knock back bottles.

Flavia kicked Marco. 'There ought to be breathalysers on telephones.'

'Come on Flave. It'll be fun. We're no good on our own with Ma.'

'Shouldn't we try? She can be tricky, though. Roger says she was dreadful to ditch. Whinged and blubbed and nearly topped herself. Poor old bat.'

Marco rose. 'Let's get our show on the road. There's the train to meet and Ma to get round.' He walked to the window and looked to the haze on the hill.

Muriel stumped down the stairs to find Phyllis in the hall. With a sly stare, she proclaimed, 'Someone to see you Mrs Cottle.'

A man, clean-shaven, bright-eyed, middle-aged and wearing an evangelical expression, thrust his hand at her and spoke rapidly. 'My good lady. I'll start by mentioning that I take an interest in old coins. Anything old. It's my hobby, you might say.'

She watched him in silence as he rattled on. 'I use a metal detector and you'd be surprised by the treasure I've accumulated. Who plays that?' His eyes went to the deathly blackness of a grand piano.

'Might I try it? My mother was an entertainer but she didn't pass the gift on. I've got one tune - or did have.'

'Did have,' she judged as he played a few bars from *Home on the Range* with many mistakes.

He sprang from the stool. 'I come to the point. I'd like to hunt for treasures in your field.'

'Certainly,' said Muriel.

With amazed eyes and soothing voice, he told her that she was a truly good woman and promised to share proceeds from any Roman coins or agricultural implements that the detector might uncover in her field with the good lady herself. He told her that he was a member of the Salvation Army and that he lived in a nearby village.

Off he went to detect and Muriel quaked with fear lest she should join the Salvation Army, buy a metal detector or find herself rolling about in a Roman ditch with this unsavoury fellow, as she faced Phyllis's wrath.

'Mr Atkins told him time and time again to keep off the land here. Now. Well.' They glowered at each other as Muriel rapped out the order for another bed to be made up. Then she made for the kitchen in hopes of finding Kitty and to explain about the arrival of Roger in time for lunch. Roger. The utterly appalling - unwelcome at any time anywhere, given any circumstance - Roger.

She walked towards the kitchen, wishing with utmost fervour that things were otherwise. How happy she might have been on that hot day, quietly acquainting herself with the dawn of a new life, enjoying the church service and the excitement of Delilah as local eyes fell upon her. It might have been rewarding to have conquered Phyllis and the rest by careful timing and the use of authoritative manners but she was trapped into disadvantage; handicapped by Marco drooling and issuing invitations to the ultimate loose ender - free to catch a train (even whilst in a plaster cast) on a summer Sunday at the drop of a hat.

Would he make it in time for lunch? Sunday trains? A leer was sure to excite his features as he congratulated her on her newfound wealth, prior to exposing and raiding her cellar.

Roger.

Muriel, during one of her periods of gloom triggered by Hugh's defection, had tumbled into a fling with Roger. Peter was particularly non-committal and she was under-occupied.

Roger had called in for a browse at Lizzie's shop during a barren afternoon when Muriel had been in charge there. After her contretemps with the press, she had maintained a certain newsworthiness that had attracted the brute. She particularly resented having to remember this as she found herself in the kitchen telling Kitty that he was to be fed and housed within the day.

Her brief liaison with Roger had been gruesome from start to finish. He had used every opportunity to stupefy or to sponge off her. She recalled vile visits she had made to him in the northern outskirts of London. On the first of these she had driven grimly, willing things to take shape, squinting at a guide to the city streets that slithered on her knee. She had passed through inelegant streets and wondered that Roger had pressed her to visit his quarters. The entrance into the building where he lived was squalid, the front door half-hidden in a jumble of tumbling dustbins and scary pieces of flying paper. Motives for the visit escaped and avoided her but she made up her mind not to linger or to look back. Here she failed and returned to the scene.

Before her finger left the doorbell, she had heard footsteps. Roger wore a blue towelling dressing gown that stopped, short, above his knees. His feet were bare. He kissed her punchily on the lips and propelled her towards a dismal sitting room. Clearly he was not a home bird. Drink, glasses, newspapers and ashtrays but no pot plant or hearthrug. No lamps. Just gleaming light from above. Roger smelt of men's toiletries. His magnetism was crude, set apart from his person. He carried it about with him in a plastic bag.

The bedroom was cramped and housed little more than a double bed. Its purpose was soon and speedily served. A short night passed before he was up and asking if she wanted a cup of tea. 'Great that you came round.' He looked at a battery-operated clock that sat on the floor. 'A cup of tea and then, I'm afraid, I must be off. Pressure of work. Dearie me. I must get dressed, but do have a bath if you want one.' There lay Roger's strength. He was interested only in his next arrangement. Women were dismissed. He knew no shame and his victims lay hell-bent upon improvement or revenge. Nothing less.

He had wished to be deposited from her car in a central part of London. He did not pinpoint the spot but proposed a certain piece of pavement near Hyde Park.

It was horrible having to relive these moments, and Muriel cleared away Roger and all those who had inhabited her head in the garden. She appealed to Kitty.

Kitty said, 'Of course. That'll be nice for you. Company,' when learning that an extra visitor was expected.

Muriel made for the telephone. What could she say to Mambles? She'd have to ring Lizzie and explain her defection from the shop. She dreaded Lizzie's deadly eagerness. Her nosiness was unstoppable. She was ill at ease when those she knew failed to remain in the slot she allowed them and the slot allowed to Muriel by Lizzie was not that of landowner. Before reaching the instrument, Muriel hummed a tune and sang words firmly under her breath.

'My story is far too sad to be told
For practically everything leaves me totally cold.'

It occurred to her that her mind was slipping in every direction. It was only a matter of time before she joined Jerome and the, as yet, invisible matron. Marco and Flavia would seize the reins and install Roger as major-domo in charge of liquid refreshment. She urged herself to take a pull. She was in a position of extraordinary power. Chatelaine.

Something warm and wet touched her leg. It was ginger and it startled her. Muriel had almost forgotten Monopoly; had supposed, without fully focusing, that he had wandered away down passages and into rooms and that he was appreciating priceless chattels.

'Oh Josephine,' she pleaded. 'Stay with me for a while.' Monopoly pushed his head under her hand. Fortified by his unconditional encouragement, she dialled the number of the grace and favour residence and asked to be put through to HRH Princess Matilda.

'How are things going,' the morning voice replied, 'in your horrid house? I can't make head or tail of what's going on. You're here one day and gone the next. What about our rendezvous? Marco rang yesterday to ask where you were. Of course I told him as best I could, but I didn't understand why he was in the dark. Why the mystery?'

So that was it. Under pressure she had given Mambles the general particulars of her whereabouts. 'Is there something fishy about it? Mummy keeps asking.'

Her voice soared and stretched as Monopoly lay quiet at Muriel's feet with his paws wrapped around her bare ankles. His presence kept her steady as Mambles continued, 'I'm having such a horrid time and you're no help at all.' She was officially angry. 'That dreary old Cunty is coming to lunch today and I always count on you when she insists on barging in.'

Muriel winced, as she always did, when Mambles spoke of Cunty. Cunty had been Mambles's governess. Her real name was Miss Crunthard and the royal family, much given to the dishing out of nicknames, had christened her Cunty early in her employment. The pet name had come about, in part, owing to the inability of King George VI to pronounce his r's.

Nobody, not even Miss Crunthard herself, had ever dared to protest and, on the whole, friends of the family had swallowed the awkwardness without too many a snigger, and the old brigade queried it no more. Muriel, though, could never quite accustom herself to the indignity silently suffered by the ageing governess.

'You know how tedious Cunty is, always going on about my first trip on the underground.'

Muriel, revelling in a hot lick from the curled-up dog, broke in. 'I'm sorry about Cunty but it's difficult here. I need a while to take it all in. As I told you, the old man isn't even a relation and it has all fallen on me out of the blue. He's not dead. Just off his trolley.'

As she said this she realised that something blocked the light and that she was in near darkness. Wheezing drowned Monopoly's soft breathing and Muriel looked to her left. It was Dulcie who had cast the shadow and Dulcie who showed no respect for the fact that Muriel was engaged in conversation. She spoke loudly to gain ground. 'For a start, I would not say that Mr Atkins was off his trolley, and when you have finished with that damned machine, I want to ring the health centre about that knife you stuck in my mouth last evening.'

Dulcie's huge, hard stomach was hideously close and Muriel, with her free hand, pushed forcefully at it and said, 'Go away. Can't you see I'm talking?'

Dulcie spluttered. 'There's one thing I will not tolerate and that is physical violence.' She let loose an expletive but, to Muriel's astonishment, charged off in the direction of the kitchen.

Returning to Mambles, Muriel explained about the hiccup. Then, 'Where was I? Yes. Off his trolley.'

Mambles whined for a while and held tight to her determination to harass her friend into issuing an invitation for, apart from her date with Cunty, she was at a loose end. Like Roger.

64

Muriel relented and told Mambles that she could come for one night. Wednesday night, with Jubilee, chauffeur, maid and God knew what. Dulcie must practise her curtsey.

Marco and Flavia had not resurfaced, as far as she knew, and she decided to tackle Lizzie before events overtook her. Lizzie was frightfully cross. She had not been dropped more than a hint by Muriel - a hint relayed by Peter with a wispy word about 'property'. Her voice was staccato and Muriel could almost hear the tic-tic-tic of her high-heeled shoe as she tapped it against the marbleised linoleum in her hall.

'I'm sorry.' Lizzie nearly always started a sentence with 'I'm sorry'. 'I'm sorry but you've got to tell me what you're up to.'

Muriel spoke softly as there was no knowing when Dulcie might steal up beside her. As well as she was able, she encapsulated her tale; it was not an easy one to synthesise.

'So. Are you frightfully rich?'

Muriel chested her cards.

'No, but, seriously, how much? Is it a proper estate? Will you be seriously rich like Lupin and Madge?'

'God knows.'

'Well. I'm selling the shop. It's worth thousands, so when the deal goes through, I'll have masses of lovely money too, like you.' A little laugh. A little 'aren't-we-all-awful' laugh.

Lizzie possessed a sharp, quick brightness and quantities of sex appeal. Age appeal too. Muriel's father had thought the world of her. 'So responsive,' he would say as Lizzie left her scent behind her in the air. Jerome was certain to fall for her. Better not let Lizzie loose in the geriatric wing.

Muriel, not perfectly confident, cried, 'Please Lizzie. Don't. I'm distraught.'

'I can't say that I'm sorry for you. Still. Once I've sold the shop, I'll be able to hold my own.'

'Your tongue. Hold that,' Muriel said to herself but, for Lizzie, she tried a burst of hollow laughter. 'You will indeed.'

At least she was not to be faced with the complication of extricating herself from helping in the shop. But Lizzie with nothing to do! Another loose ender! Then came the words, 'I'm sorry but I've got to come and see. When would be best for you?'

Best? Marco, Flavia, Mambles, Roger and now Lizzie.

'What about the weekend?' Muriel fervently hoped to have ousted the others by then.

As she broke off she heard noises in the hall. Marco and Flavia, dressed to the nines in summer wear, appeared agog; lively and eager.

'Hi Ma. Have you chilled out? What about breakfast? Have you found a train for Roger yet?'

It was past ten o'clock and the matter was urgent if Roger were to lunch, however late, at Bradstow Manor.

'Look Marco. Do it yourself. I'm frantic.'

Barbarism ate at her sensitivities. A roughness of revenge, long hidden, took charge of her every instinct. She was a mouse that had learnt how to bite.

'Go to the kitchen and ask Kitty for a cup of coffee. Breakfast is off.'

Dulcie stood indefatigably amongst them. 'Coffee's off too. Cooker's gone out and as for trains....' She knew the timetables by heart; back to front. Not that she had ever travelled. Sundays, holidays, changes in the clock. She spouted as she looked at the ceiling. Marco jumped at one of the trains that she mentioned; one that could transport Roger to the local station by one-thirty. That would fit, given leeway with a late luncheon. 'I'll ring him now,' said Marco, pleased to be acting with efficiency.

Flavia faced her mother-in-law. 'So, Chick. What got into you this morning?' She gave Muriel a hug as one bestowing forgiveness. 'Cheer up. You don't mind about Roger any more. You told me so yourself. After all, you introduced us to the guy in the first place. We could hardly help it if we became friends.' Muriel was being blamed and it was most unjust.

Flavia was twisting things; laying everything at the door of Muriel's misery, when the feckless Roger of her shame had been so warmly taken up by her son. Tears formed in her eyes as she turned away. They would never cease to torture her. Dulcie had followed Marco to the telephone lest he needed prompting when it came to train times, and Muriel explained to Flavia that she and Monopoly were going out for an hour or two. They were to visit Mr Atkins. 'It's the least I can do.' She sighed and hoped that her words would show Flavia that there were strings attached. Flavia merely replied, 'Righto. I'm going to do some mega exploring. Wheee.'

She pirouetted in her pretty frock.

Back at the bin, Muriel left Monopoly in the car; thinking to open a window. She walked into the hall to find it unmanned and wondered whether, on a Sunday, they were short-staffed. She passed the deserted reception desk and went on down towards a wide passage where kidney bowls and dressings lined the walls, but no nurse, most certainly nobody gorgeous, came to greet her. She had learned from Arthur that there were both wards and private rooms in this hospital and that Jerome occupied one of the private ones at great expense. (Great expense? So quick to be totting up her outgoings.)

Dawdling down the passage she looked to the left and then to the right in the hope of spotting her benefactor through the glass. Half way along, through an open door and in a cubicle, she saw him. He wore a dressing gown and slippers and sat in the clanking chair in which he had been wheeled away the week before. His head was slumped forward to rest on his chest. His hands, both chalky white, clasped at the rails. A motionless tableau.

Muriel tiptoed towards him and touched a hand. He blinked and jerked his head up to face her. She felt sick. Slowly he loosened his grip on the arm of the chair and held out one hand to her. This she took whilst bending down to put herself at his level. She looked into his face and said, 'I've come to visit you.' No answer. As she continued to look at him she noticed that his teeth were larger than she remembered and that the top row stuck out over his lower lip so that his mouth was not exactly open as she had first believed. His hair had been smarmed down and his head appeared smaller than it had on the day of their one and only meeting.

As she held his hand she began to wonder if she had entered the right cubicle. Most certainly she would not, under any other circumstances, have recognised him.

'Is there anything you need?' she asked, as the pressure of his hand increased but remained feeble. Muriel was convinced that he was smaller than the man she knew by sight; that he came from a different mould. She was not inclined to waste a morning chatting up someone else's uncle - not that he was hers. It would be a complete waste of time. If, on the other hand, he was Jerome, it would be appropriate to stick it out a bit longer.

She unwound her hand and left him alone while she searched for somebody in authority. Again the passages were empty, but when she reached the hall she met a big, bustling woman wearing a cotton coat and skirt. In spite of her dress she turned out to be the matron in weekend mufti. Muriel, not keen to expose her doubts, feigned to have not yet visited the patient. 'Can you kindly tell me where to find Mr. Atkins?' she asked. Matron beamed and led her straight back to the same silent figure with white hands. 'Here you are dear. A lovely young lady to see you.' Perhaps matron was rather gorgeous.

Muriel reinstated herself level with his knees, re-clasped one of the hands and thus remained in silence for three quarters of an hour, during which time she did not look at him but readily fancied how he looked. That was that. When she came to rise she was racked with pins and needles.

Monopoly, patient since his character change, marked time in the scorching car. As they drove away from the nursing home, past the bright flower beds and the grey grass, they turned to each other for company. Monopoly had shifted himself, scattering hair onto the passenger seat.

How strange, she meditated, that I could have failed to love this dog; any dog.

She put it down to Hugh and to his rascally excluding methods of conducting himself. His soppy handling of the dog had enraged her, particularly the foolish expression he adopted when tending him. There was something about Hugh, the combination of Hugh and Monopoly, that gave her the creeps. It was almost as though, at pinnacles of infidelity and falsehood, he considered that his unswerving love for this dumb creature exonerated him from other deeds.

Monopoly, of course, had irritated her too; had seemed to have no sense of her suffering but existed to promote Hugh's profligacy. Then there had been his interminable search for Hugh; even scouring the lavatory. She had found that disgusting. Now all was forgiven. Monopoly had changed sides. What, though, if Hugh were to return? Her brain, again, was buzzing with bothersome images as she drove home.

As she stepped from the car, dog at her heels, dread overpowered her but she knew at once that Marco had left for the station - for his car was not to be seen. She willed it that Flavia had accompanied him on his grizzly mission.

Dulcie, who had, to all outward appearances, forgotten about the punch-up, greeted her at the front door. 'Well. How was he?'

What was to be done about Dulcie? Did she have total freedom in the house? Where did she sleep? Had she always been permitted to enter any room, at any time, to make use of the telephone even when it was in the hands of another? To spurt blood over the furniture? What was this letter that she referred to with mysterious conceit? These questions were to be among the first to be put to Arthur the following morning.

'Not too good.'

'I knew it. I knew that the day you put him away he would disintegrate.' She pronounced the word clumsily and swayed in delight. 'If I'd had my way you never would have done it.' Muriel ignored Dulcie's superiority and headed for the kitchen. Kitty's magnetism spirited her there.

Muriel had asked Phyllis to prepare a barren room on the top floor of the house for Roger. Now she remembered with rage that his leg was in plaster. 'Kitty,' she said, 'I made a mistake about the room. Could I...do you think it would be possible...could Phyllis make up another one? The guest, the friend of my son, his leg is in plaster. I forgot.'

'Phyllis is off. Always was on a Sunday after midday. I used to take over with Mr Atkins for the rest of the day. I'll do it. Lunch is late and I've loads of time.'

'Hasn't the cooker conked out?' Kitty smiled and said, 'That was Dulcie I'll be bound. Don't pay attention. She says things as they come into her head. Then she'll forget them just as quick.'

'Where does Dulcie sleep?'

'Oh heavens. You poor dear. Nobody's told you anything. She sleeps out in the paddock in her van with the cats. Has done for donkey's years. Ever since early days when Mrs Atkins ran the show. They say she could wind Mrs A. round her little finger.' Kitty wiped her hands on a blue cloth and went about the business of attending to comforts for undeserving Roger on the first floor.

There was at least an hour before the party was due back from the railway station and Muriel gloated over the prospect of peace. While Kitty worked she would peruse her paradise uninterrupted. She would not answer the telephone, nor would she agree to be summoned to it. Dulcie could deal with Lizzie - or with Mambles come to that.

She willed her head to clear as she dwelt on the glories around her. Roses bulged in tubs and vases. Who picked them? Who arranged them?

She placed herself in the hall in a winged armchair furnished in frail chintz, and crossed one leg over the other. The struggle reflected in her face began to evaporate as, with an effort of will, she ceased to be tormented by delirious imaginings. Placing her hands at her sides, she gazed upwards to a large portrait that hung above an oriental wooden sofa opposite to where she sat. It showed a languid lady dressed in lace and muslin, seated out of doors on a fine day under a spread of dark branches, one hand at her beaded throat whilst the other caressed a miniscule dog, smaller than any that Muriel had encountered.

Her expression was carefree and vacant. Muriel, faced with this untroubled creature, felt firm and blameless. For all she cared Monopoly could do as he pleased. He was nowhere to be seen. He was at liberty to chase cats, bother Dulcie, roam freely. Muriel intended to freeze out all interlopers with authority. Not a soul disturbed this period of time. Her will kept Dulcie at bay. She sat for a long while under the portrait to be disturbed only by the reassuring sight of Kitty who came to say, 'It's two o'clock Mrs Cottle. I see they're not back yet but there's no need to worry. Lunch will keep.'

Two o'clock. They were late but that was nothing new. Nonetheless, at any second, she must expect the presence of Roger, as championed by her son. They were likely, all three, to be alarmed by the change in her manner, by the power of her newly-formed presence. Recollections of the jauntiness of Roger's gait and manner, of his seeming to be untouched by any sense of shame, swam before her as quickly as she strove to suppress them.

As her resolves multiplied, she heard the unruly roar of Marco's car outside the front door. This she had kept wide open to let air into the house as she ruminated. Here she had erred for the hall was cool and the outside air was hot and humid. She would never make a proper country person.

She rose and walked to the spot where the car had pulled up, scattering gravel.

Roger, unmistakeable, sat in the front passenger seat, Flavia behind. At a glance Muriel could tell that they were all a trifle tipsy and deduced that they had stopped at a pub on the way back from the station, disregarding the lunch hour. Forewarned that lack of enthusiasm in her reception of Roger would place her in the dock, she muttered 'kind but firm' under her breath, as both Marco and Flavia raced to where Roger sat and made to help him out of the car. Plaster; crutches; smug infirmity. He was, unsteadily, on his feet and she saw that he wore a long white caftan and sported a pair of orange crutches with shiny metal tops. Recollections of her fling with Roger enraged her as she looked straight into his steely grey eyes, and as he gave her the sidelong attention of an intimate enemy. Poised between comedy and tragedy, she planted a kiss upon his face and uttered a vague greeting. A longing for decency, for respectability, flooded her soul and she wished to heaven that she were young and a virgin.

'Hi Ma. We stopped for cocktails. Roger needed one for his leg. He's pretty impressed already.'

'Certainly am, Madame.' How he vexed her as he fumbled for his crutches.

Muriel said, 'I'll leave you to get yourselves into the house while I go and say that we can start lunch.' Firm.

Marco had spoken out of turn when he reported that Roger had shown himself impressed. In fact Roger strained every muscle, in plaster or not, to appear to take calmly the twist in Muriel's life. For him it was a maiming sadness that he had been born with 'no background' and now he strained with the effort to appear at ease and untitillated by Bradstow Manor. For, many were the manors where he knew the ropes, and many were the cellars where he had lubricated his expert lips.

With scuffles and grunts from the wounded visitor, the party congregated around the table where the three had dined the evening before. Unconfrontational supremacy. That was Muriel's aim.

The hatch went up and Kitty cooed, 'All vegetables fresh from the garden by the way.'

Flavia, too tiddly to talk, sat silent, a fragile china teacup filled to overflowing. Marco, tiddly too, jabbered ceaselessly. He wished for Roger to be aware that these were early days; that things would be looking up; that vulgar voices rising from a hatch were soon to be things of the past.

Muriel's scheme was put to the test as she kept up lively conversation with Kitty, engaging in deliberate mateyness as example to her son. It was, in some ways, fortunate for her that the three had returned from the station the worse for wear so, rather than reprimand them, she increased the dosage, aware of her own rashness; there was every chance that she encouraged them to swig a fortune's worth.

'Try this Roger,' she ordered. Holding a bottle of red Burgundy and reading from the label, she announced, '1959 Château Cheval Blanc. Could be good. You'll be able to tell us.'

Roger, whose eyebrows had shot up, sipped and said, 'Squisito'. He held up his hand, pressed forefinger to thumb, closed his eyes and whispered, 'Mmm. Soft and sweet.' His face was wet and waxy but his eyes, when open, continued to swing in wariness, professional excitement and calculated opposition.

Flavia slipped away.

'Touch of 'flu.' Marco beamed as he pushed at his plate and held his own glass out to Roger who was lurching and had allowed his orange crutches to fall to the floor. The men, with sacrilegious haste, polished off two bottles, declined to eat sugared currants and, with maximum kerfuffle over the sorting of Roger's crutches, left the room. They had sat at the table for less than twenty minutes. Marco called, 'We're both going to lie down. Don't, for God's sake, let that transvestite disturb us.'

Muriel ate as much as she could and called to Kitty that the others were unwell, not that the cover-up was necessary for Kitty had observed enough through the hatch. She replied, 'That'll give you some time to yourself. You haven't even seen round the whole house as yet. I'll make you a cup of coffee and then, if you want to that is, I'll take you on a guided tour.'

That, thought Muriel, is perfectly true. Jerome's bedroom for a start. Had he ever shared one with Aunt Alice?

To her surprise Dulcie stood stock still in Jerome's room, a cat curling round the khaki of her calves. She did not move but watched them both as though allowing for an audience. Jerome's room was dark. Curtains were drawn across the casement windows and the air in there, as had been his suit, was distressingly rank. Kitty drew back the curtains, closed since his departure, and Muriel's eyes made for the bed which prompted her to think that, apart from the smell of decay and various accoutrements of decrepitude, the room might have belonged to a boy. The iron-ended bed was narrow and mean, unmade and provided with but one pillow. The sheets were grey; Phyllis's laxity exposed. Bowls, basins and rubber cushions rested on a commode in an arbitrary corner of the room, and on a table beside the bed, half- hidden under a torn lampshade, bottles filled with pills congregated; a small army of aperients. It contrasted with the luxury elsewhere on that landing.

'My Aunt?' Muriel turned to Kitty. 'Where did she sleep?'

'She was before my time. I did live in the village then but I've only been coming in for two years. I believe she kept her own quarters; the ones your son and his wife are resting in.'

Dulcie remained still and silent but the cat continued to curl. At the window they looked out through small panes and spied Muriel's new friend, the man with the metal detector, wearing an unseasonable cap and scouring the field. As they watched they spotted a huge woman striding over the grass to join him and, for a while, the pair appeared locked in argument.

'That's Joyce.' Kitty defined. 'Don't mind her. She thinks she owns the place; has done ever since Mr Atkins allowed her to keep her sheep in the field. It'll be good for her to find that you're in charge. Outdoors as well as in.'

In charge.

They left Dulcie in Jerome's room. 'Searching for some letter,' Kitty explained. Bypassing occupied rooms, the women toured the house, Muriel's euphoria mounting. On a long wall over the stairs on the top floor, was a handsomely mounted array of antlers. Their owners had been shot decades earlier. The heads of warthogs, kudus and dwarf buffaloes looked glassily down at her. The rooms up there were dirty and smelled of cat. 'Dulcie has reared a few litters up here,' said Kitty. 'Hyacinths. They say that hyacinths do the trick. It's only by putting them in a room that you can get rid of the smell.'

As they stood on the top landing a loud 'Cooee' reached their ears. Muriel started and Kitty said, 'We'll have to see the rest some other time.'

'Cooee. It's me. Delilah. We were sorry not to see you in church. Dawson's outside. We were taking a walk. We usually do on a Sunday afternoon and Jerome has always allowed us to roam around his grounds. Gorgeous place. I just popped in to ask if we are able to carry on as usual.'

Had the young ones not been drunk they would have been awoken by this interruption, so clear were Delilah's tones. Curls and teeth came close. 'We heard that your son and daughter-in-law were here. What did I tell you? You never lose them, do you? And a friend, Dulcie tells me. Lovely when they bring their friends home. My boy, one of my boys I should say, Geoffrey, is down for the night. Could you bring them all round for a drink this evening?'

'Where is Dulcie? She was upstairs a little while ago.'

'Dulcie? Oh she usually goes out on her motorbike at weekends. In the week too, come to that. You should see it. Huge great thing. Actually she has several. Keeps them in beautiful condition. She has friends over at the cat sanctuary in Winspey. They are very good to her.'

Through the open door Muriel saw Dawson drawing on his pipe.

'Oh dear. Not tonight. There's so much to do, what with the meeting with Arthur tomorrow morning. So many things to see to. By the way,' she wished to be seen to have done her duty, 'I called in at the home this morning.'

Delilah was agape. 'What a kindly act! How did you find him?'

Muriel told her, acknowledging as she did so that she had barely registered the dramatic decline that had affected him in so short a space of time.

'He'll pass away, then, before long. Lost his spirit. I'll get Dawson to pop over. He's lovely with the dying but then, as I mentioned, he's an academic. Now, what about tonight? It would do you good to take a break. I've never been one to recognise the age gap. You're as old as you feel, don't you agree? I'm sure you do. All the same it is lovely for young people to get together sometimes. Does your son have any hobbies? Our Geoffrey was thrilled when he heard you had young down here.'

Muriel's mind wheeled to the three who slumbered through the afternoon of superb sunlight.

'Unfortunately their friend has had an accident. His leg is in plaster so he can't get around.' She added, 'Other than with difficulty,' to cater for Roger's arrival by train of which Delilah was certain to have heard. How was the woman to be kept at bay? 'I think, if you don't mind, we'll lie low for a day or two. I'll ring you up as soon as I can see the wood from the trees.'

'What a lovely expression.' Shaking her curls and rattling her teeth, Delilah followed her husband to the edge of the lawn. She was bitterly disappointed not to have lured the new occupants of the big house before anyone else grabbed them, but Dawson replied when she told him the sad news, 'It takes all sorts.'

Muriel was trapped. She could not explore the garden for fear of bumping into Dawson and Delilah, or the field for fear of confrontation with the metal detector or the woman who kept sheep. It came to her that she had no right to allow the metal detector to detect in the field. She was, after all, only heir to the place. She was not yet the owner. It would have been appropriate to have waited until after the meeting with the sweetie before dishing out permissions.

After eating so much lunch she was near to vomiting and resentful of having had to swallow dishes disdained by the drunkards; anxious, too, about the potentially startling contents of the cellar. Just then there was a noise of juddering feet at the door and the frame was filled by a man of fearsome build. She tuned to a nearby looking glass and took a peep at herself as she advanced upon the visitor. It was a relief that her legs remained long and her hair still bouncy. Had she not, at that moment, seen her reflection in the glass, she would have been hard put to believe that her general appearance had survived.

The man, who was dishevelled and smelled of cowpat, wore soiled dungarees zipped up in front and he carried a can.

'Put it this way. I would have come along before, but my wife said to give you time to settle.'

'I haven't.'

Her snappy reply alarmed him and he twitched and moved his feet upon the mat.

'It's like this. I thought I'd give you time to settle before coming along. As you know, I'm head gardener here. Have been all along – back in the days when they both took an interest.'

Muriel brightened. Perhaps he was to be illuminating.

'She told me to have a word with you. My wife did. She heard from Dulcie that you'd taken charge.' He treated her to a sad expression as she offered excuses. 'If you're not in charge then who is? That's what I need to know. That Joyce, thinks she owns the place – ever since he said she could keep her bees down by the greenhouse. They block the entrance. Can't get in or out. Not without danger to myself. That and the sheep.'

Muriel mentioned the meeting with Arthur and told the man, whose name was Eric, that he would be advised as soon as somebody knew what to say.

'Is there somewhere that Mr Atkins, er, saw people? An office or something?' It was unimaginable that Eric should enter the house caked in cowpat.

'Never saw no one. Not in recent years, that is. Not unless he got buttonholed.'

She closed the door on him and made for the chair where she had known peace but, before she sat, Kitty called that she was wanted on the telephone. A woman. Without a shadow of doubt the woman on the other end of the line was hysterical.

'I'm his wife and I'll stand by him,' she bellowed through thunderous sobs. 'I do. I've always stood by him. Wouldn't you stand by your husband?' Muriel, wondering whether she had been rumbled already, said nothing. 'It's me what told him to come and see you. Has he been along?'

'He's just left. Eric you mean?'

'Eric. That's him. He's not appreciated. It's her - that Joyce. Tells him he isn't doing his job.' The sobs became harsher and more unruly, no longer allowing for words. Muriel embarked on her spiel concerning her uncertain position.

Kitty wished to know about supper; if it would be in order to leave something for Muriel to heat up or whether they would be content with a cold meal. She didn't normally stay late on Sunday evenings. Mr Atkins usually took high tea then watched television until bedtime; no matter what was showing.

'Phyllis will come in but I think you'll find she'll go straight to her room.'

Muriel said 'yes' to everything but was too tired to ask advice. She wondered if there was a washing-up machine. No good asking the ne'er-do-wells to lend a hand.

'Sufficient unto the hour…' She spoke quietly, realising with alarm that in recent days she had taken to talking to herself. From a window she watched Monopoly sniffing at shrubs.

Kitty made matters in the kitchen plain, and together they laid the table in the dining room. There were many questions that Muriel wanted to put to Kitty but weariness suffused her. She clasped her hands behind her back and, cracking at her finger joints in taut snaps, paced the floor and remembered that, as yet, her legs were still long.

A few minutes passed before she found herself followed. The coin-collector was at her side, gleefully emptying the contents of a linen pouch onto the surface of a leather-topped drum table.

'Charles the Second,' he announced in rapture, as he held up a blackened coin for her inspection. 'Buckles, pennies, a farthing or two. I have to tell you, my good lady, I've seldom indulged in such happy hunting. It's the history that gets to me. Just think of the people from the past who have wandered on your land. Now I shall go home and polish these bits up. One thing, though, I must mention. I was, I don't like to say it, treated like a criminal out there by a lady who came to see what I was doing. Making holes in the grass - she said I was. That's not true. No. Here I tell a lie. I do have to make a small hole but I always fill it in behind me. Meticulous I am about it. I'm a Christian gentleman as I said. One more thing, my good lady, before I go,' his voice conspiratorial, 'I would be grateful if I could reserve the honour for myself.'

Muriel tried to coax a crackle from her finger joints but she had performed the trick too recently for any noise to emerge.

'I said to her. Said it straight, that you had given me permission and, well, I don't like to tell you this but, er, well…' Muriel halted him with her hand.

Through the open door she saw Dawson and Delilah on their return to the rectory. Their heads were close and it was clear that something of importance was under discussion. They were planning one more intense effort to persuade her and her young to socialise. She waved the man and his metal detector away and returned to the looking glass. She wished to take advantage of further investigation to prove that, whatever else, her body stayed stable. As with effort she tightened her belt by one notch, she noticed that a figure stood beside her; reflected in the glass.

She turned round and found herself eyeball to eyeball with Joyce who wore shorts, exposing red legs and a shirt too tightly buttoned. Her face was pinched which was unexpected given that the rest of her was solidly fat; her hair short and greasy and her overall impression most unpleasing. Was she another of Aunt Alice's recruits? Was a letter of promise lurking in some cranny for her too?

Eyes pink and frenzied, Joyce smashed the silence. 'I saw that Eric had been here. Had to get his word in first, I suppose. I've been allowed to keep my bees down by the greenhouse since heaven knows when. He's been at them with a stick and now I've got two angry hives on my hands. I don't know if you have any knowledge of bee-keeping?'

'Not much. I'm Muriel Cottle, by the way.'

'I assumed as much. Was it you who told that dreadful man he could hunt for coins in the field? Heavens above! We'll never get rid of him now. He's no better than he should be.' Muriel might have perpetrated a massacre judging by the look this woman gave her. 'We've been trying to keep him off the land for donkey's years. Holes in the field. A sheep could break its leg out there.'

'Whose sheep?'

Joyce coloured to a sultry mauve from her chin to her hairline. 'Mine, as a matter of fact. And, in case you didn't know, I provide this house with free honey.'

Muriel mounted the stairs and made for the bathroom. As she closed the door she heard the telephone trill in the distance. Soon she was shoulder deep in water.

Chapter 7

Airily dressed for dinner, Muriel left a message on her American friend's answering machine. He was called Jackson and she urged him to join her in time for Mambles's visit. Then she checked on potions in the drawing room, where coarsely-carved Elizabethan grapes divided the ceiling into moulded panels and where the walls were rough and bumpy and almost entirely obscured by paintings in faded frames. As she counted glasses on a wooden chest behind a sofa, she heard the frantic attempts of Roger as he descended the stairs unattended. What were Marco and Flavia up to? She was doomed to spend time alone with him. His efforts were noisily emphasised and expletives sounded out at every step.

Muriel made no attempt to go to his aid but stood, smoking and looking out of the French window (added, she supposed, by the Victorians in sensible desire to let in light). At one moment she pressed her hot forehead against a domed glass lampshade.

When Roger came into the room, Muriel turned to acknowledge him but uttered not a sound. He was white from head to toe. The plaster that encased the lower part of his left leg was, not surprisingly, chalky in its brightness. But the rest of him! His hair, she saw for the first time, was white – if thick – and not unlike Jerome's. He wore a white shirt and white shorts. His face, damp, shone a ghostly ivory and only his crutches stood out in fiery hue.

'Very comfortable bed. Not bad, eh, this place?'

'No. No. Not bad at all.'

Roger, unnerved by Muriel's constantly altering manner towards him, folded his crutches and, with maximum manoeuvre placed himself upon the sofa, still stained with Dulcie's blood despite vicious scrubbing by Kitty. He shifted and, with both hands, humped the injured leg to a position of better comfort.

Muriel knew, for she had been party to his paltriness, that he was not a man but a machine; an inferior one. Bits of his brain were missing. It shocked her to remember that she had driven a thousand detours immersed in amorous dreams to ease his practical burdens; lifelessly alive, fetching and carrying with tense energy. She had waited long in pubs for his late appearances, preoccupied with passion. He had taken her to the races and told her that she was the 'tops'.

She handed him a glass of whisky poured from Marco's bottle, and asked, 'Are the others awake?'

'Absolutely. I heard merry prattle coming from the magnificent bathroom.' He chuckled as, remembering the wine at lunch, it occurred to him that he might do well to re-hook his hostess. Had he not always deserved the prop of a country estate? He would take up shooting, fishing maybe; hunting was not out of the question. Tally-ho.

'So. Tell me Roger. How did you break your leg?'

'Thereby hangs a tale.'

Again he chuckled as he picked his nose. It came back to her that he had always been a nose-picker and it vexed her that he should, in the past, have winced when she cracked her knuckles. She had never reprimanded him for his habit; deeming it too grave to be mentioned.

His eyes lit on a copy of *The Sunday Times* that had been set upon a stool near the window. He signalled to his companion, 'Wonderful woman. The paper please. I left mine on the train. Crutches. Ha. Ha.'

Muriel, interested to note that she supported such a weekly paper, rolled her eyes and took it to him, thinking how incorrigible he was - picking and pleading and sipping in washy white. Although his mannerless scrutiny of the newspaper irritated her, it was better than having to talk.

After twenty minutes spent thus, they were joined by the pair from above. 'Heavens Ma! Had you forgotten that the fridge is stuffed with champagne for this evening? You've started Roger on whisky. Swig it down, old man, then we can get on with more serious matters. Receptacles on the way. Me and Flave'll go for the nectar.'

They left the room as Dulcie appeared, bent as a croquet hoop, whiskers brushing an array of engraved champagne glasses arranged upon a tray. She plonked it down, with a series of shuddering tinkles, on a chest where the bottles vied for space. As she did so, and as she straightened up, she chortled, 'About time too. I've always maintained that what this place needed was a bit of appreciation. Now, when Mrs Atkins was alive, - Alice, she was to me - there were regular celebrations. Absolutely regular.'

After a pause she resumed reminiscence. 'Not with him. He never had the faintest idea. Not the faintest.'

Roger hastened to polish off the whisky in his glass. He flinched to be seen to exude disapproval, to show that he knew how country houses were run. Not in this way. Not with scope for insubordinates in the drawing room. Dulcie went to the window; wishing to witness the subdued popping of corks. The champagne, several bottles, arrived and Dulcie made no move. Roger said, 'Ahem. Ahem. Muriel,' and pointed at the onlooker.

Muriel ignored all signals as Marco exclaimed, 'How about this?' He reassured the company. 'Don't worry about lack of flying corks. This is ancient stuff. Hardly a bubble in it.'

Flavia, glass in hand, made for Muriel. 'Come on Chick. We're all on for a piss-up. Don't be uptight.'

Muriel recognised a distant whiff of old age rising from the orange contents of her glass as Dulcie moved from position of spectator and made for the door. The route she had chosen, a circuitous one, was blocked by Roger's leg that stuck out before him like a giant slug.

'If you will kindly move that leg of yours, I'm off to do a mile or two on my exercise bike.'

Roger, who had already absorbed several glasses of champagne following fast on whisky which had followed on a long and drunken sleep, was not alert to the mixture of reactions that romped around him. Most certainly he was not going to inconvenience himself by attempting to provide a passage for this creature.

Yet Marco, it was manifest, had decided to make a feature of Dulcie. Did she not constitute a cabaret? Did not an aristocratic estate, by divine right, possess a jester? A jester was as good as a ghost. He pictured some of his friends in stitches at the sight of the androgynous creature pedalling on her exercise bike.

Roger ordered, 'Marco. Please can you explain to the good lady that my leg is painful. Ouch. I suggest that she finds an alternative egress.'

'What the hell is an egress, I'd like to know? I've never appreciated fancy words. Now. Let me pass.'

Dulcie moved the leg herself, twisting and contorting it with savagery as Roger winced, swore and sweated. Then she headed, powerful with purpose, for her bike; Doc Martens upon Aubusson; wry smile on her lips.

After Dulcie's departure, the room, apart from the sounds of constant pouring and clinking, seemed half empty, for those left behind remained consumed with thought.

Roger, irascible and hazy, determined that Muriel pull herself together and eradicate absurdity from the place. He began, even, to imagine that with his support this transformation might come about. He looked shiftily at Marco. But Flavia put her money on Muriel as she considered a rosy future. 'You know what, Chick. You ought to try corrective green. It's a sort of face powder. It would make you look a trillion years younger – not that you need to.'

Marco was ebullient. 'Listen, Ma. Is there a billiard room? And what about a library? Haven't seen a single book since I crossed the threshold. I'll get Dulcie to set up a conducted tour tomorrow and I wouldn't say no to a ride on one of her bikes. Zoom. Zoom.'

He was unsteady on his feet but his words flowed easily as Muriel panicked about dinner. It was after nine o'clock and she thanked her lucky stars that she had opted for cold meat and salad. It was certainly beyond her to set about heating dishes and carrying them around after this painful stretch of the evening.

Soon she must order them all through into the dining room where another empty example of wastage lay ahead. She was scared and ashamed. It was difficult about Dulcie. Half of her agreed with Roger that the woman's odd presence must be rooted out; but the other half acknowledged that it amused her, and when things were organised perhaps she might make an ally of the old retainer. She wanted to swat Flavia. Grinning and sucking up and calling her Chick and telling her to use corrective green.

She looked at her boy. She loved him and at least he was outgoing. He did not camouflage his thoughts or represent them as other than they were. Once again she picked up scattered pieces of her past. Like stop-press news from a remote star, a vision appeared. Marco, twelve years old, picnicking in spring on a southern slope of Monte Albano. Dark watch, too large for his thin wrist. Stars of Bethlehem grew amongst coarse grass and tall campions stood out, mauve, against white blossom. Marco had tugged her into a roughly-built house, reputed to be Leonardo da Vinci's birthplace. Her boy had been alive. Now she chided her son vehemently for allowing Roger to be there, drunk and clad in white, when she was all at sea; drowning in complexity.

Supper was, as Muriel feared, a repetition of lunch. Little was spoken and less eaten; plenty drunk. Again she stuffed herself with Kitty's fare and again she wondered whether or not she kept chickens. Eventually she left them to it with fine wines, and went to her room where she found Monopoly sprawled across the foot of her bed. It was a tonic to see him there but, since the night was hot, and never before had she slept with a dog on her bed, she manoeuvred him cautiously, uttering nonsensical blandishments, into his basket.

She lay down under a light cover and thought of the ordinary things that many mull over before sleep. In the morning she would be downstairs at an early hour; she would beat them all to it and clear away corks from pots, vases and from under chairs. Bottles, too, must be hidden before Phyllis's acid eye led her to accept that her fears were confirmed.

Then there was the dining room. More corks and bottles and a mountain of food to be concealed. Yet again she longed to know whether or not she kept chickens. If not, she meant to do so. Not long before, she had seen a cluster of Black Silkies when staying with distant cousins in the country. They were small birds and their heads were crested; their feathers a mixture of fur and velvet. Very dark. One of her cousin's Silkies had won second prize at a Poultry Club show.

Imperceptibly these considerations transformed into grotesque images as in the darkest chapter of a children's book. The usual tranquillity of her pillow let her down as she tried to recreate her own sanity in the maelstrom of her mind. Her head felt light, as though from the depths of sleep she was entering an unhealthy and dangerous situation.

Roger, wearing an indigenous mask, stood at the bed. A flow of boiling saliva escaped from a corner of his mouth. His eyes were rheumy and his wounded leg stood out in clarity; a traffic signal in the fog.

Without warning his form was replaced by that of Marco, smoking and wearing a dressing gown. He stood beside Muriel in front of a triple mirror and, as each scrutinised the other's multiple reflections, a sunny, silver-framed photograph that she always carried with her, of the boy, aged seven or eight, amidst flowers, was reflected, too, in the glass, and took them both wandering back to early days when they had known happiness alone together.

They had headed for Volterra. Muriel at the wheel, they drove past flocks of black sheep; spindly and spare, and through fields of sunflowers; huge heads bowed on leafless stalks like nudists dropping their heads in modesty. The boy smiled and, uncorrected, sucked his thumb. As drought dried the countryside, tractors ploughed the chocolate earth scattering cornflowers and butterflies while men and women toiled across miles of burnt-out hillside. As the car shot forward the climate changed. They crossed a dry river bed, then climbed golden hills; orangey-rust as the champagne from her cellar. Fields rose in ridges beyond clumps of coarse corn, shining ilex and feathery acacia trees. Figs were ripe, splitting open to display the moths of a thousand tiny sharks. They drove into the town through a thick wooden gate, hammered with nails, onto uneven flagstones.

No trace of Hugh.

Out of the blue came the most petrifying insult of all. Marco turned on her. The balding, smoking Marco. He bawled at her for her failure to rear him correctly, for his weaknesses and limitations, adding a torrent of complaint about the collapse of her marriage, her foolish affair with Roger, her futility when it came to the commanding of a household.

As the tableau misted and her gatecrashers dissolved into specks, she turned on the light beside her bed, looked at the clock and waved her legs in the air. Monopoly breathed easily and Muriel slithered out of bed and went to the basket. She laid her head upon the moulting back of the dog where she found reassurance, then returned, with equilibrium, to bed and to practical plans.

She determined that there was to be no false dawn. She fell asleep again.

Chapter 8

Muriel lay in bed after her mouldy night following a mouldy day. Screech owls had kept her awake for a while even after the nightmares had dissolved. Monopoly slept throughout.

She and her dog started early in the morning. It was a shambles downstairs but she hit on a method of making light of the work. Every time she retrieved a champagne cork or cigar butt, she stared at the empty space and pretended that it had been spirited away by unseen hands. She did this rhythmically in time to noiseless music, suspecting that she looked pathetic.

When the ground floor was tickety-boo, when she had unshuttered all windows and taken Monopoly for an airing, she stood tall and marked time, pending a battering. With a cup of coffee in her left hand, she sat at the kitchen table and wrote lists, mainly of queries for Arthur.

Phyllis came in looking tarty in a shiny navy frock, high-heeled shoes, mouth wet with lipstick. Her hair was pulled back and tied in a ponytail. As her arms wheeled, buttons on the navy frock came near to popping and Muriel sat, tense, hoping once again to avoid the subject of breakfast. Heaven alone knew when Marco and Flavia, let alone Roger, were likely to be ready for it. Her evasions were interrupted by a call to the telephone. It was Dawson, and Muriel fancied Delilah to be prompting him.

'Once you've got this meeting with Arthur behind you, we're hoping for a bit of a get-together. Plenty of beer down here; or plonk if you prefer it.' Plonkety–plonkety–plonk.

'Now. About the school. A report at the last meeting indicated a predicted overspend of three thousand pounds....' He droned on. 'Well. This, prorated 'til the year end, gives a predicted underspend of one thousand pounds. However the underspend is likely to be eroded. The overspend predicted at the last meeting was mainly associated with equipment. This biased the spend to the first half of the year – hence the elimination of the predicted overspend.' She treated him to a mumble and, as she rang off, heard the unmistakeable sound of Roger floundering down the staircase. He charged past Muriel, heading for the kitchen. She did not try to delay him but remained rigid by the telephone. Uttering many a curmudgeonly and roundabout phrase, he reached his destination as his hostess followed, slowly, behind him. She hid herself as he advanced on Phyllis and demanded a boiled egg.

'The freshest you have – and coffee –freshly-ground too if you please.'

She heard the buzz of Phyllis's petticoat as it rubbed against the nylon of her navy frock, held her breath and listened to the pair at play.

'Wonderful woman. Wonderful woman.' Worst fears confirmed. Roger was making a set at Phyllis.

'Another thing. A fork. Is there a long-handled fork? There's an itch. Down near the bottom of my plaster on the inside of my leg.'

Phyllis bustled off in search, perhaps, of an ancient toasting fork laid aside since the reign of Aunt Alice. A chair scraped and crutches squeaked against linoleum as Roger pulled himself towards the table and awaited the services of Phyllis. Muriel would have continued to eavesdrop but the telephone rang again.

It was Delilah. 'It's about the fete. I believe that I mentioned it to you briefly but the day draws nigh. We're all very anxious to know whether you will be willing to hold it in your grounds. The village is on tenterhooks. We keep the trestles in your shed, the triple-bay, we call it. Teapots, cups and saucers are all in the cupboard below your back stairs but I'm sure you know all this. I've told Dawson that you are prepared to do the fortune telling and he thinks it's a lovely idea.'

Partly because it was uncomfortable standing in the passage with the atmosphere of hideous flirtation wafting from the kitchen, and partly because she wanted to shut her up, Muriel interrupted. 'Yes. I don't see why not but I haven't had the famous meeting with Arthur yet. Can I mention all this to him?'

'No need. It's up to you. Arthur has never meddled in these matters. Might you help with the teas? That is to say, between telling fortunes. I run the fete committee and it's a terrible job filling slots. Dulcie sometimes lends a hand on the day; not that she'll commit herself in advance which makes it awkward, and then there are those who don't like to take their cup from her but, while we're on the subject, Dawson would be most grateful if you could let him have a bottle of plonk or suchlike for the tombola.'

Muriel promised to ring her when the meeting with Arthur had been consummated. Delilah answered, 'You do have a sense of humour,' as Muriel put the telephone down.

Roger's voice sounded out. 'Wonderful woman! Now my back. Here. Here. Lower down. Lower down. No! Higher up. Perfect.' Turning away, Muriel walked to the hall. Let her scratch him silly. She stood whiling away the time; aggrieved and in revolt against all responsible demands, wondering whether to order Arthur to revoke Jerome's crazy will. As she wondered, Roger, preceded by Phyllis, crashed into view. He had abandoned his crutches and depended on her shoulders, which he clutched from behind. Upon her face was a manifestation of triumph mingled with pain. In this tandem they made for an armchair where, with hurly-burly, Roger was lowered into the seat.

'Wonderful woman,' he uttered in jerky notes as Phyllis drew up a chair behind his and, entranced, scrutinised the visible part of his forefinger as the rest of it worked its way into a nostril.

'Phyllis,' Muriel asked, hell-bent upon shattering the spectacle, 'Where are we to hold the meeting?'

'Normally it would take place in the dining room.'

'Come with me then. We'll set it up. Mr Stiller will be here at ten o'clock.' She tried with deliberation to take her down a peg as she made to preen her way, via conquest of Roger, into a position of supremacy. Was it not her own aim, but via nobody, to arrive at that point?

'Very well.' Phyllis's red lips pulled together and her body stiffened as she rose to follow her mistress.

'How many will we be?'

'It's up to you.'

'Well. There's me and Mr Stiller. You and Sonia, I presume. Not Dulcie.' She was firm here. 'But it would be very useful to have Kitty with us. That'll do for this time round.' She had not yet met Mavis, the cleaner.

'What about your son? Shouldn't he and his wife be in on this?'

'They'll be asleep.'

'I could wake them. Roger, your gentleman guest, he'll be wanting to inspect the cellar shortly. I'm willing to give him a hand but I can't, can I, if I'm to be dragged into this business?'

Roger's play upon the sensitivities of this unnerving woman was indefensible and made her long to kill him with an orange crutch. She told Phyllis to arrange chairs around the table, to put out biscuits or whatever, to see to a round of coffee.

Knowing that she looked scrawny and unappealing, Muriel returned to Roger. 'For God's sake Roger, leave Phyllis alone. Can't you see what a foul position I'm in without your little tricks?'

'Lady of the Manor. Haw. Haw. Nothing the matter with your position. Take your cellar for a start. I rather like her. Sorry for her, you know. All these changes. Can't be easy. Calm down.'

It was hot again and her wits were trapped; darting as silver fish behind a pane of glass.

'Listen Roger. Just sit here. Don't move or wake anybody or invade the cellar or make up to Phyllis or pick your nose.' She had said it and he was startled.

'Sorry if I'm not wanted - but worry not! My plaster comes off on Wednesday and I have to be in London for that mid-morning. Marco and Flavia can drive me. I'm not taking the train again in this heat - or this condition.' Reprieve. They would all be out of the way before Mambles's arrival.

'Meanwhile I shall have to get down to work on that cellar of yours. Marco can help me when he stirs his stumps and, er, Phyllis, when you've finished with her.'

Nothing in particular was accomplished at the meeting even though Muriel had believed everything to hinge upon it. It was decided that Phyllis was to stay on as housekeeper, Sonia as secretary, Kitty as cook, Mavis as cleaner and Dulcie as watchdog for a three-month trial run. Their duties were defined by Arthur and Muriel, and it was determined that a similar meeting take place the following week to sort out problems connected with those who worked out of doors.

No doubts were expressed by Arthur as to the validity of Muriel's ownership. No questions were asked - other than by Sonia who sat muffled, her face barely topping the table. 'About the dog? How long is he going to be amongst us? It can't go on indefinitely.'

Arthur, who Muriel, too, had begun to consider a bit of a sweetie, replied, 'Sorry, Sonia. Mrs Cottle is within her rights to say that the cats can't stay indefinitely. If she wishes to keep her dog with her then, I'm afraid, you will have to make your own arrangements. Simple as that.'

So. She held the reins.

For the most part Muriel failed to concentrate during the meeting and allowed Arthur to burble on. The overall management of the house, repairs, locks, keys, roofing and so on, seemed to rest as before, in the hands of Sonia and himself.

When the meeting wound up and when Arthur had taken his leave, she walked with Monopoly in the garden. She wondered whether, in her awkwardness, she came across as haughty. Arrogant? Why did the healing of internal scars hinge, in her awareness, upon her changed position of power? Anti-democratic perceptions struggled with democratic ones, for had she not been trained to subservience? Images of both her draconian father and her weary, snobbish mother scoffed at her from the sky, and memories of Hugh and his disgrace came back to bother her. She was not, would not be, subservient. On the other hand was she comfortable with hierarchy? Mambles?

She was truly unhappy as she indulged in fantasies of revenge. Roger, the destabilising menace of recent years, must be banished. But might not any victory over him prove to be a pyrrhic one? Might Phyllis, during Mambles's visit, spy upon her and hasten to provide Roger with gossip for columns? And what of Marco? Beloved but confusing. Peter was on hold.

Muriel's situation had devolved upon her but she feared that this power might have already become more important to her than any relationship - or did it merely relate to relationships? The house. The garden. The peculiar pickle. Houses depended on people inhabiting them. Why was this happening?

Marco, Flavia, Phyllis and Roger spent most of the second half of the day in the cellar; Phyllis pounding to and fro with trays, glasses, bottle openers and cushions for comfort. As some of Muriel's inner conflicts gathered force it became clear to her, even in her semi-ignorance, that the cellar was of unique standing. She had heard of wine being sold off as death duty payment. Roger must not consume the nest egg.

From time to time she caught catches of laughter and complaint, of appreciation and contentment gushing and oozing from the depths of the building as her loneliness intensified and her hand lowered to touch the head of her dog.

In bed that night she thought back to Roger's bare sitting room in North London. There had been no photographs, no sign of normal life. He had lived, and probably still did, in a well of anonymity. There had been a packet of Alka Seltzer and a book about hangovers. Little else. He would need both after the spree in the cellar. If only Marco and Flavia had let Roger be. She willed them not to speak of her. Willed that their conversation be of nothing but gossip columns, horse racing, food fads, drink and hangovers. She knew, full well, that Roger, however little power he had over himself, had the power to make others warped and unaccountable.

The following day the house was thick with action before Muriel and Monopoly made their morning descent. Roger sat in the hall at a low, velvet-covered table on top of which rested a computer-like contraption and at which he pounded with several fingers as his eyes rotated to a heap of notes by his side. He had unshuttered two of the windows, the ones necessary to illuminate the patch where he sat. It would not, Muriel thought huffily, have crossed his mind to have lent a hand in any area other than one that served himself. In steely motion she completed tasks as Roger held up a defensive hand.

'Sorry. Can't talk. Dates. Vintages. Treasure trove it must be said.'

Phyllis, still tarty but this time in pink, sneaked in upon the scene bearing a tray supporting a boiled egg hidden under a pale flannel cosy and a pot of coffee that smelt of Volterra in spring. She told Muriel, icily, that two letters lay for her upon the kitchen table but her attention remained with Roger.

'There. Down there.' He pointed to a small octagonal table and dismissed her with a few words triggering the familiar buzz of her clothing as she waltzed away on tight shoes.

'Roger. How dare you order Phyllis about?'

'I'm a houseguest aren't I? I think you'll find that in most statelys houseguests are expected to express their wishes to the staff. Brace up Muriel. I've already told you - I like her and she likes me. Anything wrong?'

Houseguests, staff, statelys. How grotesque he was. Between each one of Roger's teeth a narrow gap showed. Muriel stared in anguish at the susceptible side of her own being. Roger and his bit-of-the-old-one-two, his sidelong, meaningful, cheeky looks. His innate cleverness, his rich, expressive voice. Tight trousers. Masculine mystery. What a weird tangle of aberration had entrapped her.

Monopoly's tail flickered over the pile containing notes on the contents of her cellar.

'Fucking brute!' Roger let out a hissing, sucking noise and sat back as if defeated. He wore a no-peace-for-the-righteous look on his face.

'When does the hapless Phyllis get a day off?'

'Roger. Please.' She supplicated as had done Sonia on the day of Jerome's incarceration; notwithstanding the knowledge that no one would ever get the better of Roger.

'Please don't disrupt my household. Please don't publish anything to further complicate my position here. Please leave Phyllis alone.'

'What are you accusing me of? What the hell do you think I've been able to get up to?' He pointed to his damaged limb. 'That's not to say,' he continued with relish, 'that I mightn't have a crack at her some other time.'

He lolled back against the padding of the sofa and, with a self-congratulatory guffaw, asked, 'Haven't you heard why they call me heroin?'

'No,' she said, 'no idea.'

He pointed to the patch where his horrible cock lay concealed. 'They get hooked. Haw. Haw.'

She writhed to remember that she had ever had first hand knowledge of the loathsome organ. She didn't consider herself to be exactly a feminist but she found his words entirely shocking. Had he said 'fishing line' the words would have been unacceptable enough. But heroin. Synonymous with suffering and death.

Muriel told him that, if his plaster was to be removed the following morning, it would be sensible for him to leave as soon as possible. She used, as lever, the unanswerable fact that Marco and Flavia would never make a start early enough to get him to hospital on time and that, anyway, she needed to be left on her own to see to various affairs.

Into this horrible colloquy darted a host of interruptions. Sonia's little person appeared and reappeared, presenting a stream of querulous conundrums and posing feeble queries. The metal detector came to display a faded florin. Dulcie, who had been lying low, returned with vigour to say that she had run out of razor blades and to ask what Muriel planned to do about it. Dawson rang. Delilah rang. 'One more thing. Our shop. The Bradstow Venture Community Shop. That is to say that Dawson had a lovely idea. He thought to add the two extra letters. Now it's known as The Bradstow Adventure Community shop. Just to make it scan. Are you a versifier by any chance? Dawson has the gift and he needed that little prefix when he wrote his lovely poem to celebrate the Venture opening.' Until then Delilah didn't pause for breath. Muriel had realised that there was no shop in Bradstow but nobody had told her of the community concern or that she might be expected to serve in it. Delilah went on. 'It's in a converted garage on the outskirts of the village. You did mention that you'd had shop experience and it would be a lovely way for you to meet the villagers. Just allow me to quote you some of Dawson's poem.

'You can buy anything from a pen to a mop,
At the Bradstow Adventure Community shop.
You can start at the bottom and rise to the top,
At the Bradstow Adventure Community shop.'

Tomorrow afternoon. That's my shift. I'll call for you and we can walk down there together. I'll be able to show you the ropes before we fit you in to a permanent slot. I think you'll enjoy it and I daresay you'll feel rewarded.'

No sooner had Delilah hung up than the head teacher of the village school rang to introduce herself and to ask for Muriel's views on sex education. Mambles rang to firm up on instructions for her visit. Muriel whispered for fear that her words might be heard by the departing trio and influence them, particularly Roger, against their decision to be gone. She hoped that one of the letters to which Phyllis had referred might be an acceptance of her invitation to Jackson, her American friend.

Eric and Joyce, from the garden, fought their battles as Phyllis huffed in and out, winking and simpering and sighing to herself and muttering that she planned to visit Jerome 'poor old dear'.

Peter rang to ask if Muriel was all right and if he could help in any way. She said she would ring back when she was calm. Marco and Flavia half-heartedly resisted her request to move Roger without further ado as Muriel contrived and connived to be rid of them.

Throughout these scenes of botheration. Monopoly, sensing disquietude and guessing - she supposed, at her inner endurance, stayed beside her and ignored all interlopers or participants in the tense activities.

She was not certain as to how, precisely, the parting came to be arranged but, by four o'clock in the afternoon, Marco, Flavia and Roger were once more seated in the positions that they had occupied but two days earlier in Marco's car and ready for departure to London.

His mother whispered to Marco as they embraced on the mat under the bird-splattered porch, 'Do come again soon. I'll ring you. You and Flavia. No friends, though, please. I'm sorry but I just can't get to grips with things. Not with outsiders here.'

He had the look of one who understood and gave her a slightly sympathetic squeeze. Flavia was dazed. She had been drunk since before lunch when she and Roger had vied with each other in a wine-tasting wager; each had consumed a fortune's worth. She barely bothered to say goodbye. Not a word to Monopoly.

Roger flourished under the guise of wounded sensitivity. 'Not often one's asked to leave a stately.' She winced. 'Sorry to have caused offence Muriel. You'll get accustomed to your position before long. Meanwhile try not to take life too seriously. One more thing. Be decent to Phyllis. She deserves a break. I'll do my best to keep in touch with her.' With that he pressed his lips against her cheek. What a cheek.

They were gone. She had twenty-four hours on her own to fool around. Twenty-four hours before Princess Matilda, Jubilee and their entourage were due to pick their way to Bradstow Manor. These hours were not to be restful ones. Had other things been equal, which they weren't, she would by then have been frantic in preparation for her royal visitor.

As she tuned back to the house after watching her son's car disappear down the drive, Muriel underwent an aesthetic stirring of the blood; a sensation of overflowing unlike any other existing in her memory. With this came the lifting of a burden and the consequent spiralling of spirits as she ran to the kitchen where she announced, 'Well. That's over. Now. On to the next visit.' Before enlarging on this overture, she opened Jackson's letter and read it with both amusement and disappointment.

'*Just the other day I heard from a friend that finger bowls are quite proper except if you have royalty to dinner. Someone might make the terrible error of proposing his toast and passing his glass over the finger bowl, which would remind the royals of the indignity of Bonnie Prince Charlie having to cross the water to escape Britain, a terrible insult to the crown. Please do have finger bowls when you're having the Princess to stay. I would hope that someone - the vicar? - would propose a toast and I would be quick to put my hand over the bowl lest I offend royalty, if the Princess was even unaware that I was saving the crown from being insulted.*

I know that a visit to you would fill pages and pages in my diary. I'm tempted to cancel a prior engagement, which is the baptism in the Greek Orthodox Church of an infant girl for whom I'm to be godfather. And I must admit that, as much as I shall miss not being with you, the prospect of a full Greek baptism and reception with singing and dancing fills me with wonder. And have I told you that I have been asked to a Chinese wedding?'

Although Muriel read quickly, there were many more pages to be perused so she scrunched it into her pocket for later; sad that Jackson had to go to his Greek baptism.

The second letter that needed her attention was local, and came with no stamp. She tore it open, anxious to get on with matters.

'Dear Mrs Cottle,' it read, *'You are new to the neighbourhood and I write to introduce myself as your local councillor. I am aware of a very malicious letter you may have received containing misleading information about my work. A Mr Gregory Gregson has attempted to blacken my character and raise doubts as to my integrity since my opposition to the use of his drive-in for a prosthetic limb factory. If you wish to ask about this vindictive character please get in touch.'*

She decided against getting in touch and returned to Mambles's visit. The resentful expressions that had dominated and charged the whole room dissolved as she, with confidence, told them of her future guest. She warned of the dog, the maid and the detective; spoke of complexities and extra duties and, whilst fearing mutiny and reprisals, launched into the eccentricities of Mambles's needs. Whisky in the bedroom for a start; ashtrays everywhere and ice buckets. She half-hesitated to mention that a chamber pot would have to be placed beside the bed. That was one of the many things that Mambles refused to do; travel on foot during the night.

As she spoke she became aware that her audience had swollen. Kitty was amongst them, introducing Mavis who had, hitherto, given Muriel the slip.

There they were; four Squirrel Nutkins changed from everyday beings into bright-eyed stagehands, agog for the first rising of the curtain upon a transformation scene. Dulcie was the first to speak. 'No earthly need to search for a chamber pot. There's one beside each bed. In the chamber cupboard, naturally.'

She added these last words with confident candour.

Questions were fired. Linen? Curling tongs? Extra protection for the windows? Security? Prying eyes? If it were true that Muriel expected a visit from a sister of the Queen - whatever else might occur under her authority? Never before had she entertained Mambles in style. She had, of course, provided her with the odd meal in Chelsea for which she had pulled out stops; solicited fellow guests and hired pairs of hands. Naturally she remembered accompanying her on visits to country houses (but not in recent years) and was always astonished by the *petits soins* deemed necessary for her comfort. Mambles never seemed to be aware of the lengths to which house owners stretched themselves, and Muriel used to laugh at them but now she joined their ranks. Flowers flew in through every door and window. The bustle was comprehensive and startling. Rooms left empty by Marco, Flavia and Roger were stripped and aired, broomed and reordered. Kitty, Mavis and Phyllis vied for tasks in animated awe as Dulcie stood, vast frame shaking, offering advice and reflecting, 'In my day the entire school would have been given a half holiday.'

Phyllis betrayed no evidence that she rued the departure of Roger as she flourished in the spare bathroom. Muriel reacted positively to the frenzy that overtook the household. It was becoming manifest that Mambles was the very one to whom she would eventually owe gratitude for hoisting her onto a pinnacle in the centre of her entourage. The prospect of the visit had almost induced terror-crazed palpitations in her but now Mambles began to emerge as a heavenly spirit.

During these hours of mobilisation Delilah called in person.

'Just to make sure all is well. Dulcie tells me that the young have already gone back to London.' She paused but Muriel knew that something important lay lodged on her mind. She understood what was expected of her; that Dulcie would have alerted the rectory to forthcoming events and that Delilah must be beside herself in a ferment of hope and agitation. Mambles was tricky about introductions and feared boredom and social effort at all times, even when 'on duty'.

'Oh dear,' she said as Delilah eyed tubs of fuchsias and tall daisies that decorated every crowded space. 'One thing after another. The young ones have gone but now I'm expecting an old friend who needs a bit of looking after. I am sorry. I've been rushed since I arrived. Things will calm down. I'll be in touch before the end of the week. We must talk about the fete.'

Her voice was harsh and false and Delilah's disappointment, which showed in every cranny of her eager face, shook her to the roots. She wished she had not mentioned the fete. Horses for courses. She had patronised her.

Nonetheless Muriel hurried Delilah out after assuring her that she could be counted on to help in the shop the following afternoon. She felt pained yet exhilarated by the power that spread from her and unsure as to whether she held it or whether it represented the power that had been thrust upon her.

As the house rushed towards readiness, Muriel experienced an intoxicating suffusion of impulsiveness within the framework of manic organisation. Everything was geared towards an occasion of unique magnitude and she, whatever else, was the catalyst.

A hostess. That is what she aspired to be. She was to become a hostess of renown. It would be bliss to live in a state of semi-permanent preparation.

'But she mustn't leave her panties in the hall, of the hostess with the mostes' on the ball,' she hummed one of Mambles's favourite tunes as she cracked her knuckles and planned to take Monopoly for a walk in the warm evening air.

They were very happy in the garden as they roamed towards the water and nosed into new corners and parts of the whole. They found an ancient, gravel-floored potting shed beside a well-kept greenhouse, the entrance to which was blocked by two battered beehives. Property of Joyce. Avoiding the angry swarm, they took a winding course, through apple and pear trees loaded with unripe fruit, down to the stream.

Three fat mallards, two drakes and a duck, swam towards them in hopeful haste. They were tame and Muriel supposed that somebody was in the habit of feeding them. As they stood and as Monopoly braced himself in interest, she sighted a queer and almost hallucinatory spectacle a few yards from her feet. Sonia, wrapped in wool, was standing with her eyes to the sky and clasping a small tabby cat. She was singing in a clear euphonious voice; enunciating as one filling a concert hall. At her feet lay a picnic hamper beside a folded rug.

'All I want is a room somewhere.' She sang piteously, with the fervour of an outcast. 'Far away from the cold night air.' It was another of Mambles's favourites.

It was not until Sonia had warbled the last moving words, 'Wouldn't it be luvverly,' that she saw Muriel with her dog at her side.

She went into a type of trance, a numbness that brought her to a rigid standstill as she squeezed the cat between her hands. Monopoly took a few paces in her direction whereupon she opened her mouth to let out, in a whispered whimper, the words, 'Spare Pussy. That is all I ask of you.'

Muriel told her not to be foolish. 'Can't you see, Sonia, that Monopoly is on a lead? Even if he weren't he wouldn't hurt your cat.'

Her eyes opened wider and wider until Muriel wondered whether they owned lids. Sonia's madness exasperated her and she determined to force her to contain it.

'I have a friend coming tomorrow and she's bringing a dog with her too. I hope you will control yourself and keep calm. We will both look after our dogs and expect you to do the same with your cats.'

At this point the wind dropped from Sonia's sails and self-interest struggled to gain over insanity. 'Would that be HRH?'

'Yes. Princess Matilda.'

'Would her dog be a relative of those belonging to the Queen?'

'Certainly. Close.'

At this she melted and loosened her clasp. Muriel thought it a miracle that she hadn't strangled Pussy in her effort to protect her. She lowered her lips to the cat's right ear and spoke into it. 'There, Pussy. We must make friends with the new doggy tomorrow.'

Kingdoms combined. The harmony that Mambles's visit was producing within the walls of the house was spreading ripples over troubles out of doors. Juxtapositions.

The house smelled of flowers, drowning mustiness, and Muriel was calm as she remembered that she had promised to ring Peter. He was entertained by accounts of happenings and more than delighted, in his reflective fashion, to hear of the effect that Mambles's visit was producing. She didn't tell him of Roger comparing his cock to heroin. Peter said that he missed her but allowed no note of clumsy reproach to mar their talk.

In the morning Muriel was woken by Phyllis and her active arms. She grimaced as she explained that the bathroom allocated to the honoured guest smelled of sewers. Marco and Flavia had been the last to occupy it and Muriel underwent a spasm of shame. What had they been up to? She'd have been pleased if it had been Roger's bathroom. 'Mice,' she said,

'mice or rats. They've eaten a cake of soap. Funny your son never noticed.'
She proposed alternative methods of exorcism. Sprays, open windows,
electric fans, joss sticks, hyacinths. Muriel didn't like to mention that
Mambles had a weak sense of smell. Spirits and nicotine protected her in
all atmospheres.

Soon after breakfast Delilah again tackled by telephone.

'Dawson and I have been thinking about you with your friend staying.
I know that it's not easy to entertain around here. Would it be *comme il
bien* if we were to pop in for a drink – say around sixish this evening? I
know that not many want to socialise in this neighbourhood and
Londoners do love to meet locals.'

Keeping notes of irascibility from her voice, Muriel suppressed Delilah
and her plans, saying that she didn't know what time her friend was
scheduled to arrive. She would not be unaccompanied and might take
time to settle; was certain to be tired, would not necessarily stir from her
quarters until dinnertime. She concocted too many excuses and knew this
as she spoke, knew, too, that Delilah was wounded and resented that she
caused her pain.

Kitty, who had overheard Muriel's part in the conversation with
Delilah and who, in spite of her kind heart, was not free from human
weakness, said, 'You stand firm with that Delilah. Wants to be in on
everything. She's snobbish.'

Muriel realised that her occupation of Bradstow was becoming
divisive. Hard though she tried to push thoughts of Delilah and her
thwarted attempts to come face to face with Mambles to the back of her
mind, they hovered above her.

As though to defeat them and in the hopes of being rewarded, she
kept her promise to Delilah and walked with her through the village,
turning left by the chestnut tree and passing rusty, distorted fencing that
prevented, but only just, cows from descending to the road . Muriel hoped
that the fence didn't belong to her. The converted garage was ill equipped;
stocked with sliced loaves, sweets and weary vegetables. 'From your garden
I believe.' Delilah was conspiratorial. 'I don't like to say this but I'm not
sure that Eric doesn't make a little on the side.' She rattled at the till and
asked her assistant to rearrange tins of custard powder. 'Ah,' she said, 'here
come your Kitty's girls. Gemma and Lara. They're lovely.' Two plump eight
or nine year olds in checked frocks bounced in, clasping coins. Gemma,

the older of the two, said, 'Good afternoon Mrs Rector.' Delilah made haste to explain that she was thus known in the village.

'Mum's making cakes for the freezer, ready for the fete.'

'Baking powder? Flour? Butter?' Delilah rushed to Gemma's aid. Whilst instructing Muriel to pack the goods in a plastic bag, she introduced her. 'Now. This is Mrs Cottle. New lady at the Manor where your Mummy works. Say "hello" nicely.' Both girls said "hello" nicely and scarpered. After that there was a long wait before further customers appeared and Delilah took advantage of the time to advance intimacy.

'Of course, Dulcie's a bit of a mystery. I think your, er, Aunt Alice always made her believe that she might eventually come in to something. That, or so I'm told, is why she spends so much of her time prowling around the house. Looking for a letter so they say. A letter that your auntie left for your uncle, something to Dulcie's advantage perhaps. But that's only gossip.'

Dulcie a pretender.

'Another little slice of wisdom,' Delilah went on, 'Dawson suggested I put a word in your ear concerning the metal detector chappie. He has a history, I'm sorry to say. Uses the coins he digs up as a front for those he steals. He has been inside in his day, but you're new here and it takes time to learn the local ways.'

Two boys, approximately ten years old, entered the shop with confidence. Delilah whispered, 'Keep an eye on them. As you know I don't like to say a word against any of God's creatures but....well. Keep an eye.'

Muriel kept an eye and satisfied herself that they had not pilfered. They didn't buy anything but shuffled out, disgruntled.

Delilah hadn't quite finished. 'Phyllis. She's a funny one. Nobody's sure of where she came from. Answered an advertisement I believe. No family I hear. That must be a dreadful thing. Dulcie, of course, met up with your aunt at a cat show. They say she was, er, well, very attached to her and moved her and her van into the paddock. There were even hints - but, no. Here comes a customer.'

She served a packet of sugar to an old man who had swerved to the door on a bicycle, then reverted to the life that was led in Muriel's house. 'Of course, Phyllis, too, had some hopes. She did everything for Jerome and they say he made her some promise. Sonia overheard words one afternoon and mentioned to Dulcie that it sounded like a marriage offer.'

Phyllis also a pretender. Marco and Flavia counting their chickens. Hugh poised? Lizzie livid. Hidden letters. Head spinning, Muriel returned to her pulsating house.

It was teatime when Mambles arrived. Her detective, Moggan, doubled as driver. A room had been prepared for him amongst the kudus on the top floor, and Phyllis had ordained that he and Mambles's maid eat with her and Kitty in a semi-abandoned servant's hall tickled up in no time for unexpected use.

Muriel happened to know that Moggan was not the marrying kind or she would have feared for further assaults on Phyllis's exposed nerves. She had not been given advance warning as to which of Mambles's retainers she planned to travel with, and, from where she stood, was not able to see who sat beside her in the back of the car. Jubilee, who crouched on his mistress's knee, scraped on the windowpane.

Dulcie was already on the driveway and charged forward to open the car door, pre-empting Moggan, doubling up and bowing from the hip to the alighting Princess. Muriel was only narrowly in earshot but could almost swear that she murmured the words 'your worship' in her greeting, then continued to murmur something about the school and a half holiday.

Mambles's eyes were fully stretched as she stared, showing that she observed an unusual example of the human species. She was at her most Scandinavian, tall and yellow. A long yellow cardigan hid, for the most part, a white pleated skirt, and signals of humour issued from her hard eyes as, ignoring Dulcie's obeisances, she creaked towards her old friend with open arms.

Partly because a group had gathered on the forecourt, and partly resulting from other diverse forces, Muriel felt more loath then ever to embark on a curtsey. Could it be that she now felt nearer to being her equal? Her superior even? She acceded to the necessary formalities; kissing and curtseying, then watched with pride as Kitty, Phyllis and the rest sank before her to the ground.

As the huge yellow sprig from the royal branch, followed by her retinue, surged into the hallway, Muriel saw, to her disquiet, that she was trailed by an elderly figure dressed district nurse-like in dark colours and carrying a briefcase. She recognised her as Miss Farthing, ex-ladies-maid to Queen Elizabeth and known, affectionately, by her employers as 'Farty,' and thanked God that Cunty, at least, was out of the way.

Mambles stood still and feasted with theatrical ostentation, her eyes upon the treasures, now to all intents Muriel's own.

'So. Muriel. You haven't done half badly.'

All onlookers regarded her in high esteem. She knew from the faces that turned to hers that they awaited orders and appealed to Mambles who decreed that both she and Miss Farthing would like, before all else, to see to their rooms and 'make themselves comfortable'.

How long was Muriel to live in suspense before Miss Farthing's pet name was revealed?

All was flurry. Dulcie buttonholed Moggan and insisted upon a minute inspection of Mambles's Daimler, watched by Eric and Joyce who had become thick as thieves, united in events.

On the staircase Phyllis whispered in conspiracy with Farty as she explained the intricacies of the master suite, the whereabouts of the chamber pot and reserve supplies of whisky, enough, even, to last Roger a month.

Mambles dismissed Muriel. 'See you later alligator,' she cried, as Farty shut the door upon her; leaving no time for the lady of the house, as custom demanded, to reply, 'in a while crocodile'.

The two passed an interminable amount of time in their rooms which adjoined each other, leaving a desolate emptiness in the house. The build-up before the arrival had been nothing short of hair-raising; the arrival itself and moments surrounding it, ecstatic. Now all was tranquil and, apart from the fortunate Phyllis who had been handpicked by Farty for the honour of carrying a tea tray to the illustrious guest, they were left at loose ends. Dulcie monopolised Moggan and bore him off to examine her caravan.

Muriel was puzzled. Mambles behaved out of character. Never before, when under the same roof, had she been allowed a single second to herself. Normally she was made to sit on the end of the bed; admire her clothes as they emerged at the hands of Farty or whoever else, from an ancient leather suitcase. She always had to entertain Mambles; chatter, read snippets from newspapers as long as they weren't 'horrid' about Mummy, to suggest and to cajole. Why, now, was she dismissed? Particularly after the days of separation about which she had complained. It must surely be the changes in her life that held significance.

Muriel went to Kitty in the kitchen where the sight of her brought back the niggle in her head that had been ousted by distraction. She dwelt on the image of Dawson and Delilah at the rectory - looping the loop in their rejection.

'I'm feeling a bit guilty about Delilah,' she said, knowing that Mambles would have upbraided her for speaking with familiarity to an underling.

'Don't you mind her. She's ever so pushy. Mark you. She was different for a bit after they'd had their troubles. Ever so nice for a while, that is. Pity she didn't keep it up.'

'Troubles?'

'Yes. Their youngest boy, Alastair. Dropped his trousers on public transport. It could have been hushed up, if his Dad hadn't been rector, that is.'

'What's he like? The boy?'

'He's queer. Ever so moody. Well, he gives me the creeps. We won't let him near our place, not with Gemma and Lara being the age they are.'

Muriel was more ashamed than ever that she had not found it in her to incorporate Dawson and Delilah into either of their visiting groups; what with their son dropping his trousers on public transport and being denied visits to local homes. From the start she had been a disappointment to them; even at the time of Delilah's first telephone call and she had to accept that, lurking in her, lay an urge to shoot the messenger. Without Delilah's intervention none of this might have happened.

It would, she knew, have been circumspect to have been on excellent terms with the rector and his wife.

Kitty and Muriel talked of supper. A card table had been erected in a corner of the dining room at which she and Mambles were to dine alone by candlelight.

When the telephone rang it was answered by Kitty. She called out for Phyllis, betraying that it was Roger (Mr Roger, she called him) who wished to speak with her. Phyllis, radiant after her trip with the tray, twirled past her, smug and buzzing. On no account was Muriel tempted to hear one syllable of her conversation with Roger. She left her to it and strode away, shuddering with rancour, to inspect preliminaries as set out for supper. Subservience to rank, as displayed by her underlings, was contagious for Muriel, not by nature a perfectionist, fingered forks and tweaked at flowers at the card table that awaited the tête-à-tête.

Farty came to announce that Her Royal Highness was much satisfied with her quarters and that she would be dressed and downstairs by seven-thirty. During this indefinite time Marco rang and his mother confessed to him without delay that Mambles was staying at Bradstow. The news titillated him.

'Good on you Ma. That'll rev your team up if anything can.' Here he paused and, Muriel fancied, gulped.

'By the way, sorry about Roger. He simply doesn't know how to behave. Me and Flave gave him a wigging for flirting with that fright in nylon. Told him that it isn't playing the game to interfere with people's servants.'

Marco, too, was affected by his mother's elevation to a state of feudal responsibility. He was reviewing boundaries. Muriel asked if they would like to return for the weekend, remembering the sympathetic squeeze he had given her on parting. He sounded vague and dithery and suggested that they play it by ear, as Muriel lost concentration and planned to invite Dawson and Delilah for a drink, a meal even, during the next influx.

Mambles, in full regalia, advanced upon her in the drawing room at seven-thirty on the dot. Muriel was alone with her, having forbidden Phyllis to attend upon them until she and Mavis served supper at the card table.

'So,' she began most majestically as she and Jubilee, who quivered in competition with the proprietorial house-owning presence of Monopoly, placed themselves in comfort on a sofa.

'Congratulations, Muriel. This certainly is the real thing. Farty is in her element. Nothing left to chance. Did you inherit the maids as well? Who was the cranky old man who bowed to me outside?'

'I think so. The man is called Dulcie.'

Again her eyes stretched as she allowed the matter to slip. 'By the way. Mummy wants to know more about your uncle. There are some ghastly people called Atkins who live in Cunty's village. They keep begging Cunty to get them through the doors of Clarence House. For some reason Mummy's got it into her head that they are connected with your lot. Next time I come I'll bring Mummy.'

The dart in her glance was duplicitous and Muriel knew herself to be on probation. How much hobnobbing, she was asking, could her friend handle?

'Any interesting neighbours? When I bring Mummy you must make it a proper house party and ask the county. They love meeting us.'

She shook her head and began, with good humour, to scrutinise all that lay before her. 'Is that an ancestor of yours Muriel?' pointing at a portrait showing a man with a double chin. Muriel replied that she had no idea but that she doubted it.

'Shall we visit your uncle? Nurses get so silly when I go to hospitals. It can be rather fun.'

Never, ever, had Muriel known her in a mood like this; so skittish; so keen to put rank to advantage. She pictured her own popularity, other than with Dawson and Delilah, to be soaring in every direction. She sneezed. Too many flowers in the house.

'Bless you twice.' Mambles always said this whenever anybody sneezed. She creaked and drank and planned Muriel's future.

'Perfect for house parties. Perhaps we should summon that horrid Hugh back. Such a problem finding men. I know that pansies come in handy but it's not the same. Can you ring for Farty? I want to change my shoes. They're killing me.'

It wasn't possible to ring for anybody since a china-handled bell mounted on a frieze of gold leaves was not attached to anything else. Muriel walked to the door and bellowed for Phyllis, Kitty or Mavis. She didn't care which or how loudly her voice echoed.

Phyllis came at speed and Mambles made her request. It was the first time in Muriel's hearing that Mambles had uttered the word Farty since her arrival.

Mambles was royal and after a flicker of astonishment Phyllis took to the soubriquet with calm but, all the same, Muriel was glad that Cunty hadn't come too.

As soon as Farty had attended to her duties and when the women had each drunk a glass or two of neat vodka, they made for the dining room followed by both dogs who, for separate reasons, despised each other.

As they sat Muriel was attacked by a twinge of envy for the less formal group in the servant's hall, presided over by a self-imposed Dulcie; Farty and Moggan creating a rare interest in those once deserted quarters.

Anxious though Princess Matilda was to promote Muriel's interests at this turning point in her life, her friend could hardly help but be aware of a wistfulness attached to her advice.

Mambles's voice tightened as she prattled. 'If only Daddy hadn't died when he did. I know that he and Mummy would have seen to it that both Princess Margaret and I were given something in the country.' As on many occasions, she removed her earrings and placed them on a plate. 'Killing me. When you think what the Queen has done for her lot. Places everywhere. Even Anne has one. After all, we too were daughters of a reigning monarch. All we have are grace and favour apartments.' She sighed deeply and looked sternly at Muriel as glasses shimmered. 'Now,' she went on, 'out of the blue, Muriel, you have all this.'

Reminding her in a whisper that 'all this' presented problems, Muriel signalled to Phyllis that Mambles's glass was empty. She never touched wine. Muriel noticed that whisky from a bottle had been transferred to a glass decanter with a silver rim and wondered if this procedure was correct.

Just then, as if a cloud had descended, both diners felt the presence of Dulcie who had lumbered in as they talked and stood menacingly between them, tummy touching the table.

'I'd like you two to sort out a point of argument. Your maid,' she flashed a sunless eye at Mambles, 'tells us that she is accustomed to being addressed by an unmentionable name. Unmentionable.' No trace of the bowing and half holiday mood of a few hours back.

'Farty?' Mambles enquired.

'That is the very one.'

Mambles replied, 'What on earth is the matter with "Farty"?' Her correct name is Miss Farthing but in my family we like to take friendly short cuts. Has that sorted out your argument?'

'No it has not. In my day that word was absolutely forbidden. If strictly necessary, we referred to breaking wind. My mother was a district nurse and extremely strict. I'm glad of it. I was brought up to observe the best of manners and I have never regretted it. Not for one second.'

She turned to Muriel, 'And if you think that just because you hobnob with Hanovers, you are able to suppress that letter written to your aunt by your uncle, you're mistaken. More likely than not you know where it is and sooner or later it will come to light. Then we'll see who's in charge here.'

Both dogs, unnerved by atmosphere, began to bark. Jubilee, furious yelps escaping from his mouth, scampered to Mambles who lifted him onto her satin lap. Monopoly stood firm, outdoing Jubilee in volume of complaint but seeking no shelter. In Muriel's view he was the braver of the two dogs.

Dulcie, put out that she should be thus silenced, stood her ground and remained otherwise content.

Suddenly Mambles shrieked. Jubilee, in fright, had forgotten himself and a warm yellow patch spread speedily over the cool satin of her frock. 'Muriel. Have that creature removed. Send for Farty. Moggan too, if necessary.'

Phyllis ran to interrupt the alternative dinner party and came back with Farty who, accompanied by Moggan and followed by Kitty and Mavis, ran to the table.

'Take her out of here,' Mambles ordered.

She held herself away from Dulcie as Moggan seized the woman's wrists, whipped her into a half-turn and, before anybody could advise, marched her from the room. Muriel wondered how Farty fared inwardly during these upheavals. She did not leave with the others but gathered Jubilee in her arms, whispered apologies to the affronted animal and withdrew, taking her soiled employer with her.

Muriel gave Phyllis hazy instructions and remembered that she had failed to ring Peter. When Mambles reappeared in alternative eveningwear and carrying the chastened Jubilee, she showed no signs of shock. Muriel detected victory in her bearing.

'So Muriel, I begin to see what you mean when you complain of problems. The sooner you banish that freak to council housing the better. I'll pull strings. I think I'm involved with something on those lines. Shelter or whatnot.'

Muriel thanked her kindly as they resumed their positions at the card table.

'We can't have her, or 'it' I should say, at house parties.'

Was Mambles planning to play a major role in the execution of Muriel's inheritance? Was she, thanks to chance, going to make amends for omissions in the last will and testament of the late King? His Majesty George VI?

The rest of the evening fell flat. Mambles, although she had shown herself to be a sport, never recovered her earlier high spirits and began to repeat herself so often, banging on about sheltered housing and the efforts she so thanklessly put in to her few 'functions' that Muriel ended the ceremonies by lurching upstairs to rouse the slumbering Farty who lay, fully dressed, upon her bed - ready for immediate action.

Farty alone went in search of Princess Matilda. Muriel was not prepared to risk the stairs twice but, as she prepared for bed, she heard the pair passing her room as they headed for their own.

The following morning Muriel tottered down the dark stairs, her feet a million miles from her head, to behold the hideous aspect of departed excitement, for even the flowers, to her eyes, had faded overnight and glum spirits lurked behind every stick of furniture, hid under the piano and lay secreted in drum-table drawers.

Monopoly looked pensive and uninterested when they met Farty who had been consigned to deal with an unrepentant Jubilee's morning needs and who was clearly shaken after the mishaps of the night before, and warned that Mambles intended sleeping late.

'She likes a lie-in when in a strange bed,' she augured as though to signify that an alien force engendered by Muriel tethered her mistress to the sheets. It was unfair since Mambles barely ever rose before noon, strange bed or not.

Kitty, normally so cheerful, was infected with a share of aggregate shame induced by Dulcie's outburst.

'She never should have done that. We couldn't stop her Mrs Cottle. Not once she'd made her mind up. No sooner had poor Miss Farthing admitted to her pet name, (it was Mr Moggan called her by it) than Dulcie was up and away.'

There was an air of intrigue about Phyllis's face that chilled but betrayed nothing. Dulcie kept herself to herself, smouldering in her caravan - not, Muriel was certain, through any sense of repentance but through belligerent desire to show disgust. Members of the outdoor team, unconscious of disgrace, tiptoed through rooms plying tubs with water from long-spouted cans with hopes of catching glimpses, as Muriel paced about and tried to build up her energy level.

Anarchy perpetrated beneath her roof the night before had, she feared, diminished any (imagined or otherwise) equalisation of her standing with Matilda for, via Farty, she was summoned shortly before eleven o'clock to take up her time-honoured position at the foot of her bed. She lay, propped by a heap of pillows, nightdress buttoned to the neck, alive to the visit and supernaturally jolly. The silver-framed photograph of Queen Elizabeth, Muriel saw, had travelled with her.

'Any sign of that transvestite maniac today?' It was clear that she enjoyed herself and wished to emerge from the happenings of the last evening with flying colours.

'No, thank God. Not a grunt. Perhaps she expired in the night.'

'Farty is mixing me a Bloody Mary with the help of that anaemic Phyllis of yours. I've ordered one for you as well. Then, when I'm dressed, shall we go and spook her in the caravan?'

'Please not Mambles. Please.'

Farty and Phyllis came into the room, each carrying a filled glass. Farty looked harassed but Phyllis appeared sinister and secret. Muriel drank her drink fast and her head started to rush as Mambles decreed that a repeat order waited for them in the drawing room. She was dismissed and, at Phyllis's side, swayed along the passage and down the stairs.

She smoked as she waited for Mambles to dress.

The rest of the events of the morning were obliterated in her mind by the onrush of later happenings.

It was during lunch, where Mambles and Muriel sat face to face, that she was summoned by a white and wobbly Phyllis to the telephone. Muriel told her to relay a message; said that she was not to be disturbed. This Phyllis went to do but, when again beside her, told Muriel that she was to ring a Mr Cottle, and that it was urgent. For a second Muriel quivered - imagining it to be Hugh. Phyllis had jumped to the same conclusion and her hands fluttered double fast. It was clear that she feared for something. When lunch was over and Mambles, Jubilee and Farty went to pack, Muriel - deciding that it was Peter who had called - scampered to the telephone.

Peter sounded anxious. 'Something rather tiresome has cropped up.' He explained that Lizzie had rung him, had read to him an article fresh from the *Evening Standard*; that he had sent a visiting friend out for a copy and that the friend was ready, if she could bear it, to read the piece down the wire - then and there.

Muriel agreed and heard the voice of Peter's friend; a certain Matthew. He cleared his voice and proceeded.

'Fine wines and chamber pots provided for royalty in little known stately of dubious ownership.' There was no doubt as to the identity of the author.

As Matthew, with the odd hiccup, rambled through the words of the piece Muriel lowered her body onto a stool that stood half-hidden under the table and reached for Monopoly who wrapped himself around her legs. It could not possibly be. As she had suspected, but only to herself and in semi-jest, Roger had collaborated with Phyllis. It was all there.

'It is not explained how the mysterious occupant, Muriel Cottle, (estranged from her husband, Hugh, the disgraced Member of Parliament, whose affair with a model caused his resignation)... She has, it seems, already put up the backs of local residents - most importantly the rector and his wife... HRH Princess Matilda's visit timed to take place within days of the erstwhile owner being shut away... Much attention paid to the needs of the visitor - including a floral chamber pot to answer royal calls of nature during the night...'

The faceless Matthew went on.

'What is more a row of a scatological nature is said to have broken out between HRH and a member of Mrs Cottle's staff.'

After adding a sympathetic comment, Matthew handed Muriel back to Peter.

'I'm dreadfully sorry my dear. I decided that you had to know as soon as possible. There must be a spy in your midst. I don't think we're pushed to identify the writer of the piece. Shall I join you? If I can be of any help that is.' He had already looked up a train and told her where to meet it.

She dashed to the back of the house where she searched in maniacal rage for Phyllis, only to find Kitty who told her that she was upstairs with Farty seeing to Mambles's preparations for departure. Foul, double-dealing harpy. She decided to call Arthur; to get out of the hellhole before they ousted her.

From that moment the telephone didn't cease to ring. Local newspapers; weeklies, supplements. Architectural magazines; even a Television channel. Reporters about to appear in the flesh waiting to capture moments of Mambles's departure. Muriel said 'no comment' more than a dozen times before leaving the receiver on the table and deciding to hasten events; to have a word with Mambles in private. She lay, formally clad, on her bed as Farty pressed garments between sheets of tissue paper and Phyllis dawdled beside a long mirror holding one of Mambles's unsoiled frocks close against her body and preening to her reflection.

'Put that down,' Muriel ordered, 'and leave the room.'

Neither Mambles nor Farty flickered as Phyllis skedaddled and as Muriel sat down on Mambles's bed and poured forth her wrath, combined with miserable apology.

'As you know Muriel,' she sat up and smiled, 'I never read one word in those filthy rags. Nor does Mummy. Why, though, did you ever allow that rotter in the house?'

She creaked to her feet, kissed her friend and said, 'In my family we pay no attention to the press. Now you really have got to do the same. You have had experience after all with horrid Hugh. Farty! Have you remembered Jubilee's bowl?'

Mambles understood Muriel's need to be shot of her, speeded up Farty's fussing and, within half an hour, they were gone.

There was no one about. Muriel found Kitty in the kitchen. Both she and Mavis were disappointed at not being alerted to Mambles's departure since they would have liked to have curtseyed and waved her off. Muriel explained that there had been trouble with the press; that the telephone was to be left unanswered; that a room must be prepared for Mr Cottle - her brother-in-law - and that Phyllis must be skulking somewhere. She dropped this as a hint.

They both showed sympathy and Muriel left with Monopoly for the station.

Chapter 9

Peter refused to carry a white stick. As a child Muriel used to yearn for one, even went to the length of painting one of her father's (for which trouble followed) and pretending to be blind, so she found it hard to understand why Peter denied himself this covetable prop, eligible for it as he was.

He walked with an air of patient gravity along the platform, arm in arm with a mossy young man, drearily clad, who had befriended him in the railway carriage. The young man, Peter told her as they left the station, had a speech impediment and worked as a medium in Kent.

'He took it up after his mother "went into spirit".'

Muriel told Peter that she would like to go into spirit.

'Don't talk twaddle Muriel. You'll triumph.'

Peter was very pleased to see Monopoly. He was easy to be with and Muriel rejoiced that he had sensed her need for his company and knew that he would not crow, despite his disapproval past and present, concerning truck with Roger.

He had, indeed, come because he sensed that Muriel needed help but had come, too, because he missed her. He revered her but counted the complications of involvement with his brother's wife. Not that, necessarily, he had huge hopes of success were he to stop counting. He realised that he barely remembered his brother's voice or his appearance. Why, therefore, should he not attempt to replace one he but sketchily visualised? Cuckold the departed? But he had not tested the water and Muriel kept at a friendly distance from him.

Kitty stood beaming on the front doorstep; staring and bursting with life. She was popping to inform them that Phyllis had done a bunk. Joyce had been coerced into driving her and her belongings to a train bound for London. Wonder that they hadn't bumped into her at the station. Poor Phyllis, Muriel thought, she cannot have anticipated Roger's treachery; have credited that he would, so flagrantly, have plastered her snippets undiluted before the world. She was sure to have expected camouflage or protection. What, she wondered, would he do with the twitching bitch when she arrived on his doorstep? The telephone, Kitty said, had been busy ever since Muriel went out. She had tried leaving it off the hook but a foul wail from the exchange that exploded like an air raid siren throughout the house had decided her to replace it. Since then she had left it ringing and, as Dulcie was still skulking, nobody had replied. It rang again as Muriel led Peter to a chair.

The unremitting jangling of the bell underlined for her the inescapable fact that calamity had struck. Her loneliness, thanks to Peter with his kind, blind face, was mitigated but shame soared to top place in her heart, shame for her son who had forced Roger upon her and who, in his turn, had betrayed Mambles. Thanks to the one night the Princess had spent under her roof the whole world now knew that she used a chamber pot.

'The buck is at the top,' she sang to herself as she thought of Mambles's uncle and planned to abdicate.

She wished that Peter didn't look like Hugh for, although taller and more dishevelled than her husband and less polished in his ways, there could be no denying that they were brothers. She expected Marco to be amongst the many callers but had no wish to speak with him.

Imaginings told her that the story was being magnified by the press; that it would hit the headlines, dominate the front page of the Johannesburg Gazette (or whatever) and send Hugh flying back complete with jodhpurs and fishing tackle.

Peter said, 'No. There'll only be a snippet here and there. They'll pursue anything but, more often than not, won't use it. Just remember how peripheral Matilda is these days - what with Diana, Fergie and the rest.'

'What about the nurses? The ones that look after Jerome? It's bound to hit the local papers. Delilah? What about Delilah?'

'They can look after themselves. God will provide. They'll love it. Early to bed tonight and tomorrow we'll face whatever music there may be. Personally I don't think it'll be that loud.'

Supper at the card table with Peter and Monopoly after a walk in the garden, where Muriel described the roses that rustled in a menacing breeze and watched Peter as he smelled them for himself. She knew, at least she thought she knew, that something between them lay ahead. Hoping it to be, but fending off details in her mind, she buried possibilities and grasped at existing essentials.

Chapter 10

The house breathed more easily without Phyllis. This constituted a bonus, but rumbling reports sent out by Dulcie that the wanton had been ruthlessly dismissed cancelled out a portion of the pleasure provided for Muriel by her absence. Peter parked himself beside the telephone and dealt skilfully with enquiries both from the press and from certain acquaintances from Muriel's past - recent and otherwise. Callers wishing to write profiles; to conduct interviews, callers who wished to reintroduce themselves to one with a position in the stately sphere. Roger, even, rang to explain himself. It had all been a mistake, he told Peter. He had scribbled a piece in fun and found it snatched from his desk before he had time to shred it. 'And,' he said, 'will you tell Muriel that I'm sending her housekeeper back.'

Delilah called, fluttering. 'The local papers. They refer to a rift between Muriel and the rectory. Might Dawson pop round to set matters right? Pastoral care.'

The gorgeous matron rang to explain how tactful she had been in shielding Jerome. Not that Jerome would have fathomed a single word.

Dulcie weighed in. Solecism behind her she waved a newspaper high above her head. 'So. You've put your foot in it. I went down on my bike for a copy of *Fur and Feathers* and this is what they showed me at the newsagents.'

It was a day of remorseless complaint and interruption and but, for the presence of Peter, one that would have sent her scuttling back to the anonymity of Chelsea. The underlying anxiety was whether, by now, the news of Muriel's inheritance along with the complications arising from it had reached Hugh's ears.

Kitty produced lunch. Mavis stared and Dulcie, with a certainty of possessing the upper hand, leered and ogled.

Arthur made a teatime appointment. 'I might be of help in this unfortunate business.' Marco rang, wailing that he had played no part and pleading, 'Surely all is not lost. Tell Ma to take a grip.'

He also said that he proposed to take his mother up on her earlier suggestion that he and Flavia revisit at the weekend. This, when relayed by Peter, reminded Muriel that Lizzie's visit loomed.

The metal detector man presented a rusty button. Joyce and Eric removed flowerpots in enraptured rage. Peter told Muriel to lie down; to retire with Monopoly to her room and, if possible, to empty her head.

This she tried to do and, during her withdrawal, Peter appeased to some extent both Dawson and Arthur. He also cancelled Lizzie's visit – but not without disgruntlement on the part of the agitated woman who caterwauled, 'Don't tell me she's chucking. She jolly well might have done it herself, considering the whole world knows that Princess Matilda has been allowed in. It's a bit mean. After all I was the one who tipped you off about the *Evening Standard*.'

Peter said, 'Another time. She's in bed. Too much,' and other desperate words before he persuaded her to drop it.

In the evening Marco rang again to say that he and Flavia planned to arrive in time for lunch and that, what was more, they were to bring Phyllis with them. He hinted that Roger had thrown himself into the centre of the action and was now, free from plaster, gearing himself to trace a pretender; a living relation of Jerome's with close claims. Anything to keep the story in the public eye.

As Muriel sat with Peter in the garden after supper, she asked him what it meant to her; retaining this poetical place as her own. He replied that there was to be no going back; that he was to be beside her in the fighting of battles and that, given time and clarity of mind, they were to succeed.

In bed she revolted against catastrophe, willing that no more follow and railing against the vacillating fibres of her composition. As owls hooted and as Monopoly cracked against the wicker of his basket, she craved chocolate, stared at beams lit by moonlight and wondered if the workmen, when fixing them, had worn smocks.

Then, without in the least wishing to, she let her mind run back as she faced her own want of responsibility and the effect such want had produced on her son - culminating in his hopeless drinking habits. He was two days old and she fed him from her breast as instructed by a nurse at the hospital where Marco had been born and where she had passed those heady days in a small maternity ward. A very fat woman of low insight and loud language occupied the bed next to Muriel's and talked mercilessly, at all hours, of pains and placentas and bursting waters. She was kind but a pill. At feeding times, as tiny piglets, the babies were pushed into the wards in square trolleys and placed beside mothers who, with varying degrees of success, placated them with nipples. Muriel found the feeding of Marco to be a painful battle, but one that she was determined to fight. He was back in his trolley, a beautiful, contented baby with black hair, when she decided to slip down the passage in her dressing gown in search of a book that she believed herself to have left in the shower room. It contained a short story that she had been reading during the early stage of labour, and had introduced her to a neurotic woman haunted by ugly wallpaper. She longed to know how it ended. When she returned without the book - it had gone missing - to her horror she found that her neighbour, Lorraine, had shifted beds and was sitting, smiling smugly, on Muriel's own. Marco's crib was empty and Lorraine cradled him and fed him with her left breast.

'Crying his heart out. I'm giving him a little top-up.'

That was all. Another woman, and only for a short time, had stuffed her nipple into his infant mouth. At the time, Muriel did not mention it - not to a nurse nor to Hugh but she had snatched her baby away from Lorraine and never spoke to her afterwards. Now she wondered whether that unhappy episode had influenced Marco in his indiscriminate swilling.

Saturday came and with it a return to peace and order although underlying conundrums plagued her - the most urgent of which was how to deal with Phyllis.

Kitty, it turned out, loathed the woman and was prepared to place herself right behind any treatment likely to be ordered.

Muriel jittered as a large packet of post was hurled into the hall by a leaping lad who drove a red van. She did not bother to inspect any of the letters, held together in a tight broad rubber band, but gathered comfort from the knowledge that it was, as yet, too soon to have heard from Hugh by post.

Peter again parked himself by the telephone and continued to field the interruptions that occupied him on Muriel's behalf.

Matron, in person, rang from the geriatric wing to say that Jerome was failing; that he was now a sorry shade of yellowy-brown from head to foot.

'That's all we need,' Peter smiled at Muriel, 'Fete and funeral on the same day.'

'The fete! Next week! Tell Delilah that Jerome is about to croak. Tell her that it would be unseemly to hold it here - especially with me dressed up as a gypsy. Say anything.'

Dulcie overheard the plan.

'You've done quite enough damage here already without letting down the entire village. Quite sufficient.'

Peter told her that she did wrong to interfere and, noisily, she shuffled away. Marco and Flavia arrived with a chastened Phyllis whose petticoat didn't even buzz as she entered the house with her worldly goods in bags and boxes. Muriel though with pity of the welcome she must have suffered from Roger.

Marco greeted his uncle with forced astonishment. He would have liked to have taken charge during these days of disturbance; was irritated by the threat of Peter's superior common sense and planned to play tricks upon him. Flavia was pouty but prepared to be lively and to put forward thoughts in respect of crisis.

'So much for Roger. Poor Chick. How can you have introduced us to such a creep?'

Phyllis went to resume her duties, showing in her pettish face that the game was up.

The menacing breeze of the evening before had blown away, leaving behind a sunlessness that was neither hot nor cold. To Muriel this was an oddity, for she had not occupied the place other than in a heatwave and had hardly had time to consider it as existing in any other condition.

As, on Peter's advice, she drove towards the hospital, she fumed on a rota of rage against each one of her assailants. The hospital, too, was a place in dull light but she was confident of recognising her uncle even if it was true that he had gone a shade of yellowish-brown from top to toe.

Jerome sat, as described by matron, in his chair - head heavily forward and hands, indeed the colour of which she had been warned, clasping at the handrail. A flutter of fear and self-disgust attacked her as she watched the dying man and wished that she had known him in his heyday, even had they disliked each other and he had willed his worldly goods in some direction other than her own. Matron joined them.

'It won't be long now Mrs Cottle. But, then, it never is. Not once they come inside. Nobody for them to worry in here. That's half of it. Nurses don't react to temper.' She held herself sternly and went on, 'Of course he didn't know anything about the papers or the goings-on at his place. We managed to keep it from him.'

How could he, Muriel was angry, have ever begun to comprehend one word; this moribund imbecile, a sorry shade of yellowish-brown?

Jerome did not jerk and when Muriel shook one discoloured hand, it reminded her of a game she used to play as a child. It was called 'Dead Man's Hand' and it involved placing one palm against the matching one and then running the finger and thumb of the spare hand up and down the outside of the clasped pair. This used to create a frisson of deadness for both participants but, since childhood, Muriel had never thought to ask anyone to join her in this antic. Peter was a possibility. Suitable for blind eyes. Feeling and touch.

She signalled to matron; asserting that she wished to be left alone with Mr Atkins. Matron did not much care for being banned and showed it with a hoity-toity turn of her heel, but complied nonetheless.

In a weird and wonky way, Muriel began to address the static figure; kneeling before him but not looking at his face, for his head was so far slumped that not a feature showed to the world outside his dressing gown. It was as though his neck had been semi-severed, that the cord running through him had perished.

'Don't you die whatever else,' she begged and squeezed his yellow-brown fingers with her own.

'Why not get better? I want you to get better. Please, Uncle Jerome. I'm in terrible trouble.' Her own words moved her and she started to cry; laying her head on a shawl that covered his knees and continuing to plead with him as her thoughts ran haywire. There came no reaction but a huge and horrible fart that cracked from him like a Chinese firework and fouled the air. The stench was stupefying and she moved her head from his knees and loosened her hold on his skinny fingers. Shaking her head to rid it of poisonous air, she stood up and walked to the window from where she saw an ancient lady, head twisted to one side, being pushed across the yard by a strapping fellow. She returned to the earlier spot where she was caught between a deep stirring of compassion for the piteous being, and a heartfelt hatred for an expiring cretin. Every fibre in her fluctuating person hurt and frightened her as once again the old man farted while his body shook in the effort it cost him to release noxious gases from his shrivelled inside.

She could bear it no more. She blew him a kiss and, with tears coursing down her face, ran the length of the corridor, pushed past matron who, in her greatly aroused interest in Muriel, desired a powwow, and crossed the tarmac to Monopoly who waited for her in her car. Time she bought a bigger and better one.

At the house Peter and Marco talked in friendly enough fashion as Marco banked the fire, for not only was it dark in the hall but unexpectedly chilly. He made a great palaver with bellows and branches as he basked in self-congratulatory pleasure and made a show of proving to his uncle that he ruled the roost. Muriel entered quietly in time to hear him say, 'So, Uncle Peter. You spoke to him. What did the solicitor geezer have to say for himself? He must know if the estate can be threatened.'

Muriel was taken aback. She had not thought to ask this question of Peter, in spite of suspicions as to what Roger might be up to. According to Marco, who had done some sleuthing in London, Roger - not clever in his cups at keeping secrets - was in search of a collateral. He had botched it with the present occupant and sought to find another.

Peter replied. 'Oh. He seems to think it will be fine. It's quite definite that Jerome had no children. Nobody appears to know if he had nephews or nieces and Mr Stiller was vague as to whether, in the absence of descendants, collaterals have any right to make claims upon a will. I asked him to make enquiries.'

The fire raged and Marco set off to re-raid the cellar, informing his mother that Flavia was under the weather and was lying down upon her tantalising bed.

'So sorry.' Muriel was distracted, and relieved to have Flavia and her pouts out of the way.

Phyllis came forward wearing on her unhappy face a fixed grin and an air of desperate willingness as her hands flew and fumbled and as Peter, sensitive to the buzzing of a skirt, took hold of Muriel's hand. Phyllis wanted to know in what way she could help. Were there any tasks? Was there anything to be washed? Ironed? Muriel experienced another round of compassion. She and Phyllis, after all, had an unhealthy point in common for had they not both, at different times but with resembling results, fallen victim to the spurious charms of Roger? The girl deserved another chance. If only she would stop that constant twitching.

Peter took stock of Muriel's change of heart for, although he could not see the forbearance in her eyes, he guessed at it. He held her hand as firmly as when he had first taken it upon the advance of Phyllis's footsteps and whispered, 'Don't be too soft. Put her on probation.' He recognised Muriel's sympathy for Phyllis as being connected with Roger and repudiated any trap that linked her with the scoundrel.

Muriel, abashed that Phyllis could thus see her and possibly use this notice to the detriment of all, stiffened and stated that a basket of clothes in need of washing lay in wait in her bathroom. She was shy of telling Peter that she feared for the outcome of this witness to their clasped hands. Roger and his columns. Hugh and his ambitions for squirearchy. Peter sensed much but feared little. 'Once bitten twice shy. The mind bends to picture what she must have been through since yesterday. There won't be any more trouble of that kind.'

Still. They had held hands and Muriel was concerned when she assessed that, other than to guide or to help him in some practical way, she had not before allowed her hand to rest in his; not that the hand-holding had brought her anything but contentment. No flutter of agitation had accompanied the sensation of repose.

When next the telephone rang it was Mambles, keen for a few words with her old friend.

'You have caused a bit of a flurry. Storm in a teacup. Mummy says so. But, frankly, Muriel you must have nothing more to do with that ghastly journalist.'

Mambles was always advising Muriel to do the one thing on which she was already resolved. It was an irritating habit but kindly intended.

'Now listen to me. Are you ready for guests yet? Proper guests I mean. I've promised to entertain that horrid Greek cousin of ours; the one with the boring wife and dreary daughters. Mummy says that she will come, with an equerry or two if that would help in evening up the numbers.' She began to count - dividing men from women and establishing that they would still need two extra men if they were to balance up the presence of the two dreary daughters of the horrid Greek Prince.

Muriel explained that Jerome was on the blink and that it would be awkward at such a time to flood the house with foreign royalty - not to mention herself and Queen Elizabeth, the Queen Mother (not that she put it in those words).

'Just for the day then. It only takes two hours in the Daimlers. We could be with you in time for lunch. Let's make it tomorrow, then if the old codger stiffens in the night, we can hush it up until the evening. What a lovely treat. We can have early supper with you and still be home by midnight.'

Tomorrow.

There were insuperable obstacles. What if Lizzie were to find out in the wake of her own rebuff? Peter would satisfy as one of the missing men but who else could she find at such short notice? Flavia was sure to revive in time for such a festival and cancel Marco out. Other than à deux, Mambles could not bear a superfluity of women. Mummy must unearth an extra walker. She was cleverer in these ways than was her third daughter.

Dawson and Delilah. They must be fitted in this time. It was imperative. Teatime?

'Please Muriel,' Mambles continued with her case. 'I just can't stand the thought of feeding them here and Mummy says her cook can't cope with the numbers at this time of year. She's usually in Scotland in July and Clarence House is half closed down. She's only in London because of that stupid piece of chicken bone that got stuck in her oesophagus and she has to be watched. Please say yes. Can you keep that she-man locked away? Mummy would have a fit if he bowed to her.'

As she wavered, Muriel felt Peter's hand upon her shoulder. He advised her to agree, whispering that matters couldn't get worse. That it might restore confidence with Kitty and co. That a happening was what was needed.

'Yes,' said Muriel. 'How lovely. We'll see you all at about twelve-thirty.'

Tomorrow.

She wheeled on Peter. 'What about Lizzie? Phyllis? Dulcie? Oh God alive Peter. What about food? Peter. You'll have to think of something. Can you turn into two men?'

'Possibly. Now remember that you are in a strong position with Phyllis fawning. Work her to the bone. Dulcie must be banned. I shall ring the rectory and ask if they have a spare son at home; with luck the one who removes his trousers on public transport. I will tell Delilah that you need him to make up the numbers and, what's more, you want them both to join you here for lunch in the presence of.....'

'What if he removes them at lunch?'

'So much the better.'

Vigour returned to the house. Kitty subpoenaed a sister or two and Phyllis's desire to please knew no bounds, although no chamber pots were needed since the royal group did not intend to spend the night on this occasion. Pot plants were trundled back by Joyce and Eric.

Peter reported on his conversation with a delighted Delilah. Alistair was, by chance, their only son to be at home. Delilah urged that Muriel must not believe any silly bits of gossip that might have circulated in the village concerning Alistair.

'Tongues will wag,' she told him, 'and, well, aren't we all God's creatures? Another thing. I think it would be appropriate for Dawson to say grace. Royalty expect it I believe. I'll make sure he wears his dog collar and I'll get Alistair into a blazer.' She didn't mention trousers. 'Nobody's going to look at me. I'm only the rector's wife. And one more thing. I've just had a lovely idea. Do suggest to Muriel that she serves us coronation chicken. It would be a gorgeous gesture.'

Marco dealt with Dulcie, offering her a fiver and ordering her to visit her neighbours at the cat sanctuary. She took the money and said, 'All right. I know when I'm not wanted.' Which wasn't strictly true.

What was left of the day passed once again in restless preparation. Flavia did not put in an appearance at supper (which was light and slight, all reserves being stationed for the morrow), but Marco, more than efficient in his zeal for the house to be seen at its best, laid bare cupboards where for years precious glass, silver and china services, had been set aside and lost to use.

Before taking herself and her dog to bed, Muriel answered the telephone to matron. 'I don't think the old gentleman will last many more hours,' she reported and sighed as though to mark her belief that Muriel was likely to be unaffected by the bulletin. Gasping that she would appreciate it if matron could ring, during the night if necessary, to keep her abreast of events, she fell across her bed and weakened into a fresh burst of furious sobs.

It was hot again on Sunday morning and Muriel woke to the conclusion that she must again give Dawson's erudite sermon a miss. This repeated lapse in her behaviour, however, was to be more than made up for by granting him permission to say grace before lunch, and she feared that he might cook up an extra orthodox one when confronted by the Greeks.

Marco worked wonders with supreme wines and accoutrements for the table, setting Kitty's sisters to work with cloths, brushes and extra leaves that enlarged a table upon which sixteen places were set out.

Flavia showed up - dressed to kill but pale, grumpy and unwilling to lend a hand in spite of the enormity of events to come. Phyllis lent wandering ones wherever needed but, never for a second, allowing the leer to lapse on her lips. Kitty cooked and Peter made mental notes on the complex matter of *places à table*.

Muriel rang the hospital to learn that Jerome was 'clinging on' but not, apparently, to his handrails since he had been bundled into bed and was expected to remain in it until his demise.

Word of the royal visit had got round and figures ensconced themselves under the ilexes and between laurels in the shrubbery; garden boys and others inclined to share the glory with people from the press.

By twelve o'clock all duties had been accomplished. At twelve-fifteen news came that Jerome was dead. Peter intercepted this blow. He told matron that Muriel had been called away and was unlikely to return until late that evening; said it would be best for all if Mr Atkins rested in peace until the following day when Mrs Cottle would put in an appearance at the hospital at an early hour.

Matron suggested that it was 'a shame' that his relative had not been there to see him out. 'But then, of course, she's been occupied with her entertaining.' She agreed, since no alternative arose, to Peter's proposal.

Dawson and Delilah, accompanied by Alastair who wore blazer and trousers, were the first to arrive.

Muriel, Marco, Flavia and Peter received them in the drawing room. Delilah was colourfully dressed and her hair, that looked to have been screwed into curlers since first she learnt of her luck, was jammed in tight rolls to the side of her face. She pushed Alistair to the fore. 'He has a lovely job now, haven't you dear? Well. Dawson got it for him. Pulled strings. He's selling at the Bible shop at Shifford.' Muriel's eyes went to Alistair's flies for she wished to establish that the zip was fastened.

Dawson asked her if she had thought any more about the school's overspend and whether or not the fete was to be held in her grounds.

Delilah interposed. 'Poor Jerome. How is he? We thought we might pop in and see him this afternoon. Dawson, as I said before, is lovely with the dying.'

Peter was beside them in an instant.

'Tomorrow might be better. He was tired out yesterday.'

Muriel frowned. It would have been an ideal way of getting rid of Dawson and Delilah, Alistair too, in the afternoon. She was frantic enough as to how to entertain her guests between lunch and supper without Dawson and Delilah hovering about, unable to tear themselves away. Was Peter becoming bossy? Interfering in this way.

Time ran out and there was no further opportunity for the unravelling of this mix-up, for Phyllis warned that a slow cortège of glistening Daimlers approached and that the first one had already pulled up outside the front door.

Mambles and her mother sat in the back, Moggan at the wheel and a tidily dressed equerry-cum-courtier beside him. The second car contained a brace of equerries-cum-courtiers, one of which sat in the back with the Greek Prince - or King. Muriel couldn't remember which.

The boring wife and deadly daughters, as portrayed by Mambles, came in the third car but no one attempted to climb from their place until Queen Elizabeth had been photographed and safely escorted to the porch where she was awaited by her hostess and her son. A group of plain-clothes detectives followed at discreet distance. It had been decided in advance that Peter and Flavia stay in the drawing room with Dawson, Delilah and their silent descendant.

A reception committee formed in the hall; Kitty and her sisters, Mavis and Phyllis - all wishing to be seen to advantage. Muriel had not instructed them to line up in this way and wondered how they had concocted such a concept.

Queen Elizabeth, in organdie, truly floated to the porch and Muriel tried not to cry for it was all a bit much. Mambles followed and soon, in a terrible rush, the entire party crowded dark corners.

Prince Alexis of Greece was a short man, dark and undistinguished but with manners of syrup. He kissed Muriel's hand and said 'charming' several times before introducing his womenfolk. Princess Roxana was also short, and old before her years. The two girls were undersized and Mambles towered above them, smiling at each, eager to promote how well her friend had done in inheriting such a place.

But Mambles's thoughts were mainly for 'Mummy' who wished to be taken to the bathroom, as Mambles called the lavatory.

At first the equerries-cum-courtiers were indistinguishable from each other in their tidy clothes and uniform politeness. They gave themselves no airs and admired everything with exemplary correctitude. Marco took it upon himself to chat-up the two undersized Greek Princesses, both of whom suffered from self-consciousness.

They giggled as he led them to the room where the earlier group awaited them and giggled as he introduced them to Alastair who giggled back but made no attempt to disgrace himself.

When all were assembled; when all had been introduced; when Delilah had become half-dazed from curtseying; when Dawson had buttonholed the Queen Mother to recount to her a rambling story concerning the behaviour of a certain Archbishop of Canterbury at some royal ceremony at which Her Majesty had been present; when drinks had been dispensed – only then did Muriel begin to believe that the game was absolutely up, that she was unfit to entertain in this fashion. Her head throbbed and she could answer in nothing but syllables as equerries, in turn, posed questions as to the precise date of the house. The whole became hazy.

Queen Elizabeth sipped thirstily at a dry martini and smiled gloriously as Delilah told her of the honour she bestowed, and mentioned that one of her most precious possessions was a coronation mug depicting Her Royal Highness and the late King in all their finery.

Dawson's grace was long and in Latin. Muriel was near to fainting as she seated herself between Prince Alexis and Dawson in his dog collar. Looking the length of the table, she accepted, despite her irritation with him, that Peter had done well with the seating arrangements. Alastair sat between the Princesses. At one point he looked to his knees and Muriel fancied that he prepared a repeat of his exposure on public transport. Delilah, happily protected by two equerries, kept a close eye on her boy and Flavia, between an equerry and Peter, continued to sulk and contribute little.

Marco, flanked by the Queen Mother and Mambles, paid no attention to his wife's sullen behaviour but pulled out stop after stop, charming, amusing and delighting the royal ladies so his mother could not but be content. Marco was, it had to be admitted, a wondrous social asset. Peter betrayed nothing but amusement.

Prince Alexis, stupefied by the quality of the white Burgundy, asked Muriel if Bradstow Manor had been her home since childhood for, clearly, Mambles had not briefed him.

'No. Only a week - if that. I'd never heard of it a fortnight ago.'

He was puzzled, judged her insane and told her childish jokes; one about an old King who thrust his bottom out of a railway carriage.

He admired a Chinese lacquered clock that ticked in an alcove. It reminded him, he said, of his own childhood and his English governess who had taught him and his brothers a song entitled 'My Grandfather's Clock'. It was accompanied by a merry air and he and his siblings had amused themselves by removing the letter 'l' from the lines. He puffed his chest and rendered in a low and tuneful tone:

My Grandfather's cock was too big for the shelf

So it stood ninety years on the floor.

It was larger by half than the old man himself

Though it weighed not a penny weight more.'

Both Muriel and Delilah glanced at Alistair who giggled with the shy Princesses, all three near to losing inhibitions. Princess Roxana sighed and frowned. Dawson, on the deaf side, clapped, for he did not hear the finer points and approved of song. Queen Elizabeth and Mambles rose high above earthly matters and, apart from Flavia in her filthy mood, all went well.

Phyllis, Kitty and Kitty's sisters tripped and trotted with extreme neatness in spite of resentment rankling in Kitty that the rectory crowd should be included on such a day and that Phyllis was still present in their midst.

Princess Roxana of Greece, not entirely unmoved by her husband's lapse in taste, swallowed her pride and sat enthralled as Dawson described his own method of brewing beer and commented kindly as he propounded the problem of the overspend on the school budget and, in lower voice, told of the head lice alert. A case had been reported in lower primary earlier in the week.

Kitty had done wonders with several chickens (not precisely cooked in coronation style but near enough to earn a beam of satisfaction from Delilah), a floating pudding and, thanks to Marco and treasures from the cellar, the enjoyment of the royal party knew no bounds.

Dawson stood to say grace. The meal was over. A hurdle scaled. Now what? What the hell was Muriel to do with them now?

Mambles suggested that Mummy lie down for an hour and volunteered to care for her if Phyllis would show them to a bedroom.

'I wanted to bring Farty but she looked so alarmed at the prospect of returning here that I let her off the hook. Poor Farty. Mummy thought of getting Cunty for the day but, sadly, she's got a gallstone.'

Alastair offered to take the Greek girls for a ramble, to which suggestion their mother agreed, believing it fitting that her girls should stroll with the son of a rector who had said grace at luncheon.

The three spare men, too, decided to take advantage of their summer day in the country and walked away, each keeping pace with the other, in the direction of the stream.

Mambles tended to the needs of Queen Elizabeth as she reposed in Muriel's guest bedroom and Flavia slipped to her own. Marco ignored her escape and proposed to Prince Alexis and Princess Roxana that a tour of the house, inside and out, might interest them.

Muriel was left with Peter, Dawson and Delilah.

'Muriel, how can we ever thank you? I shall get Dawson to write a prayer of thanksgiving. What an honour to say grace in the presence of royalty. By the way, was that wine from Jerome's cellar? How gorgeous that you've taken the plunge. He wouldn't have a bottle touched you know. Sacrosanct. Not that we minded. Plonk is quite good enough for us as you know.'

Dawson said, 'I wonder what those young ones are up to,' upon which Delilah lost her lustre and suggested following them, 'keeping our distance of course,' to the bushes.

Dawson returned to the project of paying a visit to Jerome and Peter decided that the time had come to reveal to them that they would find but his mortal remains in the hospital bed.

Delilah shouted, 'How tactful! How very tactful. You were keeping it quiet, I suppose, until royalty returned to London.'

Muriel was grateful to Peter for his common sense for she knew how differently would Delilah have viewed the subterfuge had she and Dawson not played their parts in the action of the day. It was a comfort to her to know that, at the rectory at least, the suppression would be treated with respect.

Jerome was dead. Should she not slip over to the hospital? What of goings-on in the shrubbery and beyond? What of Queen Elizabeth, the Queen Mother, asleep on one of her beds?

Peter told her to do nothing; absolutely nothing until the next day. 'Then,' he agreed, 'you must go straight to the nursing home and I, er, or Marco will ring Arthur and the undertaker or whoever.'

Delilah, intoxicated, agreed to everything and Dawson began, as they spoke, to prepare a sermon for the funeral.

'Saturday today. Normally the funeral would be round about Wednesday. Nothing going on in the church that day as far as I can remember without my diary. I have one or two little anecdotes up my sleeve that might be appropriate.'

Delilah butted in, 'There goes the fete I'm afraid. I don't imagine it would be appropriate for you to go ahead as Gypsy Rosalee. It will have to be in the school grounds. Never mind. Next year and, Muriel, I've just had a lovely idea. What about getting Her Majesty to come down and open it for us?'

With her reflective faculties at a low ebb, Muriel walked to the window and saw Dulcie, in helmet and leathers, bending fiercely forward as she guided her Suzuki over the gravel. Marco's fiver had not bought more than a few hours absence.

Expecting Dulcie to steam on in the direction of her caravan, Muriel half turned her head to the remaining band who sat on sofas absorbing the news, but quickly turned it back again for the motorbike stopped with a crunch at the front door.

Within a minute, a wrapped figure; red and black as a spy from the devil, filled the width of the drawing room doorway. 'Don't tell me you haven't heard that Mr Atkins is dead. They told me over at the cat sanctuary. One of the girls there has a cousin working at the nursing home.' She was cock-a-hoop. 'And what is more she tells me that this house was fully informed at exactly twelve-fifteen. Now what, I would like to know, is a fleet of Daimlers doing outside the front door on the very day that the old man meets his maker?'

This was a long sentence even for Dulcie and, having uttered it, she shrank in her suiting to await results.

Delilah looked at the clock and yelped that, owing to the short notice given for the lunch invitation of the day, she had been unable to cancel the organist who proposed to bring his mother to tea at the rectory, and cakes were still in the freezer.

'I'm sorry,' she squeezed Muriel's arm, 'to leave you here with these problems. Don't pay any attention to Dulcie.' Here she lowered her voice and, breathing close to Muriel's ear, whispered, 'She's one off you know. A law unto herself. But then, of course, it takes all sorts.'

They took their leave, apologising for failing to take their leave of the distinguished visitors; offering praise and humility as they pushed past Dulcie who still half-blocked the doorway.

Delilah took stock. 'By the way. Can you send Alistair back as soon as they return from the ramble? And, er, if somebody could keep an eye on them?'

'I most certainly will,' offered Dulcie. 'That boy should not be allowed out of your sight. Not after what he did on public transport.'

Delilah, notwithstanding her uncondemning ways, threw a fearful look at Dulcie betraying that the thrust had detracted from an otherwise unclouded day.

People came and went.

Mambles sent word that she and her mother, due to residual tenderness resulting from the chicken bone so recently lodged in Queen Elizabeth's oesophagus, intended to spend the rest of the afternoon in the spare room. They simply requested that tea be served to them up there; tea and either jelly or blancmange.

Equerries popped in and out of the house raising praise before paintings and investigative patience before china objects. They talked fluently in quiet tones as they admired all in sight and offered assistance where none was needed.

Alastair and the Greek girls returned, breathless, from the garden before six o'clock. Nobody had looked for or kept an eye on them (other than Dulcie who spied unseen and unseeing - for her eyes were weak - through well-worn field glasses).

All three were in good condition and the girls explained that they had persuaded Alistair to throw in his job at the Bible bookshop and to follow them to Cap Ferrat (where, when not travelling, they lived with their parents in exile). Alistair wriggled in quiet euphoria. Whatever had taken place in the shrubbery had been nothing less than therapeutic and each wore a successful look.

The senior Greeks, upon their return, announced that they had spent a fruitful afternoon under the guidance of Marco. They had visited the church which boasted an interesting marble or two. There was nothing, though, to equal the pleasure when they discovered that their mouse-mute daughters had made successful contact with the rector's son. What was more they had met him through the auspices of their royal relations and were barely able to express how welcome he was to be made at Cap Ferrat.

Behind this pleasantness and in the company of Peter, Muriel suffered underlying anxiety. Marco and Flavia were clearly at odds. Whatever hollowness invaded their union they had, hitherto, been in it together; had always supported each other in their useless way of life.

Greeks and equerries wished to 'tidy' themselves and were shown to bath and washrooms by Kitty's sisters - for Phyllis busied herself with jellies and blancmanges.

When he and Muriel were alone together, Peter said, 'I think Flavia's pregnant. Does she wear that telltale look? That look of being gnawed at from within?'

Muriel said that she hadn't noticed and that such an eventuality would not, surely, but make Marco more attentive rather than less.

'Perhaps he's against it. Perhaps he made it a condition of marriage. People do you know and, to Marco responsibility is a very dirty word. Perhaps he's not the father. One has to think of everything.'

'Not Marco's?' Something dawned on her.

There had been a suspicious weakness in Marco's reluctance to let go of Roger - possessing, as he did, the knowledge of his mother's continuing dismay in her awareness of the intimacy. Marco was feeble. It was likely that Flavia had dominated in determination to include Roger in combined activities. The chance that her grandchild, were there to be one, was sired by Roger came as the final piece of ill fortune before the end of a tiring day.

Then came a glimmer of optimism. Had not Flavia, only the day before, chastised Muriel for introducing them to Roger in the first place? She imparted this splinter of hope to Peter who became pensive and replied slowly. 'I shouldn't have put the idea into your head. I daresay it's all tosh but, in my view, Flavia knows which side her bread is buttered. Not only did she witness Roger flirting with Phyllis but, er, since all this,' he pointed at the plasterwork ceiling, 'she may consider Marco to be a better bet than the scribbler.' Peter disliked speaking Roger's name.

Guests reassembled and Marco revealed that Flavia had flaked out and sent apologies and, although Muriel doubted the truth of the reported nicety, she was touched by her son's attempt to cover up for Flavia.

A sense of rebirth controlled the group as Phyllis made known that Mambles and her mother were shortly to appear and that they would both appreciate a vodka cocktail. There was a thrill of oncoming rush and, as each member of the party stiffened, Queen Elizabeth, closely followed by Princess Matilda, entered the room.

Mambles's face was luminescent. She had monopolised her mother for three whole hours without interference from the Queen or Princess Margaret or indeed from any of the younger generation who pulled the wool over the old lady's eyes.

Queen Elizabeth carried a large signed photograph of herself which she handed to Muriel and which Muriel recognised as a replica of the one taken to mark her ninetieth birthday; the one that she had seen in a silver frame on top of Mambles's piano. Muriel thanked her and vowed that she would display it worthily. Mambles, vigilant throughout the transaction, interposed, 'Mummy doesn't usually give a photograph unless she's stayed all night. Still. We were in the spare room for over three hours. I suppose that counts for a bit of a night.'

Queen Elizabeth asked after Muriel's dog, for Monopoly had stayed upstairs in his basket, and said that she missed her own.

'Another time,' she said, 'I'll bring Sir Walter Raleigh. Matilda mentioned that you keep cats. Sir Walter enjoys a cat-hunt but seldom gets a chance. My daughter, the Queen, cannot abide cats.'

Muriel asked herself how Sonia would respond to the sight of a corgi-shaped Sir Walter Raleigh chasing Kitty or Corin as cheered along by the mother of the Monarch.

Supper was more manageable than lunch. For a start there was less noise without Dawson, Delilah, Alistair or Flavia (not that Flavia had contributed verbally but she had clattered cutlery).

Without Alastair, the Greek Princesses lacked vitality but they did both smile at intervals as they anticipated his arrival at Cap Ferrat in the not-too-distant future.

Marco continued to enchant and Queen Elizabeth, forgetting all painful effects of the rascally chicken bone, told him in confidence that her favourite song was 'Drink to Me Only'.

When they had all departed and shortly before darkness fell, Muriel's powers gave out. She sat upon a shallow step of the solidly-built staircase, placed her head between her hands and asked of Peter and Marco who themselves began to think of bed, 'Tomorrow, when I go to the hospital, will I have to kiss the corpse?'

It seemed to her that she floated from a drifting sea that was never still, onto an alien shore where she knew nobody and where her daily props were to be forever denied her. In this no-man's-land she found that there was no corner-shop, nowhere to lay her hands on a Mars Bar or a Crunchie; no quick crossword; no battery for her headphones to move for her the pages of a talking book, designed to tether her thoughts during sleepless nights. The list grew longer. No ready-made sandwich, no crisps, no ribbon for her hair.

It hit her fair and square that the remoteness from which she suffered, both in sleep and in waking hours, was one that had dogged Mambles's childhood and her first trip, oft-described by Cunty, on the underground.

Chapter 11

It was early when Lizzie rang on Monday morning. Muriel was up and conversing with Monopoly who enjoyed freedom after his banishment of the day before. He promised, with a wag, to keep her company in the car when she visited Jerome's relics.

'I'm sorry. It's a bit much, Muriel. There's a piece in the *Daily Mail*. It's just come through my letterbox. Listen. I'll read it to you.'

Muriel begged her to desist.

'Please Lizzie. Let me off the hook. Whatever that stupid paper says, do believe me. I had no control.'

'I'm sorry but it says that your uncle, if he is your uncle, died before you entertained the Queen Mother, Princess Matilda and half the Greek Royal family to lunch in his house. It also says that your caretaker, a Dulcie-something-or-other, aged over eighty, gave an interview from the nursing home, having ridden there on a motorbike after learning that the Queen Mother had put her feet up on your spare room bed.'

'It is sort of true, I must admit.'

'So. Why did you get that blind brother-in-law of yours to chuck me?'

Lizzie ranted and Muriel knew that she had been mistaken in bidding Peter to lay her off.

'Lord protect me from my friends,' she silently quoted as she did her best to atone with a series of rash promises.

The country was dry and fields almost white after, apart from one brief thunderstorm, weeks of drought. Muriel and Monopoly looked out from their separate windows, aiming to acquaint themselves with landmarks in the locality. They passed cattle, cottages, horses and hedges as they neared the nursing home. To the side of the road, jutting from a half-hidden entrance, a hand-written sign read 'Pick your own' and Muriel thought of Roger.

At the home, a nurse presented Muriel with Jerome's rank suit and a pair of dusty shoes. She also handed her a gold signet ring rubbed bare of lettering.

'There's his overnight bag to follow,' she informed with a briskness that compounded Muriel's misery.

'Would you care to come along?'

Muriel followed her as far as the closed door that barred her from looking into the cubicle where her dead patron lay. There they stopped and the nurse (Muriel supposed her to be the one with connections at the cat-sanctuary) asked if she would care to take a last look. She nodded; sensing such behaviour to be correct.

Jerome lay, clean and cross, no longer senile but forbidding. Muriel wished with vehemence that the nurse had not followed her into the cubicle for she knew that the woman expected her to kiss the blue lips that tugged her eyes towards them.

'Should I kiss him?' she asked.

'Just as you please.'

'What do people usually do?'

'It depends. It's up to you.'

Thus they wrangled as Jerome, all but his face hidden beneath a sheet, lay doornail-dead and powerless to advise.

The curious thing was that, later, Muriel was never able to remember how she had resolved the dilemma. She never knew, even in old age, whether or not she had bent to kiss the lips of Jerome Atkins; deceased.

Slipping the worn ring into a cotton pocket of her frock, Muriel's mind turned to other gems that might, by chance, be hidden in the house. Aunt Alice, had she possessed any treasures, was unlikely to have bestowed them on Dulcie. Dulcie in a tiara. Was there any limit to the possible depths of her all-probable inheritance? Jerome, most decidedly, had not lasted the seven years that Arthur had recommended to free his heir from death duty. She ruminated on this and other matters as she drove back to Bradstow where, without time to take stock, she found herself incarcerated with an undertaker who waited for her in the hall with a show of limitless patience.

His name was Mr Cabbage. Chuck Cabbage. He was tall and wore a long grey mackintosh suited to the solemnity of his trade. His high, domed head boasted but a few strands of sticky black hair.

With gravelly intonation and infinite understanding, he clasped Muriel's right hand in both his own.

'Mrs Cottle. I am grieved Mrs Cottle to hear of your tragic loss. Now, Mrs Cottle, if there is any little thing Mrs Cottle - such as a favourite hymn of the deceased, Mrs Cottle.' She could not believe her ears. Never, particularly, had she cared for the name that Hugh had landed her with but, until her meeting with Mr Cabbage, had not realised that it was downright absurd.

'He will be with us by now Mrs Cottle, in our Chapel of Rest. The main question, Mrs Cottle, is whether it's to be burial or cremation Mrs Cottle.'

They cleared up many points.

It annoyed her that Chuck Cabbage, with his exaggerated use of her name, had succeeded in reminding her of Hugh and it struck her that, were she to divorce Hugh and marry Peter, her name would still be Mrs Cottle. It was hideously unfair.

Ushering Mr Cabbage to the front door, her heart turned over, rendering her giddy - for this was the first time that she had allowed for Peter in her plans. Of all the haunting disturbances that had put paid to her peace of mind of late, this created the greatest havoc and puzzled her (for by nature she was impatient) that Peter's blindness did not bother her, other than for the uncomplained-of distress that it caused him. He was furnished with his own radar system and seldom broke or bumped or found himself far from his intended spot. Hugh was one to point out faults; specks, untidiness and such like but she shuddered as she weighed Peter's incapacity as a point in his favour and took mental advantage of it.

After despatching Mr Cabbage to his duties, she found Peter in the hall and palpitated lest he read her mind. He gave no sign of having done so and suggested that the time had come for her to visit Flavia in her bedroom. 'But,' he continued, 'dismiss our irresponsible musings from your mind. Just ask her if she needs anything.'

Marco had not surfaced and, when Muriel knocked on the bedroom door, it was he who grunted out permission to enter. The pair lay entwined as she had seen them there before, putting paid to imaginings.

'How's Flavia today?'

'Don't know. She hasn't woken.'

Marco jumped from the bed in creased pyjamas and said, 'I'll tell you what Ma. I'll be down in a jiffy,' remembering how his mother loved that word. 'Let's take Monopoly for a walk.'

As she waited for her son to dress she anticipated confidences and thought to ask Peter if he would join them outside since, with all she had to fathom, the fear of extra burdens loomed intolerably and a third party would undoubtedly keep revelations at bay.

Peter, however, was nowhere to be found and Muriel, Monopoly and Marco made for the rookery beyond the stream.

'So Ma,' he said, half addressing the dog, 'I daresay you've guessed. Flavia, I mean. A little one. A baby in time for the New Year.'

'My darling,' her voice was forced and fragile. 'How exciting? Are you pleased?'

'Sort of,' he replied, his voice half-drowned by rasping rooks. 'Flave's not though. It's put her in a peculiar mood. It's going to be a problem, what with me being hopeless, no job and all that.'

'Perhaps I'll be able to help. Have it down here or something. You can come at weekends. Kitty might have a sister.' She was carried away by schemes.

Marco brightened and turned towards her, lines of weariness escaping from his white face. 'Might you Ma? You must hang on to this place at all costs. I'll tell Flave. It'll cheer her up. I'll try to get myself sorted out - work or whatnot.'

Untroubled by suspicion.

He smiled and said, 'Good old Gran,' and stretched himself as though to express a view that problems had been shelved.

They returned to the house where Muriel's attention was grasped by those who sought instruction.

'It's likely to be a large crowd.' Phyllis used her hands indicating a mob. 'Mr Atkins was well liked before he went funny. There's the church group; school managers and the rest. They're not going to want to miss out.'

The funeral was planned for the following Thursday at midday. Then there was to be a buffet lunch hosted by Muriel for an indefinite number of guests.

Interminable confabulation with Dawson ensued. 'It's come at a bad time - what with the fete. Now Delilah. She's an expert on flower arrangement as you know. As a matter of fact, she's known as the Constance Spry of the Midlands around here.'

Peter undertook to sort out the order of service with the help of Kitty and her pencil. Joyce and Eric wheeled in pots and Muriel considered it unseemly that the very same blooms appeared and reappeared with little to show for their journeys but the explosion of the odd extra flower or the removal of the odd piece of fading foliage. It would have been more festive to have shown different displays for different types of occasion.

Dulcie humped logs.

'He liked a fire at all times as I have previously mentioned.' Once again the weather was scorchingly hot.

Phyllis came, breathing conscientious effort, to ask if Muriel cared for her to bundle up Jerome's clothes in time for the fete.

'Joyce would be pleased to have them. She runs the rummage.'

Whilst assenting, Muriel inspected her image and accepted that there was every chance that criticism would arise. Jerome's clothes flung from the house to be unravelled upon the village rummage stall within days of his departure from the world.

Flavia kept to her room.

The telephone began to ring in earnest although more often than not the calls were put through by Dawson or Delilah offering suggestions. Muriel realised how little she knew of Jerome and his earlier doings. Had he, for example, ever earned a decoration? OBE or something.

Arthur came in person to the rescue, happy to be of service and exaggeratedly civil in his address to the lady of the house.

On the morning of the day before Jerome's funeral Muriel paid a visit to the Norman Church of which Dawson was the rector.

Waterproof sheeting, spread to cover the width and half of the aisle, was heaped high with flowers and greenery where three elderly ladies chatted as they sifted and arranged under the directions of Delilah whose hair was gathered in a flimsy net and who called 'Cooee! I'm in my element. Flowers!' She pronounced the word 'flahs' and pressed her face into the prickle of a rose.

She introduced Muriel to her companions. 'My team,' she termed them with pride.

'Now team. This is Muriel. Muriel Cottle. You'll find her a tremendous kindred spirit.'

The three elderly women gazed at her in boundless curiosity for there were many reasons to excite their wonder. Not one amongst them was free of the knowledge of wines, chamber pots and royalty, and the affair of Hugh and Miss Ingrid Malone, too, had been doing the rounds. Whatever appeasement offered by Delilah in her assurances that it took all sorts and that Muriel was likely to be a tremendous kindred spirit, they had their doubts.

'How kind. How very kind. Can I help? A vase or something?' Muriel tried in the face of scandal.

The women started and stared and one ran to a cupboard that stood in a dark corner behind the organ and beneath bells. Muriel, in the knowledge that she was held in disrespectful awe, was anxious not to make a hash of her flower arrangement. Delilah made almost as free with Muriel's first name as had Chuck Cabbage with her second. The woman who had run to the cupboard returned with a large glass vase that she handed to Muriel, saying, 'Let me know if you need any help. Oasis or wire.'

Delilah took charge.

'What about down there? Just below the pulpit. There. Gorgeous. Make sure that Dawson's surplice won't brush it when he passes on his way to deliver the address. Lovely one by the way. A bit above my head, I fear but you'll appreciate it and, er, some of your London friends. Might any of them be coming?'

She threw a conspiratorial look that radiated upon her fellow florists and sent their colours rising as Muriel filled her vase with a tangle of roses and honeysuckle, squashing them together and tousling them around until they presented a blob of untidy bravura.

Standing back, she stared at them; much pleased to have produced such a delightful effect. Delilah was beside herself; full of praise.

'I can see that you're a natural with flahs. But, I'll tell you what. A little tip.' She squatted and started to tweak at the masterpiece. Using both hands she twitched at stems to the left and to the right of the vase. As she gave her concentration, the shape of the arrangement altered, becoming flattened and fanned.

'There. That's all it needed. It's a little something I learnt. Women's Institute as a matter of fact. Might you be persuaded to join? We had a gorgeous girl down. Constance Spry-trained. She passed on the knack.'

Muriel guessed that she was unlikely to be collared as a member of the

Church flower rota and offered thanks and wild appreciation as she left the ladies to fan to their hearts delight and walked back, the length of the village, to resume other duties.

There were those who stared at her as she passed and to each, unseeing, she threw a dazed smile of warmth.

At the house, goings-on had reached a peak. Marco, with unnatural ebullience, raced around with a silver cleaning cloth tucked into the belt of his trousers and Peter continued to make mental notes. There were those, he had been advised, who would expect to be placed in the church; Arthur, gorgeous matron, Delilah and so on. Muriel and Marco (Flavia, too, if she were to attend) must, of course, sit in the front pew, right beside the corpse.

Chuck Cabbage crossed the carpet; unexpectedly, silently and clad in a light grey mac.

'Last minute details Mrs Cottle. You, Mrs Cottle, as chief mourner, along with your son, Mrs Cottle, if you so wish, will be expected to enter the church behind the coffin. We, Mrs Cottle, that is to say myself and my lads, will bear the body Mrs Cottle. I'll tip you the wink when we are about to leave. Just outside the porch that will be Mrs Cottle. There was a time, Mrs Cottle, when it would have been our job to carry the body up the church path, Mrs Cottle. The lads today, I'm sorry to say Mrs Cottle, aren't what they were and, consequently Mrs Cottle, we draw the package as far as the porch, Mrs Cottle, on a truck.'

Muriel registered that she was to be tipped the wink as soon as the coffin had been shunted from the truck and, with misgiving, accepted the part she was required to play.

Phyllis passed on the way to an outhouse - carrying black bags stuffed with Jerome's clothing as Marco called out to her, 'Steady Phyllis. There might be some interesting things in those bags. Waistcoats and whatnot. Let's have a dekko before you throw them out.'

Muriel stood mortified. It was bad enough to be jettisoning Jerome's effects. Worse still the proceeds were to be sidetracked from fete funds to increase the lining of Cottle pockets. Never before had she so disliked her name.

Flavia came down to breakfast on the day of the funeral and, although her aspect was wan, she forced a smile and bid Muriel, 'Good luck Chick.' Marco showed her some attention as they gave the impression of a pair who had recently ridden a storm. Breakfast was cleared at top speed, for those in charge of the kitchen wished to deck themselves in black. Outside caterers had been hired to produce luncheon for an indefinite number and flowers accompanied by cards inscribed by unknown (to Muriel) authors, were delivered at an alarming rate.

Muriel, as she changed into a grey frock that matched perfectly with Mr Cabbage's mac, spoke aloud to Monopoly who lay on her bed.

'I'll be better, old boy, when this is over.'

Monopoly replied with an uncertain and unsatisfactory movement of a paw.

They gathered in the hallway; Phyllis, Kitty, Mavis and a sprinkling of Kitty's sisters; soberly dressed and carrying black handbags, each looking as if it had been in store since winter.

With the crash of a closing door, Dulcie, in a pinstripe suit of thick cloth and a navy peaked cap, lunged to the centre of those who gathered, 'He'll be bloody mouldy by now in this heat.'

Near to the time for the great occasion, Muriel shooed them all, including Peter, from the house, explaining that they were to go ahead to take their places in pews.

She, Marco and Flavia remained; intent upon timing.

The three spoke together in agitated nervousness, Marco observing, 'It all looks pretty smashing Ma,' and Flavia echoing, 'Yes. Well done Chick. I wonder if the rector's son will be there - or has he left for Cap Ferrat?'

Marco put his arm round his wife's waist and said, 'Hope he doesn't do anything funny in church, Flave. You're not to look. Not in your condition.'

Muriel, cracking at her knuckles before placing a finger to her lips, implored, 'No jokes kids. Not 'til later,' and, in harmony they headed for the church.

Bells clanged as they made their way, entangling with other mourners who had left their cars in a field on the opposite side of the road to the house. Ladies tested the ground for firmness under their high-heeled shoes and darkly dressed gentlemen saw to the locking of their vehicles. The three chief mourners dawdled, allowing for strangers to pass them by in the hope of being unwatched when tipped the wink by Mr Cabbage. There were stragglers who stared at the coffin; flower-laden and resting behind the glass of a glistening hearse.

Mr Cabbage and his lads wore grey macs of identical cut and Muriel regretted not having donned black.

There was an indefinable flaw in the atmosphere that made Muriel afraid for she was not certain where it came from. The colour of a car? A half-recognition? Monopoly's discreetly doubting response to her suggestion that the worst was nearly over?

She found Mr Cabbage's sepulchral confidence reassuring. He wore the mask of one who had buried a million stiffs a minute, year in year out, including bank holidays.

'Now Mrs Cottle. You wait here by the hearse while we get the coffin onto the truck Mrs Cottle.' He advised her, then, to walk a few paces ahead of the truck and to halt beside it as they decamped the cadaver by the porch. All this took an age and further latecomers passed them in haste as they accompanied the truck, but paused to peer at Muriel.

Organ music, selected by Peter, wheezed out into the open and attendants, one of which was a fully and sombrely clad Alastair, handed out service sheets. Dawson stood, pleased and surpliced, in the porch as he fiddled with his hearing aid.

'Pretty good turn out,' he addressed Muriel. 'Many unknown to me, though I daresay Delilah will be able to identify most of them for you. She's a walking address book.'

The walking address book already sat upon a privileged pew.

Headed by Dawson, the procession moved slowly through the body of the church. He raised his face to heaven and without stumbling and in a resounding voice, half sang the words, 'We brought nothing into this world and it is certain that we can carry nothing out.' Muriel knew that all eyes were upon her. Everybody in the church had heard of her good fortune in inheriting the something that failed to accompany Jerome. Head half-down and wrapped in morbid thought she, with Marco and Flavia, followed Dawson's lead. On a reflex she allowed her eyes to swivel towards her vase, the flowers in which stood fanned and to which sprigs of feathery fern had been added.

When Mr Cabbage and his team had deposited Jerome upon a wooden frame that had been set up for the purpose, he signalled to Muriel that she and her two companions take their places in the front pew on the right-hand side of the aisle. This had been left empty for them and she saw, as she turned to obey orders, that a partified Delilah in mauve stood immediately behind it and that beside her, in dumb fury, huffed Dulcie. No more faces could she distinguish for she faced the front, and Dawson announced the first hymn. 'Fight the Good Fight.' Muriel remembered Jerome as he walloped the ambulance men.

As the congregation sang the first verse Muriel entertained, for an unbelieving second, the instinct that her fears were being confirmed.

A male voice, a strong but wavery alto paying much attention to vowel sounds, overreached those of fellow singers and burst from a pew not far behind her. During the following verse she strained more earnestly to listen and the weak fears that had first aroused her belief made way for an indisputable truth - that the voice belonged to Hugh. She clasped at the wooden arm beside her and mustered force to remain upright as Delilah reached out from behind, laid a jewelled hand on her shoulder and said, 'Are you overcome? There. It speaks well for you Muriel. Try and cling on until Dawson's address. Then you'll be able to sit and, though I say it, you'll find it stimulating.'

By the time Delilah stopped talking they were all well into the third verse.

'Cast care aside...' How could she? Hugh's vowels came across powerfully and with punch. Marco stirred and laid a hand upon one of his mother's. They faced each other and he mouthed the one word 'father' with astonishment and amused interest. He passed the word to Flavia who turned right around and, visually bypassing Delilah and Dulcie, set her eyes upon the singing face of Hugh, then turned back to inform Marco that his mother's suppositions were corroborated.

'That's all we need. *That, That, That's* all we need,' sang Muriel to music as the fourth verse commenced. The singing of that first hymn completed, the congregation sat and waited for Arthur, in morning coat, to take to the lectern for he was to perform the first reading. It was obvious that he had rehearsed this solo several times, and in front of a long looking glass.

He cleared his throat most traditionally, looked from the front to the back of the church and began.

'Call me by my old familiar name. Speak to me in the old easy way which we always used. Put no difference in your tone, wear no forced air of solemnity or sorrow.' He ended with the sinister words, 'I am but waiting for you, for an interval, somewhere very near, just around the corner.'

Muriel continued to tremble as the second hymn, providing even greater scope for Hugh and his vocal feats, struck up. She attended to no voice but his and the knowledge of his nearness brought her close to passing out as it dawned on her that he was certain to expect to be invited to spend the night at the manor. He was, in fairness, her husband and it was unlikely that he would even consider an invitation necessary. She thought about Monopoly and resolved to send the dog to the devil were he to resume his loyalty to Hugh.

And what on earth was Delilah going to make of this unheralded and unexplained arrival? Introductions all round. Hitherto, the companions of her new life, whatever their suspicions, had been tactful in their reticence concerning Hugh - and Hugh was likely to take it amiss when he discovered his brother to have become, practically, a piece of his wife's precious furniture.

These disturbances flew about her as she allowed the darkness of the service to rush past, although, during Psalm 147, she shuddered as Hugh's voice soared to the words (in reference to the Lord) 'Neither delighted he in any man's legs.' She was glad that the Lord delighted not in Roger's recently-plastered leg. Jerome's were safely in the box liberated from rank trousers. Whether erudite or not, Dawson's address was tedious. It related largely to the school and its predicted overspend. He did produce an anecdote or two about Jerome but threads were hard to follow. One of them concerned an incident at a school manager's meeting upon which Dawson and the deceased mistook each other's hearing aids for their own. It was a feeble example of wit and Muriel wondered why the aids had not been firmly plugged into the appropriate ears.

After the service, Dawson announced that Mrs Cottle had invited the whole congregation to take lunch with her and, he added, 'I think this is an appropriate moment to welcome the new owner of Bradstow Manor into our midst.'

There were no noticeable noises of assent but necks craned and Muriel thought of nothing but how this public recognition of her new role might be affecting Hugh; his own name and connection unmentioned as he rested his voice.

The mackintosh men entered and lifted the coffin from the wooden frame and hoisted it upon their shoulders. Walking with the procession, Muriel at last looked about her but did not turn to the spot from which Hugh's voice had soared. Their meeting was inevitable and sure to take place within a short space of time. She turned to the opposite side of the aisle and spotted Roger. His grey eyes stood out in startling contrast to the black suit he wore. Each failed, deliberately, to catch the other's glance but Muriel, as she passed, took stock of a female at his side. The fleeting impression portrayed a small, plump and heavily decorated woman who wore a black hat with a veil which covered half her face.

Muriel was truly dumfounded. Roger had never clapped eyes on Jerome and had been as good as asked to leave his house. He had betrayed every person connected with the place, including the housekeeper, to the extent that even the omnivorous Marco had called him to account.

Dawson led the troupe through the church and out into the open where the sun shone and where many began to suffer from the heat in their funeral outfits. They followed him to a corner of the churchyard where sections of artificial lawn surrounded a deeply-dug hole and contrasted with the brown dryness of summer grass.

Standing by the orifice, eyes turned once more to heaven, Dawson crumbled between his fingers a handful of earth. He scattered grains over the coffin which had been speedily lowered and, speaking for the people, let loose a last farewell, '…earth to earth, ashes to ashes, dust to dust; in sure and certain hope of the Resurrection to eternal life, through our Lord Jesus Christ who shall change our vile body….'

Poor Jerome with his yellow-brown body and ripping farts.

Delilah was the first to squeeze Muriel by the hand and then to follow up the gesture with a kiss, anxious in her wish to introduce the chief mourner to everyone in sight. Here her reputation as a walking address book belied facts as she scoured around for many minutes before she could collar anybody of her acquaintance. During these minutes, Hugh made his approach.

Muriel's first impression was one of stupefaction for he was nothing if not over dressed. This was a new departure. In their earlier life together he had made a study of casual clothing; to the extent that his sartorial deficiencies were, occasionally, and justifiably, mocked. He used to be accused of attempting to 'make a statement.'

A very different statement, if statement it were, was now made.

Hugh reddened hotly in a thick morning coat; traditional stiff collar, black tie and pearl pin. Only Arthur and two other elderly men wore similar outfits. Others wore black suits or, particularly the younger members, grey or pale cotton.

'You look smart,' she ventured.

'Hired it. This morning. Just flown in from Johannesburg and thought I might be needed.'

He looked at her most attentively and Muriel sensed that not only Delilah but others, Dulcie in particular, watched and listened.

'I hope you will be able to come back for lunch.'

Hugh, at this, was greatly startled.

'Lunch Muriel? I'm back. Back for good. We'll discuss it later. I've come to give you support. Don't tell me you don't need it - or have things been plain sailing?'

'Plain sailing? I wouldn't say so. Later Hugh. When the guests have gone. Later. I'll explain.' She had no idea what she was going to explain as she turned her back on him.

There was nothing at that juncture that she was prepared to say and, most surely, she had no wish to introduce him as her husband to baffled funeral guests. General rejoicing might ensue. Delilah and Dawson, in Christian joy, would jump to clamp the pair together; happy family at Bradstow Manor; that and royalty. It could not be.

Peter and Marco greeted brother and father. Peter with reticence and Marco with great good humour. 'Hello Dad. Here to share the spoils? Don't blame you. Ma's done pretty well for herself.' He forgot where he was but paused as the head teacher showed him a look of ugly reproof.

Muriel, after turning her back on her husband, found herself eyeball to eyeball with Roger who made, unsuccessfully, to kiss her on the cheek as she held him at bay during a muddled moment with neither one knowing how to handle the next phase of the encounter. The podgy woman who wore cosmetics and who Muriel had noticed as she passed the pew, was definitely Roger's date for the day. She appeared to know nobody and held her body close to Roger's as one who wished herself to be considered protected.

'Aha. Yes. Aha. This is Judith. Judith Atkins as a matter of fact.'

Atkins. Atkins. They stood but inches from the dead and buried body of Jerome. Jerome Atkins.

Muriel refused to react to this heinous introduction but muttered, 'Hot isn't it?'

She dared not seek the company of Peter for he continued to talk to Hugh as the graveyard group disbanded down the church path, heading for the house. Delilah was her only hope. Together they walked, clear of the rest, through the village; Delilah jubilant to have carried off such a prize, Muriel praying for Jerome not to be waiting for her, somewhere very near, just around the corner.

After the occasional interruption, (a farmer here, a friendly neighbour there - one keen to earn points for broadmindedness) they arrived hotly at the front door of the house that stood, supposedly, threatened by Miss Judith Atkins.

The party, if such constituted Jerome's wake, got off to a loud start. People arrived, one on top of the other, none having come but the short distance from the church. The house was, within a short space of time, jammed with darkly-dressed men and women who, in the heat, grabbed gratefully at glasses filled at Muriel's bidding, and contrived to meet their hostess. Cold luncheon was served in the dining room where guests helped themselves and then wandered to sit with whom they pleased. Muriel left the duties of hospitality to Marco who gained pleasure from bestowing instant commitment with fluency and ease of manner.

She had a double task. It was imperative not to have truck with Hugh until the visitors had departed and it was equally imperative to have none, at any stage during the day, with Roger or Miss Judith Atkins. She knew the executions of these evasions to be unrealistic for, were they not there to confront? What purpose did Roger proffer in the production of this woman?

She flew up the stairway, sledgehammers beating at her head, and hurled herself upon Monopoly who slumbered on her bed. How dare Hugh shock her in this way? She decided, then and there, to hide the dog and looked for cubbyholes. Her main desire was that Hugh and Monopoly should not come face to face. She planned, if necessary, to lie to Hugh and to explain that, in his absence, his pet had died a natural death. Pined.

The end of her world threatened if Monopoly were to change allegiance. Of Peter she was sure there was no likelihood that he would support his brother in favour of herself or encourage her to mend her marriage, but dogs were different and she had never been able to fathom their secrets - for Monopoly was the only dog ever to have held a place in her anti-canine heart.

Exhaustion subdued her spirit as she lay with her head buried in Monopoly's fur but she knew it was imperative for her to preserve outward composure and to rejoin the wake.

Downstairs, she cold-shouldered Roger, as did Marco - which impressed his mother for, normally, he had no talent for such tactics. Flavia held herself aloof. Phyllis, red and runny, refused to travel in the direction of her seducer as Miss Atkins clung closer and Roger, glued to the female, strove for an interview with Arthur. He recognised the latter from his earlier visit to Bradstow when Arthur had passed him by as he picked his nose in the hall.

Guests ate and drank as Delilah, social predator, contrived to mix with all she met. As befitted her sense of responsibility, she spent a word or two on Phyllis and beamed upon Sonia who sobbed, but her true energy targeted meatier quarry.

Roger, on the point of accosting Arthur, took her attention for he wore the look of one who came from far afield.

She tackled him. 'I always think it's permissible to introduce oneself at a funeral don't you? After all - we do have one thing in common. We are all here because of Jerome. Are you, by any chance, a relative?'

'Ahem. Not personally, but allow me to present Miss Atkins. Miss Judith Atkins.'

His face was both blanched and livid as he reached for further refreshment from a tray carried by Phyllis, who had no wish to prevent the consequences of such a transaction.

'Miss Atkins! You must be a relative! Don't tell me you're not. Where's Muriel? She would hate to miss the opportunity of meeting a relative.'

Failing to find Muriel, she plumped for second choice and seized upon Arthur who munched nearby, scattering rice onto his morning suit.

As she performed the niceties, Delilah's higher ambition was to identify the strange man talking to the blind and puzzling Mr Cottle, Muriel's brother-in-law.

'Miss Atkins? May I call you Judith? Christian names only, down here. Rule of the village. This is Mr Stiller. Arthur. He's a sweetie. Jerome's solicitor.'

Roger showed signs of becoming the worse for wear and looked hazily on as Jerome's solicitor, now to all effects Muriel's, came face to face with Roger's nominee.

'Pleased to meet you. Sorry. Can't shake hands. Always a bit of a problem at these do's you know. I can't say that I ever heard Jerome mention any kin; other than Mrs Cottle, that is to say.'

For the first time Miss Judith Atkins spoke. She signalled to Roger for support but without result for he had become bleary.

'I was not aware that Mrs Cottle was his kin.'

'Not his own, perhaps, but his wife's.'

'Mr Stiller. I plan to spend the night at The Bear at Shifford. I have reason to believe that a meeting between you and I might be beneficial to us both. I am free at any time during the day tomorrow and will presume to ring you at your office in the morning.'

The length and content of her sentence weakened Miss Atkins and she turned to Delilah for reassurance. Delilah, both flabbergasted and uneasy at witnessing such divisive insinuation, commenced, uncharacteristically, to panic. The woman who confronted Arthur was neither young nor old. She was unclassifiable in that respect but, under Delilah's scrutiny, passed as something near to fifty.

Muriel, having braved her re-entry and expecting Jerome to be lurking just around the corner, came into view and Delilah hailed her, confident that with her royal connections, she was certain to triumph.

Before Delilah could capture her, a vast female face, property of an ageing widow, swam as from an aquarium, to meet Muriel's own.

'You won't know me. Well, how could you? My name is Angela Swann. My late husband, Godfrey, and myself used to enjoy good times here in the old days and we're all anxious to know if you're going to make any alterations. A little bird has hinted that you're planning to call down a London decorator.' In claustrophobic anxiety, Muriel inched away, creating some space into which a reply might be fitted between their two mouths, but such a reply was not to be allowed for. Another face wedged itself in there and opened its mouth.

'I can't help wondering if you received my letter. I'm your local councillor. I wrote several days back, as a matter of fact, concerning a vindictive element in the neighbourhood.'

'I'm hopeless, I'm afraid. Disappointing everybody. It's early days. Nothing's certain.' As she backed and backed - she backed, as it happened, onto a patch of carpet near to where Roger, slowly and noiselessly, sagged and crumpled to the ground. He had passed out. Delilah sidestepped the body and clove to Muriel who had only guessed at Judith Atkins's intentions; guessed, too, that Roger would not have selected the gauchely-attired creature for this inappropriate outing other than with nefarious motive.

Half the party ate in the dining room; some in the hall and the remainder, not more than twenty at the most, sat or stood supporting glasses and plates in the drawing room. Among this number sat Hugh and Peter whose heads touched in the bow window. Their conversation, to Muriel as she scanned, gave the impression of earnest compatibility.

Delilah came very close.

'Muriel I must ask you something. That man talking to your brother-in-law. There's a resemblance. Can you throw any light on his identity?'

'Him? Hugh. He's my husband.'

It had to be told.

Arthur, scattering rice, mulled over the words of the half-veiled stranger at whose feet Roger groaned, and agonised as to which side his bread was likely to be buttered.

Delilah, ignited by Muriel's tidings, wondered who to inform as guests began to leave. Those who had not already collared her sought Muriel with the desire to shake her by the hand and to invest in the future life at Bradstow Manor; royalty and all. She allowed for politeness and willed them with sincerity upon their ways. Then, as though their presence had been but imaginings, they were gone.

Roger lay, secretion oozing from a corner of his mouth, prostrate across the carpet as Judith Atkins looked daggers in his way; her supporter rendered useless by champagne. She had, in fairness, gained permission to put through a call to Arthur in the morning but, at present, failed in further audacity without a hand from her champion.

Arthur left, and those present in the drawing room dwindled to the following figures; Hugh, Peter and Marco in confabulation, the inert Roger, Judith Atkins, Phyllis and Kitty, a brace of Kitty's sisters clearing plates and glasses, and Dawson and Delilah. Alastair had beaten an early retreat in order to see to his packing for he planned to leave for Cap Ferrat the next day.

Muriel pre-empted Delilah; thanking both her and Dawson for the gorgeousness of the service, the flowers and for their general assistance and saying that, before long, she would arrange a get-together.

With curiosity and reluctance they took their leave and, as they did so, Muriel's heart failed her. The die was cast and at any second she and Hugh would be tackling immediate plans. Longer ones must be shelved.

151

Chapter 12

The confrontation that she had held in trepidation, longed for, dreaded, imagined and rejected was on the point of taking place. Hugh was at her side, smiling and aiming to touch her, absurdly narcissistic in morning suit and with a glass or two of champagne inside him. Marco and Peter remained by the bow window.

'Muriel, sit down. You must be tired.' He enraged her. The cheek of it. Feigning to worry on the instant as to whether or not she was tired after months of desertion. She might, during those months, have dropped dead on a million occasions without his footling concern.

He made to avoid the motionless body of Roger that hindered his gallant attempts but the manoeuvre forced him to stumble and trip; to lurch and grasp with one hand at the arm of the sofa and with the other to clutch at the wrist of Miss Judith Atkins. She was not displeased. The reverse, and stated archly as she complained, that she found sequences hard to follow.

'I'm not thick, though I say so myself. In fact I tend to be an insightful person.' She smiled contentedly as she helped Hugh to gain his balance and then to sit.

'I mean – who is who amongst you all?'

'And who,' asked Muriel, 'are you?'

'I am Judith Atkins. Niece of the deceased. My father, Archie Atkins, was his brother. Two years younger. That is to say, they fell out. The dynamics went wrong in the nursery and they never made it up. My uncle made a posh marriage and believed himself too good for us.'

'So. You are here as Jerome's niece. How come you brought Roger along?'

They all looked at the figure on the floor.

'That is to say he brought me. Had it not been for Roger, who is a new acquaintance,' here she smirked, 'I would not have been informed of my uncle's demise.'

Muriel, wondering where Miss Atkins had picked up the use of such queer language, pressed on, pleased to postpone a set-to with Hugh.

'Why did Roger think fit to bring you to your own uncle's funeral? He and Jerome never met.'

Miss Atkins showed signs of anxiety. 'Well. That is to say, I assumed he knew my uncle. He told me he was well in with you Cottles.'

Hugh jumped at the word 'Cottle.' After all, he was one. His hour had come. Clearing his throat as he had done in church when exercising his vocal chords, he decided to take charge.

'Am I to assume that neither you or, er, Roger have ever met Mr Atkins?'

'Correct. Have you?'

'As a matter of fact - no. I didn't meet him but I am married to Muriel; Muriel Cottle. Mr Atkins's, well, sort of niece.'

'Not as much of a niece as I am, I have been led to believe.'

'Possibly not but, well, now the funeral is over, will you be returning to London? Did you come from London this morning?' He was muddled, and floundered as he adjusted his position on the sofa.

'The Bear at Shifford. That is to say that I would have stayed at The Bear at Shifford with Roger.' Roger showed no sign of life.

'But, well, perhaps a bed here would be forthcoming? If I could ask for assistance in getting Roger up the stairs, we would not expect a meal.'

Big of you, thought Muriel as she organised their departure in her mind.

'Sorry,' she said. 'That won't work. We'll have to revive him. I'll send for Dulcie.'

She still entertained the whisper of a wonder that Roger had fathered her forthcoming grandchild. Were that so, he had, at some point, held a carnal position in the lives of most of the women in the house.

After leaving the room, she walked to the kitchen where she asked a gloating Phyllis to fetch Dulcie and to tell her that help was needed for the task of resuscitating the inebriated Roger. Phyllis rallied with twitching zeal. Roger unconscious. Roger about to be banned from the house; Roger's new lady friend about to be banished alongside him.

Dulcie had removed her suit and tie and made it clear that the summons was welcome.

'What did I tell you? They are nothing but a bunch of alcoholics.' She ignored the presence of Muriel. 'That son of theirs is not much better and, I have been informed, that gentleman in fancy dress is the long-lost husband. Ten to one he's another alcoholic.'

With relish, she marched into the drawing room, sent Miss Atkins spinning with the slap of a hand and kicked Roger in the buttock. Hugh, who had not yet met Dulcie, sat back in uncertain terror and watched and wondered whether he did, in reality, wish to become a feature of the household.

Muriel watched too, but from the doorway. Peter and Marco had disappeared and Miss Atkins, veil askew since Dulcie's rap, was the only other observer.

Dulcie bent stiffly and, with a filthy finger, lifted one of Roger's eyelids. Then, with her sleeve, she wiped away some of the saliva that continued to trickle from his mouth.

'Water. One of you.? Fetch me some water. Perfectly useless, the lot of you. Totally useless.'

Hugh, in his tails, rose and ran from the room. Miss Atkins cried, 'You'll kill him if you're not careful.'

Dulcie had straightened up and was kicking again.

'You'll kill him.'

'Yes and I'll kill you too if you don't stop that snivelling. And what is more I'd like you to remove that silly hat.'

When Hugh returned, gingerly carrying a glass of water, he found that Muriel had deserted her post by the door.

He took the glass to Dulcie and, during a moment when she desisted from administering kicks with her boot, handed it to her before she rounded on him.

'Are you totally useless? What am I supposed to do with that? It's a bucket I need. Just you go back to the kitchen and fill me a bucket.'

He returned, collar stiff, to the kitchen where Kitty filled a pail.

As he set off, back towards the drawing room slopping water and sweating badly, he was almost prostrated by his own and his wife's futility.

He was tired, too, for he had travelled a long way during the past twenty-four hours and the spectacles that had greeted him were a far cry from those of his imagination. He had accepted that his duties might lie in a certain and not unpleasant direction; that of helping his wife deal with a bunch of hidebound old retainers. A kindly word here and there; a suggestion or two; the easing of an old favourite into retirement.

Carrying a pail of water through a gloomy house for an androgynous maniac to slosh over the face of an inebriated seducer in the presence of a la-di-da claimant to the property he had planned to control, did not encourage him.

Then there was his brother; his poor, blind, dithering brother. He had an eerie instinct that Peter was more intimate with Muriel than was appropriate. During their conversation in the bow window, Peter had given out an unprecedented atmosphere of confidence; acting as one who knew more than he was prepared to share. He thought these thoughts and spared one for the dog as he handed the pail to Dulcie.

Roger had not stirred and Miss Atkins sat blubbing, hatless, and claiming through heaves, 'I cannot abide to witness physical cruelty. I have always been an insightful person. It's my profession but it doesn't pay. It is for that reason that I anticipate a slice.'

Here she broke down and threw the bulk of her body into the armchair.

Dulcie snatched the pail and, holding it in both hands above her head, allowed the cascade to crash over Roger's face.

She stood back, well satisfied, as Roger opened his eyes, moved his hands and uttered 'fuck' several times.

'I'll give you fuck. Get up on those two legs of yours; that is to add, if you are capable.'

He was capable but only just. He clutched and grasped and stiffened before rising, swearing as he did so. Hugh held out a hand to him, pining for the duties he had dreamed of.

Dulcie propelled the empty pail towards Miss Atkins and said, 'When you've stopped that idiotic snivelling take this bucket back to the kitchen. Whether or not you can drive a car I don't know.' This was put as a question and was answered in a dismal negative.

'In that case, I'm phoning for a local taxi. You wouldn't get far with 'im at the wheel.'

Hugh filled no role.

'Now.' Dulcie manhandled Roger, twisting his arms to test flexibility and waving a big finger before his rheumy eyes. 'Now. We want to get you as far as the front door and there you will have to wait. As far as your own car goes, and I gather it is no more than hired, you can get another taxi out here tomorrow to fetch it. If you have sufficiently sobered up by then.'

Roger commented on the heat but did not hide confusion as he waited, swaying and wet, for the return to the room of Miss Atkins.

The very fact that her swain was upright brought about a return of her previous liveliness and, addressing Hugh, she made a farewell speech.

'Tomorrow I am to see Mr Stiller. Well. Phone him that is to say, in the hopes of a powwow. I have a right to improve the quality of my life and I have it on good authority that I might be entitled to a claim over and beyond your wife's. I was never provided for and, as I said earlier, my work satisfaction doesn't tally with the pay.' She lifted the black hat from the chair and placed it on her head.

Single-handed but using both fists, Dulcie orchestrated the departure of Roger and Miss Atkins; filling the driver in with warnings of his passengers' behavioural problems and pleasing herself with praise for her own capabilities.

It was not long after five o'clock and Hugh, alone, fell to reflection. He was still dressed as he had been for the morning ceremony and the heat was gruelling. Worse than South Africa. There was not, nor had there been since his arrival, any sign of Monopoly. Nobody had shown him to a bedroom. Peter was clearly ensconced in one, as were Marco and Flavia, but none amongst the bevy of helpers had offered any of their help to him – and Muriel had disappeared.

Dulcie blocked his way. 'Now. If you have nothing better to do you might as well empty that mousetrap in the back passage. There's a mouse in there. I heard it scratching. What you have to do is this.' She gave long and complicated instructions. The entire mousetrap had to be taken to the garden and emptied. The mouse then had to be assassinated. Hugh queried the method, pointing out that if the mouse had to be murdered at some stage, wouldn't it be more labour-saving and humane to use a conventional death trap?

'You'll find it gyrating beyond the telephone. It must be a gigantic mouse to get the whole trap bouncing up and down like that. Gigantic.'

Gravely Hugh performed his task, granting that it was imperative for him to act with correctitude. Task over, he asked Kitty to take him to a room where he could change his clothes and eventually sleep. Kitty had wondered whether Mr Cottle planned to snuggle up with his wife and worried that Muriel seemed to be attached to the four-poster bed; suitable for one occupant.

She showed him to a small room that, in old days, had served as dressing room to the more stately one occupied by Marco and Flavia and one that, he accepted, would have to do for the present.

Muriel, in her room, confronted a crisis in the shape of Monopoly. She knew that she had no right to imprison him indefinitely but rebelled against the risk she courted in allowing him to brush with Hugh. It struck her as ridiculous that it mattered nothing to her that Marco should greet his father in friendly fashion. She had smuggled up provisions but there were other problems. Late that night she and her dog would sneak out together, and hope not to find Sonia weaving spells with her cat by the stream.

Before supper, in the drawing room, Muriel, Hugh, Peter, Marco and Flavia foregathered. In semi-silence they sipped from glasses. In semi-silence they ate the first course of supper. In semi-silence they waded through the main course (left over from the funeral lunch) but, during pudding, (also left over from the funeral lunch), Marco burst out, 'So. Dad. What's your game? Have you come back for good?'

Hugh, casually dressed with studied precision, gave an artless reply.

'Well spoken Marco. I wondered when someone was going to break the ice. Your mother, I appreciate, has had plenty on her plate today.'

He looked tenderly at Muriel but the overture was met with no response, whereupon he decided to put his cards on the table for the benefit of the ears of the four who sat around it.

'When I heard of - all this, I decided to pack in Johannesburg. Mum,' he spoke through Marco, 'didn't want to join me and, well, I missed you all. By the way, Muriel, how and where is Monopoly?'

Whatever the planning that went before, she had never been able to hold facts back.

'In my bedroom.'

'Good God. You mean to say that my dog is in this very house and that, as yet, I have seen neither hound nor hair.' He liked his words and braced himself for action.

'If I may, I will run upstairs and find him. Muriel - er - where is your bedroom?'

Muriel, provided by nature with tenderness, was not always discriminating in her methods of bestowing it. If the strings of her heart were touched it was in her to extend support in likely directions so, when her time came to be ill used, she had no machinery with which to withhold it. She fought her own causes as fiercely as she fought those of others. It was during one of her bouts of tumbling into this trap that Marco and Flavia had labelled her a 'whinger'.

She stood tall in her grey cotton dress, unchanged since the funeral, hair bouncing as she raged against her husband across the table.

'What do you mean by calling Monopoly your dog?' Her voice was tinny. 'You left him in the lurch. You knew that I didn't like him, or any dog. You knew that he could do nothing but complicate my life. I jolly nearly had him put down.' Here she offended herself and hesitated; it sounded too awful.

Hugh, stunned in his bright blue shirt, interrupted, held up a hand and appealed to his brother.

'I said she'd had a tiring day but I don't understand. Has she come round to Monopoly? I hoped she might. Company for her. Perhaps, Peter, you can persuade her to go to bed?'

Muriel still standing but shaking and drawing hungrily on a cigarette, resumed her attack. 'Why the bloody hell do you treat me as an imbecile? If you wish to talk to me, do so, but don't carry on as if I were a photograph. Stop addressing me through Peter and Marco.'

Flavia, shirty, left the room and Marco, master of ceremonies once more, hushed his mother and ordered his father to lay off.

'No point in telling the old girl to go to bed. Never is when she's in a state. What's got into you Ma? Father only asked if he could see Monopoly.'

Muriel sat down, having stubbed out her cigarette. 'He's mine. I'll make him a ward of court.'

'Who's talking about wards of courts Muriel? I'm back. We'll share him. I've told you. I plan to stay here and help you in every way.'

She shuddered and her eyes evoked Peter who did not see. Marco, not wanting to be defeated for this was a seminar and he intended to arbitrate, scolded both.

'Look here Dad. It's your first day back after a year and all you two can do is fight. Hadn't you and Ma better mull things over tomorrow? Fancy squabbling about a dog after all these months - and, as for that Dad, Ma has a point.'

Anger diffused by this shred of support from her son, Muriel wept more helplessly.

'Go and get him,' she wailed. 'Marco. Take your father to my room. I hope Monopoly bites him.'

Hugh, sensing that there was danger there, for dogs, in his experience, did not always take kindly to returning heroes, rejected the suggestion.

'No. No. Not tonight. But I hear what you say Marco.' Again Muriel shuddered. Hugh used awful expressions. As bad as Roger and Miss Atkins. Peter pulled himself into the fray.

'Most certainly it has been a tiring day for us all. Hugh has come from Johannesburg and the rest of us - well - it hasn't been easy. Poor Flavia in her condition.'

'Condition?' Hugh was startled anew. He had not confronted or anticipated a role as grandparent and did not like to hear of such tidings from his brother.

'Well done Marco old boy. On that happy note, let's get cracking. I, for one, am ready to hit the hay.'

Hugh and Marco walked together to the door, waved a vague goodnight, and left Peter to pet Muriel.

He elected to take Monopoly, who seemed not to have sniffed his erstwhile master's presence in the atmosphere, for his evening stroll. After half an hour in the garden he returned him to Muriel, pushing the dog very quietly through her bedroom door but nothing woke her.

Muriel's first task on the day after Jerome's funeral was to see to Monopoly's airing. His mood had not altered in any noticeable way and his affection for her showed strongly as they set off for the shrubbery. She no longer tethered him; her fear of Dulcie having initially waned and subsequently disintegrated.

He roamed off and left her to look back upon the house as thoughts raced through her brain. Hugh was asleep behind one of the windows, tired, no doubt, after his journey.

Roger and Miss Atkins, she remembered, hovered in a nearby hotel, planning their attack.

Marco and Flavia were, doubtless, intertwined in bed; Marco in all likelihood, lacking the drive to think to the future or to ponder on the paternity of Flavia's foetus.

Then came an unquiet thought. Peter was somewhere in the house; cleaning his teeth or battling with his clothes.

She wished with every fibre in her that he would appear; that he would beat the others to the day and stroll with her in the garden before the complications of breakfast arose; not that Phyllis made complaints any more. She, like Monopoly, had come to heel.

In wishing it seemed that she had also willed for, coming towards her across the grass, Peter walked faster than usual. As he neared, her flesh crept for it was not Peter but Hugh. Their brotherly resemblance was a curse.

Hugh stood a foot or two away. 'Muriel,' he held out both hands in supplication. 'I'm sorry. I was insensitive.' His eyes were watery; drenched by sincerity. 'You must have been done in and I was pretty knackered myself. Today we will have plenty of opportunity to talk things over. I must say, Muriel, before I go any further, this really is a glorious place.'

Her thoughts were flying for, at any moment, she expected Monopoly to bound back with news of discoveries.

'Hugh.' She hated the sight of him. 'Monopoly is running somewhere near.'

She planned to rant but the thread was broken by a thwacking sound and a rustle in the leaves but a short distance away, and in an instant Monopoly was at her heel, rubbing his nose into her calf and letting loose faint twitches. Hugh, a foolish leer crossing his face, made for the area of the calf with outstretched hand. Monopoly's twitches erupted into shakes and Muriel bent to console him whilst, in governessy warning, let Hugh know that he would be wise to make himself scarce.

As Hugh stepped back, speaking to the dog with soppy softness, Peter emerged from the house. He listened before being drawn to the group by a combination of the sound of Monopoly's yelps and Hugh's drooling. The dog gave way to calm as Peter came near and ambled towards him, offering to lick his hand.

Peter had not intended to vaunt his superior position or to be seen to supersede his brother. He wanted to retreat but Muriel took his arm in hers and half laid her head on his shoulder. Could it be that she was drunk? The symptoms were identical. Left-over alcohol from the evening before maybe? It was not impossible. Monopoly watched this display with wisdom in his eyes. Finding himself to be a piece in a picture that he had dreamed of for an age Peter tugged her closer to him. She kissed him hotly. Hugh turned back and stared at them. Phyllis stood at the front door and stared at them. Peter thoroughly enjoyed himself but, nonetheless, thought fit to steady her.

'Later Muriel. Later. Not now.'

As she sobered she became, in a twinkling, miserably depressed; repentant, tired, hollow and confused. The energy trickled from her and all she knew was mortification. She hated both brothers; all Cottles and that went for Marco too.

Phyllis said, 'Phone call for you Mrs Cottle; that is to say if you are at liberty to take it. Mr Stiller. He says it's urgent.'

She followed Phyllis's summons and spoke on the telephone to Arthur. He began by explaining that he knew it was early but he felt she ought to know that he had already been telephoned by Miss Atkins who had hurried him into making an early appointment at his office.

'We didn't go into the why's and wherefore's,' he explained, 'but the bare gist of it seems to be that she feels that she is, at any rate, entitled to an - er - slice of your inheritance. I do not know at present whether or not she has her eye on the whole.'

'Do you believe her to have a genuine claim?' Muriel spoke haughtily, out of tune with her earlier feebleness. Arthur said that it was too early to predict.

'Thank you. Please let me know of the outcome. Please ring me as soon as the meeting is over.' Arthur said that he would do so.

As she replaced the telephone it sounded off again splitting her ears. It was Mambles.

'I thought I'd give you time to get over the funeral. Now you must be having a lovely time. Really in charge. Mummy asked me to thank you for introducing those poor girls to that nice young man. Apparently he's arrived at Cap Ferrat and everybody is delighted with him.'

'So glad. Actually Mambles; things are a bit tricky.' She lowered her voice. 'Hugh turned up, out of the blue, in time for the funeral.'

'How simply maddening. Shall I come down? I can come tonight if that would be of any help. The only trouble is that I don't think I can ask Farty to come. Shall I try for Cunty? She's passed her stone. She's an awful bore, but better the devil you know and Jubilee is used to her.'

'Why not? Yes. Do come. I'd love it.'

Mambles said that she would be with her friend in time for supper that evening.

162

'Things are looking up,' Muriel sang as she wondered where to turn.

The household was to spin again and Mambles's arrival would divert Phyllis from the spectacle she had witnessed on the lawn. Hugh, alive to rank, was likely to take notice of Mambles's interference and Peter would have no time to remind her of her indiscretion on the lawn.

Marco's energy would come into play with wines, and Kitty and her sisters would delight in entertaining Moggan once again. Moggan and Cunty.

Mambles, if necessary, was more than capable of dealing with Roger and Miss Atkins. Send them to the tower. Indisputably she was a godsend. Before long both Peter and Hugh hovered in the hall and, instead of facing facts with either, Muriel was able to say, 'Right boys, Mambles on the warpath. We've got our work cut out.'

Awkward as she felt with Peter and much as she wished to avoid an opportunity to repeat the kissing into which she had ensnared him, Muriel did not, as the morning wore on, entirely abominate him but wished that she had not been the one to have perpetrated the passion.

She had no desire, moreover, to find herself alone with Hugh in his country squire's outfit. Could he but find the tact, she thought, to depart without farewell, she would be relieved. Were Peter to do the same she would, she realised, be aggrieved.

Mere hazy thoughts on these matters did not control her as she ran from room to room and demanded that the time-honoured pot plants be positioned by Eric and Joyce.

As the bustle increased and as the brothers, each feeling very differently to the other, walked silently in the garden, Monopoly stayed close to his mistress, shunning independence.

When the telephone rang again it was Arthur who presented himself to say that the meeting with Miss Atkins had taken place. He was not capable of enlightening Muriel with views on any outcome for he admitted himself baffled. He burbled and padded and owned himself confused.

'Of course, it has to be said, she is very much more closely related, or was I should say, to Jerome than you are, er, were. Her friend, a Mr Roger something-or-other (I forget his name for the moment), came along too with a bit of bumph about him relating to what we call "collateral claims".'

Muriel interposed. 'Look. We're very busy here. As you know I've never gone into any of it. In fact the whole thing has unsettled me.' Inwardly she blamed her present unsettledness on her exhibition on the lawn. 'I never fought or contrived for the place and I now rather resent being challenged over it. If the woman really believes she has a grievance, then she should come and talk it over with me before taking professional advice.'

Muriel was wound up and believed herself capable of talking for several hours without interruption if need be. In fact she found it difficult to desist.

'Before you go any further it might be worth your while to delve a little into the history of the ownership. It is likely and I believe it to be a fact, that the house was originally the property of Jerome's wife, Alice.' Here she remembered with a spring of optimism, Miss Atkins's reference to her uncle's 'posh' marriage. 'She was related to me, albeit not closely, and had no blood tie whatsoever with this Miss Atkins.'

She wished that she had, at any stage, ever listened to any word that her parents cared to utter and smiled as she hoped that, one day, Marco might suffer the same regrets. She was reasonably confident that she had learnt from her mother that the house had came through her family before finally devolving upon her Aunt Alice. The homosexual Alice Atkins.

Arthur was still on the line.

'Now, this woman and her friend are staying at The Bear at Shifford. I don't know how long they plan to remain there and I, of course, can do nothing to assist them. I have told them that their best course of action, that is if they persist in their, er, quest, is to put a solicitor of their own in touch with me. That's all they can do for the time being. Meanwhile, Mrs Cottle, I take your point about the original ownership.' He distanced himself from her by the use of her surname.

Muriel knew that she was unlikely to learn anything of account from Arthur, in view of his intelligence being limited and his values unsound. She decided to hand the entire problem over to Mambles who only had to put through a call to her own solicitor to hold his entire attention for as many hours as required.

Flavia, terrifically dressy but wearing a hunted expression, (could it be, Muriel asked herself, that Flavia feared Roger to be in the neighbourhood still?) sidled to Muriel and called her 'Chick.' Muriel's fundamental clemency flowed as she hugged her pregnant daughter-in-law with mighty strength.

'Well done Flave. You look great.'

Together they toured the house, enjoying details in bathrooms and on landings as well as in the more important rooms.

In Muriel's mind, however, remained the problem of the two men who looked alike and worried her in different ways. She forgave Peter utterly for the kiss she had given him which, she decided, was big of her. If only she had let things be. The moment of excitability that had motivated her was to be regretted but, all considered, she began to realise how fortunate she had been, through propinquity, to pick Peter and not Hugh as victim. It might have been Dawson or Dulcie if they had been inconveniently near to hand. Peter's response, too, had been undemanding, not withstanding the fact that he had been delighted. It had, on reflection, been satisfactory and worthy of repetition.

She cheered up as she checked the house with Flavia at her side and absorbed, with shock, that she had not, in person, commented to Flavia on the subject of her condition. Only to Marco. On the dark landing she brought the matter up; congratulated Flavia; offered any help that might be needed.

Flavia said, 'Thanks Chick' and started to cry.

They sat together on a long Queen Anne sofa that took up a large amount of space on the landing and was not particularly comfortable. Flavia laid her head on her mother-in-law's knees and thanked her for kindness. Both women knew that the other was aware of possible complications but nothing was stated.

Monopoly joined them and comforted both by sharing his favours amongst all four legs, brushing himself against them in turn but, all of a sudden, he stopped and growled, as Hugh, with sprightly step, lent his presence.

Muriel entreated, 'Oh Hugh. Can't you go away? Can't you see we're sort of busy?'

Monopoly snapped at one of Hugh's legs and Muriel's heart began to bleed for Hugh in his insensitivity.

'Don't be daft Monopoly. Can't you see it's only Hugh? Your old master?'

Monopoly eyed her inconsistency with suspicion as Muriel continued to address her husband.

'Don't worry Hugh. Dogs are always like that when they haven't seen someone for a bit. He'll come round. Only don't try too hard. It won't work.'

She tried to reconcile the dog to its former owner. 'It'll all come right. You shouldn't have come back so suddenly. Taken us all by surprise.'

'That I certainly did.' He referred by a look to the scene on the lawn. He did not, however, seem cross but grateful, humble and pathetic as he left them on the landing and went towards his small bedroom.

Flavia said, 'You're kind Chick. I hope it all comes right.'

Downstairs Peter was nowhere to be seen and Muriel imagined him to have taken an interminable walk. It could, of course, never be said that Peter had supplanted Hugh for Hugh had not been there to uproot.

Marco worked at niceties as the friendly pot plants reappeared. Phyllis flapped and plans proceeded without hitches.

In the meantime Delilah rang to congratulate Muriel on the smooth execution of Jerome's funeral. 'Your flahs looked gorgeous. We did wonder what your, er, husband thought of Dawson's sermon. As you heard, along with all that scholarship, he does know how to make a little joke. Might your husband be back for good? We'd love to welcome him down here when you both have a moment.'

'How very kind. By the way. I was going to ring you. I hear from Princess Matilda that the Queen Mother has been in touch with the Greeks and has heard that your Alastair is a huge success in Cap Ferrat.'

'Bless you for that Muriel. We have been anxious but we didn't care to ask. He didn't leave an address and we would so like to write to him there. In fact we would like to drop a line to the Greek, er, Queen, is she? Dawson would actually write the letter and I would put my name next to his.'

Muriel had to admit that she did not have the address of the Greeks upon her person but she promised to provide it when possible. Delilah said 'bless you' many times but offered no hint that she had heard of Mambles's proposed return to Bradstow. Nor did she renew her invitation for Hugh to take plonk at the rectory. News from Cap Ferrat had given her plenty to feed on.

Mambles's arrival was thrilling. She came with Cunty in the Daimler, driven by Moggan, and reached the house in the early evening. This time she was dressed in navy blue with bright white accessories; a well-trained social worker. Muriel interpreted the outfit thus for, never before had her friend worn navy. Mambles had donned a makeshift uniform for the purpose of underlining her authority whilst sorting out the pickles at Bradstow.

There was plenty of kissing and curtseying as she was ushered in.

She stared at Hugh who showed great politeness. 'So. You've decided to return. We'll have to see about that.'

To Peter, who ill disguised his dislike of her, 'You're looking smart. On top of the world if I may say so. What has happened to perk you up?'

Peter was bashful and Muriel appalled.

They walked, Jubilee tucked under Mambles's arm, through the hall and to the drawing room and Muriel noticed that she did not turn her feet in, or drag them. She was lit up.

'So Marco,' she turned her attention to him as glossiness glittered in her eyes. 'I'm sure that you've been a great help to your mother over all this.' She waved a ringed hand about and continued to be strict. 'And a help to Flavia too. I hope that you're taking all these new responsibilities very seriously.' Then she demanded a cocktail and asked if she and Cunty were to occupy the same quarters that she had shared with Farty on her former visit. Muriel explained that Marco and Flavia had commandeered that room, and that Hugh slept, as had Farty, in the dressing room. Another set of chambers, however, which Muriel said she hoped 'were perfectly OK' had been made ready and Mambles, in no mood to quibble, took the news on the chin.

'Can someone tell Phyllis and Cunty to see to my things?'

Marco sped away, clashing with his father who attempted to perform the errand. Mambles rounded on Flavia.

'So. When is it to be? I shall be godmother. That'll keep things in order.' She wore a firm but humorous look as one anticipating defiance.

Flavia, scared, said, 'Gosh! Why not?'

Muriel had seen Mambles in this mood before. It sometimes came upon her when she had a role to play; when she inspected troops.

At dinner they were evenly matched; three men and three women. Mambles sat between the two brothers; Muriel between her son and her husband; Flavia between her husband and her husband's uncle as Mambles took charge.

'I was delighted when they brought back general conversation after the war.'

Flavia hissed, 'Who's he?' at Marco who signalled that she keep silent.

'For anything less than eight, I always insist on it.' Mambles warmed to her theme.

'So, Hugh. What made you turn up for the old boy's funeral without warning anybody?'

This question was left hanging in the air for, all of a sudden, there was an earthquake, an upheaval, a volcano, a thunderstorm, an orchestra on the loose. A pistol shot. A reverberating drum as Dulcie, gloating and glowering, entered the ring. In her hand she held a large square envelope that she waved triumphantly before Mambles's face.

'Before you go any further,' her words charged with glee, 'I would like you to know that I have located the missing document. His Lordship, no doubt, believed that he had it well and truly hidden but, thanks to Fourpence-Halfpenny's asthma and his persistent scratching in the cabinet in 'Sir's' bedroom, a front portion of the secret drawer came away from the framework.' Here she stopped passing the envelope to and fro across Mambles's motionless face and held it up for the rest of the party to see. 'The enclosed might quite possibly make a considerable contribution to the matter presently under discussion.'

'I suggest then,' Mambles at her most royal, 'that you hand the letter to me. I shall open it and read it aloud. After that I shall decide whether or not any action should be taken as a result.'

Dulcie looked delighted.

Mambles put on her reading glasses that had lain in a gem-incrusted case beside her at the table. Slowly and clearly she started to read.

' "Dear Jerome, I leave this letter for you in the hope that you will take some note as to what I say. I knew that, were we to have discussed the matter verbally, we would have been certain to argue. I know that poor Dulcie has long been a thorn in your flesh." ' Here Mambles stopped and stared at Dulcie who feigned not to listen. Continuing, she read, ' "If I die before you do, she would be homeless. As you know she gave up her job as linesman at the tennis club (where she lived in her van) to come here to help me with the cats. All I ask is that you allow her to go on living in the paddock, to have some access to the house, (hot water, the occasional use of the telephone and somewhere to dry her clothes in poor weather. Some shed or other in which to store her bikes, too. Preferably the one she has always used.) I am sorry if this request is distasteful to you but I sincerely hope you will pay attention to my wishes. Other than that everything I own will be yours unconditionally." '

Mambles returned her reading glasses to their case.

'I wonder,' she said, 'why Mr Atkins hid this unopened letter. Perhaps he feared worse than this simple request. So,' turning to a dismayed Dulcie, 'you need not have wasted quite so much of your time in tracking this document down. It seems to me that it makes no difference to your situation whatsoever. You still live as you did in the days of Mrs Atkins and I am certain that Mrs Cottle will do little to alter the position although she is within her rights to change the conditions somewhat if you take inconvenient advantage of her.' Dulcie made a curious curtsey and bounded from the room.

Mambles turned her attention back to Hugh who was by now deeply depressed by all he had confronted since his arrival, if mollified to a small extent by Muriel's earlier gentleness on the landing.

'I heard of all this,' he said, fingering a silver spoon, 'and I decided that Muriel might be in need of my help.'

'Have you given her any?'

Mambles was drinking whisky at a great rate.

'Not so far, I suppose. I only got back yesterday and, well, we haven't had time to talk things over.' He thought of the mousetrap.

'Let's do it now.' Her eyes danced as she lit a cigarette. Muriel, frozen by events and the recollection of her pass at Peter as witnessed by Hugh and Phyllis, pleaded, 'Mambles. Must we? I'm not sure that I can face it.'

'Nonsense Muriel. No time like the present.'

Peter joined in.

'Why not after all? We need a master of ceremonies Muriel. You change your mind about everyone the moment you feel sorry for them. Why not let Princess Matilda draw a straight line for you?' He was coming round to Mambles.

She bestowed a grave nod upon him.

'Well spoken Peter. I gather that creep, Roger-something-or-other, is in the neighbourhood and has produced a pretender to Muriel's kingdom. My family knows all about these things, has done through the centuries. None better. I suggest that you turn these impostors over to me.'

She looked comical; clown-like almost as she drew on her cigarette.

Muriel could not, for the life of her, guess how Mambles had picked up this piece of information.

'Servants,' she said to herself. She knew now what Mambles and her family had to contend with. Phyllis, in all likelihood, was in daily confabulation with Farty or whoever on the telephone. All the guards outside Buckingham Palace in possession of the facts of Muriel's pass at Peter.

Mambles must know of it. That was why she and Peter were in cahoots. Anything was possible.

'Muriel,' she enquired, 'do you have cottages? You know what I mean. Dower houses or whatever?'

'Haven't the faintest idea.'

'Bound to. I think that, for the time being anyhow, you must put Hugh into a cottage. There's sure to be a barn or a stable block. After all, he's come all this way and given up whatever – or whoever – ,' here she stopped and stared at Hugh, 'he did in South Africa. We'd better fit him in somewhere.'

Hugh looked tragically grateful. He had, as Mambles pointed out, blown it as far as Johannesburg was concerned and if Muriel was not prepared to make him her consort, he was pleased to settle for accommodation. That, at least, would solve the problem of Monopoly, for once the dog saw sense he could trot daily between establishments. It would solve the problem of Marco and the grandchild too. He was ready to compromise. Muriel unnerved him and he disliked the way she cracked her knuckles and smoked. Peter was welcome to her.

'Now,' Mambles turned to Peter as Muriel's stomach lurched. Since the morning's episode she had lost sight, through shame, of her true desires and she dwelled in dejection upon the inconvenience engendered by that mad hormonal rush.

'Now Peter. How do you wish to be handled?'

'Me?' He was calm and exceedingly at ease. 'Me? I'd like to live here with Muriel. She is sure, as soon as we can liquidate Miss Atkins, to be able to provide some little study for me. I do a certain amount of recording you see. There are rooms galore here and I think I can give her the support she may need. Then, another thing, I dote on her.'

Mambles, well pleased, fixed her gaze on Marco.

'There. That's those two dealt with. Now. Marco and Flavia. When is this baby due to be born?'

Marco gabbled, 'January, Not till January.'

'I think you had both better decide to be delighted. Far too many unwanted children in the world. I ought to know. I'm always trailing round those care centres. Just look at the slums. Both of you must be delighted and I'm sure that Muriel will be able to fix you up with an outhouse or something. London is not the place for a baby. This can be a commune. That's how families ought to live. Look at me after all. Kensington Palace is a grace and favour.'

Phyllis swirled into the room and headed for Muriel. Bending over she whispered, 'That Roger and the woman are in the hall. I tried to send them away but Miss Atkins insisted that you told Mr Stiller that she was to speak to you in person before "taking action".' Her petticoat buzzed.

'Tell them we're at dinner. Tell them to wait in the hall and, Phyllis, you'd better give them each a drink; strong ones.'

Phyllis, although loath to pander to Roger in any way, departed to do her duty, carrying the satisfaction that, before the evening was out, he and his lady friend were sure to be defeated.

Muriel, to the table, announced this bit of news; news that caused Mambles to clap her hands.

'Shall we have them brought in?' she proposed in exultation. 'No.' She changed her mind. 'Let's keep them waiting for hours and hours.'

Muriel was thankful that she did not sit next to Peter for her head revolved as she thought with joy of the future as mapped out for them all by Mambles. Had she been beside him she would have felt the need to comment privately and she knew full well that all but general conversation was forbidden.

'Everybody happy?' asked an excited Mambles as she scanned the faces before her.

'Now we must turn our attention to the next project.'

Her voice was clear and steady in spite of the amazing amount of whisky that she continued to pour down her throat.

'I think we should interview them in here. When we have finished dining, Marco, I'd like you to collect two more chairs and place them on either side of me. Then,' she paused and held up her glass, 'they must be plied with plenty of this. It's all right for me. I can drink any amount and be none the worse for wear, so can Mummy, but they are made of lesser stuff.'

Everybody agreed and championed her as they considered the roles she had dished out to each in turn.

As they drank coffee, Roger and Miss Atkins were ushered into the room. Roger, having previously and from time to time encountered Mambles, was outwardly and determinedly unfazed by her presiding position. Miss Atkins knew no such restraint and quaked in her shoes and made to curtsey. She did so after a fashion and found it neither easy nor rewarding, for Mambles failed to notice the act since it was performed only for the benefit of her profile, sitting, as she did, at table.

Speechless, she perched upon the chair provided by Marco, all but touching the frock of HRH Princess Matilda; wedging herself between the Princess and Peter. Roger was presented by Phyllis who had ushered them both into the room to the chair on Mambles's other side 'twixt her and Hugh.

Nearly all, during those first moments of Roger and Miss Atkins joining the table, of their eight eyes met. Roger's grey ones held Flavia's flickering dark ones for a second, then they roved and caught those of Muriel who let her own drop.

Mambles (never forgetting the General who returned after the war) addressed them all for she did not wish for time to elapse or for her power to dwindle.

'So. Mr, er, Roger, I shall call you. Can we be told what this is all about? For a start what has any of it got to do with you?' Roger was not sober and, in spite of the cavalier attitude he adopted in the presence of Mambles, was exceedingly intimidated.

'Justice Ma'am. Quite simply justice.'

'Justice for whom if I may ask?'

Here he failed to reply.

'Quite so.' Mambles was in her element.

'You don't know. Now I shall question Miss Atkins.'

She turned to the gibbering female on her other side and asked, 'Do you, too, wish for justice?'

'Indeed, Your Honour. I have been informed that I have a right.'

'Have you consulted a lawyer?'

'No Madam. Only Mr Stiller. We paid him a visit this morning and he advised a word with Mrs Cottle before further procedure.'

'So. That is what you are doing now. Having a word with Mrs Cottle. Go ahead. Tell her, in front of all of us, what it is you wish to say.'

The woman, near to retching, appealed across the table to Roger but Mambles interposed. 'No. Tell Mrs Cottle what it is that you are after.'

Miss Atkins wriggled on her seat and turned in torment to Muriel who offered mercy.

'Please Mambles. Can't you see she's terrified.'

'Sorry Muriel. None of your shilly-shallying. Carry on Miss Atkins.' She spoke as someone with something up her sleeve.

'As I said, I had been informed that I might be entitled to my uncle's estate – or a part of it.'

Before Muriel could say a word, Mambles again seized the reins.

'Your informant was wrong. You have no claim whatsoever,' adding with semi-mocking steeliness, 'I happen to know. Cunty told Mummy that you have never at any time had any claim whatsoever on Muriel's property.'

Miss Atkins whimpered.

'Cunty's sister, another Miss Crunthard, who you may well remember, lives in the same village as the other Atkins household.' She swigged and drew herself high. 'Your foster parents; that is to say you took their name when you went to them at the age of thirteen but were never legally adopted. You might have been had you not been a bitter disappointment to them both.' Muriel ached with clemency and Mambles took pity.

'Muriel. When this dies down and you have full control of your fortune, I suggest that you make Miss Atkins a little pressie. Ten thousand pounds will do. At the very most. Now, I don't think we will hear much more from these two visitors. Show them out.'

She spoke imperiously and looked as if she had never been happier. Looked as though the evening was making up for the many moments she had wasted whilst wishing to have been born an only child.

Both hangdog and neither sober, they left to drive the distance to London in Roger's hired car. That was that.

Mambles stared at each male member of the gathering in turn. 'I know that you are each saddled with the name of "Cottle". In my view it is not particularly euphonious and I'm quite certain that Muriel is heartily sick of it. She would do well, in gratitude for her inheritance, to take up the maiden name of her Aunt Alice – whatever that may be. I might have suggested the name of Atkins had it not been for that grizzly Atkins relation who has, I hope, now left the premises.'

She then announced that it was time for bed. Cunty was summoned and Jubilee removed from her lap where he had sat, inert, during the period of his mistress's arbitration. Monopoly, who had also lain silent but in a corner of the room, gingerly approached Hugh but did not stop beside him; merely enquired.

Muriel and Cunty took both dogs out for their evening adventures and, when they returned, there was no sign of human life in the house. Everybody, without exception, had retired to bed and Muriel was confused, imagining that Peter, at least, might have stayed up for her.

She lit a cigarette, speculated as to what her aunt's maiden name might have been and fell to wondering whether Mambles had done right at the same time as appreciating that she had put an end, if only temporarily, to the presence of Roger and Miss Atkins.

She was happy about the solution regarding Hugh; if a shed could be found for him, that was. But Peter. She did not fully understand how matters had been resolved. In any case it was odd that he had not waited up for her. Extremely odd. Smoking her cigarette to the butt, glancing about her and tugging at Monopoly, she said goodnight to Cunty who had been collecting some necessity from the kitchen, and trod the stairs with muddled brain.

Slowly she prepared for bed, hoping to recapture all that had been said. Monopoly curled and writhed in his basket as owls, nocturnally alert, hooted and again she wondered whether, in erecting beams above her head, the workmen had worn smocks.

As she lay in puzzlement, the door of her room slowly opened. Although the turning handle made no noise, she witnessed the outline of the invader by the light of the moon for her curtains were not closed. A tall man, Peter or Hugh, (which, she could not distinguish) entered; not that Monopoly showed interest or even bothered to stir. Rotten watchdog.

Lying, worrying about workmen and smocks, Muriel failed to focus. Whatever was happening was happening. It had nothing to do with her. She offered neither encouragement nor resistance. Hugh was shortly to be banished to a kennel. There was nothing for them to discuss. The matter was dead.

Her awakened mind, as the figure drew near, retraced events to a night, years back, that she had passed in a temperance hotel during a cold snap in Norfolk following a family wedding. She, in her early twenties, had lain stock-still as the door to her bedroom opened. On that occasion she had not known, until it became obvious, which of two potential suitors approached; not had she particularly cared. She had always tended to passivity. She did remember, though, that the man who joined her in that hotel room had been Hugh.

Now it was Peter who sat upon her bed. That was excellent for had he not said, in general conversation, that he doted on her?

'So', he said as she extricated herself from nightwear, 'Muriel pulls it off.'